A Little Night Magic

Magic

NEW YORK TIMES BESTSELLING AUTHOR

ANGIE FOX

This is a work of fiction. Names, characters, organizations, places, events, and incidents are either products of the author's imagination or are used fictitiously.

A Little Night Magic
Copyright 2016 by Angie Fox

This edition published by arrangement with Moose Island Publishing.

Moose Island Books

First Edition

ISBN-13: 978-1-939661-31-9

More Books from Angie Fox

The Southern Ghost Hunter series
Southern Spirits
The Skeleton in the Closet
The Haunted Heist

The Accidental Demon Slayer series
The Accidental Demon Slayer
The Dangerous Book for Demon Slayers
A Tale of Two Demon Slayers
The Last of the Demon Slayers
My Big Fat Demon Slayer Wedding
Beverly Hills Demon Slayer
Night of the Living Demon Slayer

The Monster MASH series
Immortally Yours
Immortally Embraced
Immortally Ever After

Short Story Collections
A Little Night Magic
So I Married a Demon Slayer
The Real Werewives of Vampire County

Want an email when the next book comes out?
Sign up for Angie's new release alerts at
www.angiefox.com

Contents

A Ghostly Gift

Chapter One

The ghost of the gangster adjusted his Panama hat, briefly exposing the round bullet hole in the center of his forehead. No doubt it would have been a grisly wound, had it not shimmered in black and white, along with the rest of Frankie Valentine's body.

The hook-nosed former thug stared down at the chessboard laid out on the floor between us, contemplating his next move with the focus of a commander planning an epic battle.

Absently, he reached for the cigarette case in his front left suit pocket.

"No smoking," I said.

He cast me a glance. "Yeah. It might kill me."

We sat in the back parlor, in the flickering light of a thick pink candle in a dish on the floor next to us. The electricity in my home worked perfectly fine. And I considered myself a modern girl. But due to money issues, I'd sold the century-old chandelier.

A fire crackled in the hearth. It was starting to get cold at night. Frankie and I had gathered the wood up onto the porch as the sun tossed orange and purple streaks across the horizon.

I'd gotten my workout in carrying the logs. Frankie had observed and made snarky comments. It cost him too much energy to move things on the mortal plane. He left that up to me.

Frankie pointed to the board. "Make my queen move diagonally, three spaces to the left."

I squinted to see what he meant. "I don't think queens can go that way."

"Of course they can," he huffed. "I'm the one teaching you, remember?"

Yes, but I didn't think he was above cheating.

Frankie also liked the pieces facing perfectly straight ahead. Not angled, not backward. Who knew ghosts could be so anal?

I went ahead and scooted his piece over. Technically, he was my guest and I found I enjoyed treating him as such.

Besides, I owed him. A lot.

Last month, I'd accidentally trapped his spirit on my property when I dumped his funeral urn out onto my rosebushes. At the time, I'd believed my ex-fiancé had given me a dirty old vase, long overdue for a rinse with the hose.

Big mistake.

Now I had a resident ghost living in my two-story Victorian. Frankie had the power to show me the supernatural world in a way that no one else could. With his help, I'd become a ghost hunter. Briefly. In order to save my house.

Now, I was trying to get back to normal.

If by normal you meant hanging out on a Friday night with a long-dead gangster.

Frankie watched me as I hovered my fingers over

different pieces. Deciding.

His urn rested on the marble fireplace, above a string of yarn draped with homemade Kleenex ghosts. Their heads were stuffed with tissue, their necks tied with string, and their eyes and mouths drawn in spooky black marker. I'd tasked my friend Lauralee's kids with making a few Halloween decorations to spruce up the place.

"When's the next job?" Frankie asked.

My back crinked a little and I stretched it out. It would have been nice to own a table and chairs, but I had only a few hundred dollars left from our last adventure and I didn't want to risk spending it. I knew what it was like to be down to my last nickel. I wasn't going through that for furniture.

"I don't want to be a ghost hunter," I admitted to him.

"I don't either," he said, taking in my bare parlor, "but let's face it, this place is a dive."

"Hey—" He was talking about my ancestral home.

"One big score and we could live in the lap of luxury," he added, as if I was never getting rid of him, as if this were his place too. "Wait," he began, without a trace of irony. "Does this have to do with you dating the fuzz?"

"No," I said quickly. "And one date doesn't mean we're *dating*." Not that I would mind. Or maybe I would. Oh, for heaven's sake, Ellis was my ex-fiance's brother. I had to get a grip.

Frankie and I both turned when we heard knocking on the front door.

"It's me," my sister called. The hinges squeaked as Melody let herself in.

I hadn't expected her tonight, but that didn't mean

anything. She passed through my empty front room and straight into the parlor. Her blond hair was up in a messy bun and she carried a Tupperware container. "Hi Verity. Hi Frankie."

I stood and gave her a hug. "How'd you know he was around?" I asked. Half the time, Frankie disappeared into the ether, or wherever ghosts went.

"He always backs your queen into a corner," she said.

Frankie groaned. "Aw, come on."

I looked back at the chessboard, trying to see where I was in trouble, but found myself distracted when Melody handed me the delicious smelling container. "Mmm…roasted potatoes, onions," I pulled open the lid, "gravy," I added with pure delight.

"I made too much pot roast," she said, as if it happened all the time.

She was lying through her teeth. Melody could barely bake a chicken. When it wasn't undercooked or scorched to a crisp, she'd forget and leave the giblets packet in the middle.

Ever since my sister found out I was living on ramen noodles and granola bars, she'd been buying ready-to-go grocery meals, boxing them up in Tupperware and delivering them to me under the guise of Martha Stewart.

"Thanks," I told her, keeping up the façade. Otherwise, she'd move on to phase two, which would be her trying to give me money she didn't have.

She chewed at her bottom lip. "I have to confess. I'm not just here to give you dinner this time." She cringed. "My friend needs help with a ghost."

Frankie barked out a laugh. "Fantastic. She'll do it."

Good thing Melody couldn't see him, or hear him. I

shot him a hairy eyeball. He looked much too pleased with himself, hovering over by the fireplace.

"This…thing I do," I said, returning my attention to Melody, "it has to be a secret." People in our small southern town already believed I was an odd duck. I'd be crazy to add to the gossip. Besides, the work was dangerous and scary. I was a graphic designer by trade. "I need design jobs."

"How's that going?" she mused, knowing the answer.

Not so well. Ever since I'd offended the first family of Sugarland Tennessee by leaving their son at the altar, my freelance business had dried up.

Now I was secretly dating his brother, Ellis.

I didn't know how things could get worse, but I was willing to bet they would if that little nugget got out.

Or if I started chasing ghosts.

I headed for the kitchen with my dinner.

Melody followed. "The good news is she can't pay you anyway."

"This is getting better and better," I mused.

Melody flipped on the lights. "She does have a nice pre-owned kitchen set she'll give you," she added, grabbing my lone plastic plate out of a drying rack by the sink. "This is my friend Julie from high school."

"I like her." Julie had always been nice to me. She owned a resale shop downtown. The store carried some fancy, high-end antiques, but much of the merchandise consisted of good, gently used items.

Still…

I took the plate from my sister and slid the entire pot roast meal onto it. "What does Julie want me to do?"

My sister leaned against the counter. "The store has always been haunted. She'll leave at night and come back to find pennies stacked up on her cash register. Or she'll open up in the morning and smell cigar smoke. One time, she watched an entire display of antique doorknobs start shaking like we were having an earthquake or something. A customer saw it too."

"Yikes." I located a fork and arranged my meal on the kitchen island. "It sounds like she has more than one ghost," I said digging in. "And if the place has been haunted for a while, they might even think the shop is theirs." Spirits tended to get possessive after decades in the same place.

I took a bite. Yum. Lauralee had ordered from the diner. I could taste the fresh meat drippings and the hint of rosemary in the gravy.

Melody frowned. "She doesn't need you to get rid of every ghost. Just the one rooting around in her collectibles case."

"What does that mean?" I asked, realizing I'd forgotten to pour myself a water. I grabbed a plastic cup and headed for the sink.

"Julie has this antique glass display case toward the back of the store," Melody said.
"It's about as tall as a person and it's full of quirky, unusual things. Lots of dent-able, breakables too, like porcelain figurines, antique snuff boxes and perfume bottles. She'll lock up at night, come back in the morning and the case is still locked, but the valuables inside are scattered. Last night, she lost the arm off a shepherd."

"That doesn't sound too tragic," I said, taking a sip.

"She might be able to fix it, but now it's a restored piece instead of an original. Julie doesn't make a lot of money in her store. She can't afford broken collectibles." Melody pushed herself off the counter. "If it continues, it could put her out of business."

"Ouch." I knew all about a failing business, and what it did to a person.

"She knows it's a ghost. Nobody but Julie can enter the store or open the case. She carries the only set of store keys." Melody crossed her arms over her chest. "She's really upset, Verity." She shook her head. "I know I shouldn't have told her about you."

"You shouldn't have," I agreed. Melody and Ellis were the only two people who knew my secret. And he probably wouldn't want me ghost hunting either. We'd almost been killed when we'd faced a poltergeist on his property.

Melody plowed forward anyway. "She's in real trouble. You are too. Let's face it, you could use some direction, or at least some furniture."

"I resent that," I told her. Mostly because it was true.

"She'll give you a kitchen set if you can get rid of her destructive ghost." My sister insisted. She glanced at my plate. "Maybe we can ask for dishes too."

That was all well and good. "But have you stopped to consider exactly how I'm supposed to know which ghost is causing the trouble?"

"I don't know," she said defensively. "You're the expert."

I barked out a laugh. "I don't know what I'm doing."

Melody didn't let that stop her. "Julie promises to keep your secret and never tell a soul."

"What do you say, Frankie?" He'd given up his spot by the fireplace and now lingered outside the entrance to the kitchen.

"Let me think," he mused. "No money and no reward." He made a show of tapping his finger on his chin. "Oh, wait. I don't have to think at all." He dropped the pretense. "No."

For some reason, that ticked me off. "What's wrong with helping someone?" I asked. And getting a nice table in the bargain. I turned to Melody. "We'll give it a shot."

Frankie groaned.

"Consider it personal growth," I told him.

Although Ellis wouldn't be happy. I ran a hand through my hair. Still, it wasn't his decision to make. Of course, I didn't want him to worry.

Curse my luck, I was seeing him tomorrow night.

"We'll help," I corrected, "on one condition."

"Name it," she said, as if this would be simple.

I dropped my hand. "We go this evening."

That way, everything would be over and good before I had to mention anything to Ellis.

Melody perked up. "She'd love that. I'll call her right now."

"All right then," I said, returning to my pot roast. I'd need the energy. Hopefully, I hadn't gotten Frankie and myself into too much trouble.

We'd find out soon enough.

Chapter Two

New for You stood in a row of stone storefronts that had graced Main Street since the early 1900's. I loved this part of town, not only for its tradition, but also for its permanence.

Julie greeted us at the door. "I'm so glad you're here." Flame red hair peeked out from under her colorful headscarf as she flipped the sign to *Closed* and ushered us inside.

A bright white 1960's modern chair sat on a 70's inspired chocolate shag rug. Antique chandeliers hung from the tin ceiling.

Julie shook my hand, and held it a little longer than I expected. "Thank you, Verity," she said, not questioning my power or how I'd gotten it. There was no distrust in her eyes, simply gratitude and determination. "I need to get this fixed."

"I'll do my best." I told her. I couldn't guarantee anything.

I adjusted the hemp bag over my shoulder. It contained a wallet, lip gloss, gum, everything a normal purse would, with the addition of Frankie's urn. The

only way I could bring the ghost with me was to sch-
lep along his final resting place. It clanked against my
keys, causing Julie to do a double take.

I merely smiled. "I like your shop."

A faint blush stained her cheeks. "I do, too. It's a
labor of love." She glanced from me to Melody. "And
sometimes it gets a bit...unusual. Come on, let me
show you what I have."

Her flowing green skirt swooshed around her ankles as she led us back into the store. "This space used
to house the oldest bar in town, a real manly place,
founded during the McKinley administration," she
said. "They didn't even let women in the door until
1952." Faded drawings in wood frames crowded the
left wall. I saw ink drawn portraits and a watercolor
of the town hall as it was being built. Julie noticed
what had caught my attention. "Those are original to
the bar. I left them up because I didn't want to disturb
the beer caps."

"Beer caps?" I asked, scanning the mishmash of
frames. "The pictures showed people." Then I saw
them. Dozens upon dozens of dust-coated bottle caps
placed on top of the frames.

"A lot of boys from Sugarland had their last drink
here before heading off to fight World War II. They'd
each leave a beer cap on one of the frames behind the
bar, and remove it when they got back. Everybody'd
buy them a drink. They'd celebrate. The ones left up
there are to remember the soldiers who never made it
back to collect their cap. We couldn't disturb that."

I found myself glad that she hadn't. I was helping
a good person, one who had respect for people, both
living and dead. "How long have you had this building?"

She smiled. "My mom bought it in 1974. She's the one who started *New For You*. At least ten years after she bought this space, you'd have these old timers — mostly men — stopping by, thinking they were coming into Doc's Ale House."

I lingered near a portrait of a doughboy being toasted in a bar by his friends. The hairs on the back of my neck prickled as a flutter of cold air descended over me. Perhaps some long-dead patrons had returned as well.

"Frankie?" I hissed. "Please tell me that's you."

"You wish," he said, directly behind me. "This place is buzzing.

I hadn't seen anything yet, and I wouldn't until Frankie lifted the veil and showed me what others couldn't see.

Julie watched me carefully. "Do you want to see the haunted display case?"

"Of course," I said, resisting the urge to point out that every inch of this place was likely haunted.

"What's happening with you?" Melody asked as we passed a few kitchen tables, a hutch, and a desk. I hardly glanced at any of it. "What are you thinking?" She pressed.

I had no answer for her. I didn't know what to expect at this point.

Julie stopped in front of a tall display case with intricate brass trimmings. "Here's where I've been having the trouble," she said stopping. The four black velvet lined shelves held an array of treasures, from estate earrings to antique pipes, perfume bottles and letter openers.

A shadow lingered behind an old-fashioned porcelain shaving set. "Do you see that?" I asked.

Both Julie and Melody leaned in close.

"What?" My sister whispered.

It could be nothing. I didn't know. Frankie hadn't even tuned me in yet and I had already started seeing things.

This place was powerful.

Both of them watched me, as if they expected me to whip out a Ghostbusters proton pack and solve the problem right there.

Julie averted her eyes and cleared her throat. "I can lock you in. You'll be safe."

From the living. She couldn't help me with the dead.

Before she left, I needed to learn a few things. "Melody told me that you've mostly had spirits move objects around, or make them rattle." It took a lot of energy for that to happen, but it didn't necessarily scare me. I worried more about destructive ghosts. It could mean a poltergeist. "Do you think the objects in the case were purposely damaged?"

She didn't hesitate. "Yes."

"I was afraid of that," I murmured to myself.

Julie's eyes widened, as if it suddenly occurred to her that I could walk out of here and never look back. Perhaps I should. I didn't know what I was doing. Frankie would certainly be happy to leave. It would be so, so easy.

"Melody said you needed a kitchen table," she said quickly. "Tell me what's happening with my display, or even how to fix it, and you can have your pick."

"I appreciate that," I said, as my sister slipped her hand into mine and squeezed.

"Feel free to stretch out on any of the furniture while you're here," Julie added.

I'd take her up on it. A comfy-looking purple velvet couch stretched out at the edge of a small forest of mismatched chairs. I hadn't enjoyed a good sit on a couch since I'd sold mine a month or two ago.

Julie drew her keys out of her pocket. "Okay, then." She handed me a slip of paper. "Here's my cell number. Call me if you need me."

"Thanks," I said, accepting it, knowing she couldn't help me with this.

Melody hung back as her friend prepared to leave. "You'll be okay?" she asked.

"Fine," I assured her.

I hoped.

She gave me a hug.

"Now go." The sooner I began my work, the sooner we'd have our answers. Besides, I didn't want to be talking to Frankie in front of anyone.

"This is a good thing," she reminded me.

I sincerely hoped she was right.

Chapter Three

The store felt darker after Melody and Julie left. Empty. Yes, the chandeliers blazed overhead. Display lamps shone on desks and hutches. Julie had even turned the red shaded one next to her cash register on bright.

But the tone of the place changed. It felt like a large, empty house after dark.

"Told you this was a bad idea," Frankie said.

"You're just mad because you can't make a profit," I said, slipping my bag off my shoulder.

"True," he mused.

He may be a mercenary, but I'd chosen this. I knew what I had to do.

"Let's open this place up," he said, from a place on my left side.

"Wait." I placed my bag, along with Frankie's urn, on the floor next to the purple couch. "Let me at least sit down and enjoy real furniture for a second before you freak me out."

The gangster chuckled as I eased myself down onto

the soft, supportive velvet cushions. "Wow," I rumbled, letting myself relax for that one, brief, golden second.

Okay, maybe two. I closed my eyes, reveling in it.

Until a chill swept over me.

Oh no.

The lamps dimmed. The sound of footsteps on hardwood echoed throughout the room.

I jerked my eyes open and watched the space grow darker. Ominous shadows bled across the ceiling, clouding the lamps, obscuring the reality I knew.

The ghost had begun to show me the other side.

"Aww, Frankie," I said, scrambling to my feet as ghostly cobwebs drifted over the piece, snagging on the velvet. The jerk was getting me back for bringing him here. "I asked you to wait."

He stood to my left, about a foot above the oak floor. "I did. I let you sit down first."

Any further argument died on my lips as an old wooden bar shimmered into focus along the picture wall.

The bald man behind it wore round black-framed glasses, and a white short-sleeved shirt paired with suspenders. He couldn't have been more than fifty. And I could see straight through him.

I gave a slight shiver. Yes, I'd taken on this job. One more job. But I didn't think I'd ever get used to it.

A mix of voices mingled together, talking and laughing. Glasses clinked.

Slowly, a collection of patrons shimmered into view. Each one of them appeared in black and white.

A man in a dark suit and fedora leaned against the counter, nursing a beer while he talked to an honest to goodness Civil War soldier, a sergeant with muttonchops and a full dress uniform.

Now that I hadn't seen before. My chest hurt and I realized I'd forgotten to breathe. "I thought this place opened during the McKinley administration." Granted I wasn't great with dates, but I knew McKinley came after Lincoln.

Frankie huffed. "What? So that means it's closed to a guy who wants a drink?"

I swallowed hard. "Gotcha," I mused, knowing he wouldn't get the sarcasm. "How silly of me."

"He usually haunts the library, so really, he didn't have to travel too far," Frankie mused.

A crowd of young men in dress pants and short-sleeved buttoned dress shirts stood near the front corner, surrounding one of their own. They laughed and patted him on the back. He wore a vintage Army uniform and took a self-conscious slug of beer.

"Hey!" A curly haired man with a full moustache and beard walked straight through the front door, arms out. He was impossible to miss. The man sported an obnoxious 1970's sports jacket that would have made Rodney Dangerfield proud.

A bunch of the guys called out, "Ringo!"

He high-fived the men near the door, and the fedora hat guy, and the Civil War soldier.

Seems Ringo got around.

His gaze settled on me. "Nice tits," he said, aiming a wolfish grin in my direction.

God, what a pig. I crossed my arms over my chest and scooted a couple of steps closer to Frankie. "Okay, how do we tell which one of these guys is doing the damage?" I'd like to do the job and get out of here. The shadows, the overload of testosterone, the other-worldliness of this place creeped me out.

Frankie pasted on a wide grin, refusing to even glance down. "Act casual," he muttered through his teeth, "stop looking at me."

"Why?" I asked. I hoped this place wasn't dangerous for him. He'd been okay the other times he'd shown me the other side. I gave him a quick once over. He wore the same gray suit and tie he always did. His complexion? Watery gray. The bullet hole? Still right there in the middle of his forehead. "Are you having a problem? Do you need me to go get your urn?"

"Cripes," he winced. "Your problem is you talk before you think."

"What?" Fear skittered up my spine as the bartender whispered something to the fedora hat guy. Both he and the Civil War soldier turned our way.

The sergeant braced his arms on the bar. "You mean she can see us?"

Oh, hell.

Loud sports jacket guy perked up. "Groovy!"

Frankie cursed under his breath. "Now you've done it. Before, you were just another one of the living, walking through their bar, pretending you don't see nothin' or nobody."

"And now I'm a girl," I said, finishing his thought.

The damage was done. Mr. 1970's strutted straight for me, like he owned the place. The bartender wadded up his towel and tossed it onto a tray, watching.

The squicky ghost smoothed his moustache while undressing me with his eyes. "Well, hello there," he said, winking. "Your name must be Lucky Charms because you're magically delicious."

I turned to Frankie. "Did he really just say that?"

"You started this," Frankie said, with no sympathy

at all. "I tried to stop you."

By talking to me. Tactfully speaking, that was a horrible way to get me to close my mouth and pay attention.

"Hey, baby, I'm the one talking to you now." Ringo swayed, like he heard some kind of music. Either that or he was trying to look cool. He unbuttoned his dress shirt to display—ew—a forest of chest hair. "Ever do it with the dead?" He drew a gold medallion out of his shirt and fingered it. "I've got a van parked outside."

"Argh," I needed a shower now. "What do you think I'm going to say to that?" I demanded. "Take me to your van?"

"Well, all right," he said, completely missing my point.

The Civil War sergeant drew up next to me, crowding out Frankie. "A thousand pardons, miss, for this… brute."

Ringo scoffed. "You were asking for lessons last week."

He tossed a withering look at Ringo. Sparks of energy danced over my arms, tingling.

"That is only because I am in need of a wife."

"Perfect," I said. "Are these people serious?" I asked Frankie.

The sergeant's manner softened as he turned to me. "I assure you I know how to treat a lady, even in times like this." I wasn't sure what time he meant exactly as he tried to lead me away. His watery cold touch seeped through me, chilling me to the bone. "Now is your father here?"

Oh my word. "That's enough," I said, edging away from them both.

Yes, it was fun to be thought of as both virgin and whore in the span of a minute, but I didn't have time for randy ghosts.

I zigzagged around the sergeant and nearly ran straight into the gaggle of 1940's guys. A tall, well-built, Matt Damon looking one at the front grinned like I was the best thing he'd seen in a year. "Want to have a drink and a smoke with us?" His friends stood behind him, eager for me to say 'yes.' "You never know," he continued. "Today might be the last. Better make it count, right?"

Not exactly. I felt one coming up behind me. Ghosts tended to shoot off chilly air. If it was Ringo, he'd better not touch me. I didn't like that watery, wet feeling.

"Okay," Frankie darted over my left shoulder and pushed in between them and me. "Break it up." He crowded the small slice of personal space the other ghosts had given me. "I get that she's a sheba," he told them, "but she's with me and I'm not going to have you acting like a bunch of drugstore cowboys."

I didn't get the slang, but I had a pretty good idea he'd just defended me. "Gee, Frankie. I didn't know you cared."

His cheeks darkened as he straightened his tie. "Can't let a dame like you run wild."

Heaven forbid.

I edged closer to the bar, away from the crowd, and tried to understand. I'd always been good with people, and so far, that had extended to ghosts. "I get that you guys haven't seen a girl in a few years," I began.

"Try decades," the bartender said, giving me a wink as he wiped down glasses.

He'd better not join in. I already had more undead suitors than any girl could reasonably stand. "Let's tone it down a notch," I suggested. "Try to be more mysterious. That works with dead girls too, you know." Because if an eligible girl ghost did wander in here, I guaranteed they'd scare her away.

I wasn't even their type and I felt like the last pork chop on the plate.

In fact, there was only one guy besides Frankie that was for sure not hitting on me.

The World War II soldier sat at the far end of the bar, nursing his drink, and acting like we weren't even there. I found that highly appealing.

He had a strong look about him, like he'd done manual labor. Maybe worked on a farm. An Army cap covered much of his close-cropped dark hair. He looked safe, steady.

I scooted up next to him, keeping an eye out for the crowd behind me. "I like your style."

"Just because I'm not acting like those clowns?" He took a swig of his drink and let out a self-deprecating chuckle. "You don't want to be like me."

I fought the urge to take a seat on the stool next to him. Its ethereal form wouldn't hold me. My eye caught a faded black and white picture on the wall in front of us, an army unit. It might very well be his. Dusty bottle caps maintained their vigil at the top. "You worried about the war?" I asked, wondering if he was one of the many who didn't come back.

He traced circles on his bottle. "That's over. Has been for a long time." He held out a hand. "Private John Cleveland."

I waved instead. "Verity Long."

"Right," he said, pulling back. "Believe it or not, it slips my mind sometimes." A muscle in his jaw tightened. "I never forget about her, though. The war cost me my fiancé."

I watched him take another long drink. "I'm sorry."

He huffed, like he didn't want my sympathy. At the same time, I could see he needed someone to talk to. "She really loved me. Only me," he added, looking at me for the first time. "But now I can't find her." He gave a long, hard sigh.

How sad. I didn't think he'd want to hear that, though. In fact, I didn't know what to say, so I just listened.

"She's not on the immortal plane," he said, appearing lost. "That means she's still alive. Somewhere. But I can't find her. It's like she disappeared."

I wasn't sure what to tell him. "Maybe your friends at the bar can help you look." They certainly needed something constructive to do.

"Ha. No. Have you seen those assholes?"

I wouldn't go that far, but he was upset.

"You don't get it. You've never been dead," he said, getting upset. "Even in death, you can feel that connection. You know someone cares." He squared his shoulders, bracing against what he had to say next. "With her, I can still feel it, but it's fading. Like she's giving up."

"You can't think that way," I told him.

"I can't afford not to. We're in serious trouble. She needs to understand how much I love her. That bonds us. It's the only way I can be with her for eternity, like I promised. It's the only way we can for sure find each other, after, you know…"

"She dies," I said, finishing for him. "She has to know," I ventured. He didn't seem like the kind of guy who hid his feelings. "Maybe you've been dead so long it's harder to sense it."

He nodded. "I'd hoped it was something like that." He buried his face in his hands, rubbed his eyes. "Then her ring showed up here last week. I gave her that ring as a promise when I shipped out. She let it go," he said, lost. My skin tingled with goose bumps. "She must have sold it. It breaks my heart."

My throat felt tight. "You saw her ring in the display case, didn't you?"

"Yes," he said simply. "It had been my mother's. My fiancé knew that. What if she's already dead? If so, she died without that loving bond. And she's gone."

Oh, wow. It didn't look good. But he couldn't give up. I wouldn't, either. "Can you tell me her name?" If she were still alive, I'd pay her a visit. Sugarland wasn't a large place. I might even be acquainted with her.

"Maime Bee Saks," he said with hope and a touch of fear. "She lives with her parents on 215 East Perlman Street, near Brandywine Park."

"I haven't heard that name," I admitted. She had to be in her nineties by now. I sincerely doubted she still lived with her parents. She might have even married and changed her name. It could be any number of things. "That doesn't mean we can't find her."

"I've been to her house, my house, her favorite places to be. I don't even know why." He gave a hard chuckle. "I can't say anything. I can't tell her how much I love her."

Lord, he was a dream. Most women I knew would kill to be loved like that.

"I can't even hold her ring," he said, folding his hands together in front of him. "I can't pick it up off the shelf."

No, he couldn't. It was a wonder he could have moved anything in that case at all. The ghost was certainly determined, or desperate.

"I'll take it to her," I promised. Surely Julie would understand.

"You can do that?" He asked, hope flaring. It both elated me and scared me. There was a very real possibility I could fail. Still, I found myself nodding. "There's sickness around the ring," he said. "If she's even still here, she doesn't have long." His eyes clouded with tears. "And what does it even mean that she gave it up? That she left my ring in a resale shop?" He saw the way that startled me. "I know where we really are. I haven't given up my link to the mortal world. Not while she could still be here. I'm so afraid I'm going to lose her forever."

"You won't," I said, making a promise I would do anything to keep. "I'll find her." I'd solve this. He deserved as much, after he'd fought and died for our country.

As to how? Well, I'd figure that out as well.

Chapter Four

"You want to do what?" My sister asked.

"Her name is Maime Bee Saks," I said, watching Julie open the display case.

I'd called Julie right away. She and Melody had grabbed an evening snack at the coffee house and I explained everything to them while they drove back to the store together. "Last he heard she lived at 215 East Perlman Street, near Brandywine Park."

Julie cringed. "That's where the new shopping center went in," she whispered, as if that would keep the ghost from hearing. I wanted to tell her that Private Cleveland stood between us.

"It's okay," I told her. "We have to find where she lives now." The redhead drew a silver ring from the display stand. Tiny blue sapphire chips clustered around a large pearl.

"Thanks for letting me take this to her," I said, as she slipped it into a ring box.

"It's a wonderful piece," she said, handing the entire thing to me. "But it's the right thing to do. Tell

Private Cleveland I'm glad to help."

"He knows," I said quietly. I held it for a moment while John drew his blunt fingers over the luminous pearl. They passed right through it.

"I hope you'll come with me," I told him.

He swallowed hard. "I will," he said. "I won't be much help. The farther I get from this place, the weaker I am."

I understood. "If need be, we'll bring her to you."

Yes, I was getting overly optimistic, but we needed to move full speed ahead on this.

I closed the ring box and stowed it in my bag. "I'll let you know what my sister and I find," I said to Julie.

Melody eyed me suspiciously. "You don't expect—"

"I need you to get us into the library," I told her. She opened three mornings a week. She had a key. "Tonight."

She planted her hands on her hips.

"This began with you," I reminded her. "I recall you saying something about how important it is to use the resources we have to help people."

"And we see where that got us," Frankie muttered from somewhere to my left.

Melody pursed her lips. "If you just want to finish this before you see Ellis, then you're out of luck. I'm not going to break the rules so you don't tick off your boyfriend."

"It isn't about that." And he wasn't my boyfriend, not yet anyway. "If Maime Bee Saks gives up completely, we lose the tie. Plus, Private Cleveland felt sickness around the ring. We don't have much time."

She wavered. I'd showed her his picture on the wall. I'd found it while waiting for Melody and Julie.

He'd stood smiling among row after row of soldiers heading off to war. We'd also found his name in hand-written white ink down below.

"Fine, I'll do it," she said, quickly. "It makes me nervous."

I couldn't help but smile. "Come to the dark side with me." Maybe I should tell her we had cookies.

* * *

The city library stood in the middle of the town square, just up the street from Julie's shop. The buildings in this part of town had been constructed at a time where every door and window was considered a work of art. And while they'd used brick and wood for Main Street, the town square was done in white limestone.

The library was one of the original buildings in Sugarland and dated all the way back to 1842. Red limestone columns flanked the entrance and the door resembled something out of a medieval castle. A spotlight shone on the right front wall, where a Yankee cannonball struck the building and is still, to this day, embedded in the white stone wall.

We're very proud of it.

It was coming up on midnight when we pulled up out front, in the shadow of the large statue of our founder on a horse. Darkness shrouded the square. It appeared a bit creepy, even before we brought two ghosts in there with us.

My sister let us in and the large wood doors opened with a loud, echoing creek.

"It's a good thing we can't afford a security guard," she said, as she led us into the cavernous lobby. I breathed in the comforting scent of old books. "I wouldn't know how to explain this one."

"Let's start with the phone books," I said, getting down to business. "For Sugarland and any cities or counties within a fifty mile radius."

"You've thought this out," Melody said appreciatively as we passed through a main hall and headed for the research area to the left.

"Of course." I said, pretending not to notice her sarcastic tone. I didn't always look before I leaped. In this case, though, I knew we were up against a time deadline.

Rows and rows of bookshelves held thick books detailing local history, census data, and phone book records. I grabbed the one for Sugarland and headed for a sturdy table. Melody took books for the three surrounding counties and joined me.

Several hours later, we'd searched every phone book for every city and county in Tennessee and the nearby states. Melody had logged into census data from 1940 through the present day.

Nothing.

I'd expected her to be hard to find. It concerned me deeply that she had no personal record at all.

"What do we do now?" I asked, worried. My voice carried in the silent library. I didn't even see the ghosts. No doubt they were conserving their energy. I'd learned from Frankie how easily they could wear themselves down, and how hard it was to maintain a presence on the physical plane.

"Come on," Melody said, heading for a section at the back, labeled Genealogy. "We'll look at old yearbooks."

Yes, but, "That's not going to tell us where she

lives."

She continued, undeterred. "It might give us a better idea of her name. Maybe we're spelling it wrong. We might be missing part."

I highly doubted Private Cleveland had given me bad information. Still, it would be neat to see what Maime had looked like.

Melody handed me the 1942 Sugarland High School Yearbook, and grabbed one from the town over for herself. "One thing I've learned about research. You keep at it. You never know what's going to give you a break."

The spine crackled as I opened it and saw a photo of the baseball team. It was hard to imagine those cocky kids had played ball at my old high school more than seventy years ago. They looked like your typical young athletes, so tough and sure of themselves.

I turned to the class pictures, to the senior class of 1942. And I saw her.

Mary Bee Saks, nicknamed "Maime."

She smiled bright, her raven hair neatly curled away from her heart-shaped face.

"Look at this," I told Melody. Then we turned back to see John Cleveland, "Johnny" in a sweater vest and a bow tie. He appeared as if he didn't have a care in the world. I almost didn't recognize him.

I'd needed to see this, to hold in my hands the undeniable truth this woman had indeed existed. But why had she ceased to exist after 1942?

I blew out a frustrated breath.

"You okay?" Melody asked.

"Of course," I said, rubbing a hand over my face. My eyelids felt like sandpaper.

We had to be missing something, a vital piece of the puzzle. I didn't know what.

"Dawn's coming," she said. A faint trace of morning light had already begun to light up the windows behind us, casting the world in gray. "I need to go home and clean up so I can open the library for the law-abiding citizens."

"Right," I said, bracing my head in my hands, unwilling to pack it up just yet. The answer felt as if it were just out of reach. Something simple. If I could only see it. I refused to believe that the woman in the book I held in front of me was somehow unreachable.

Soon it would be too late.

"Get some rest," Melody said as we stood. "Take care of yourself."

That wouldn't help Private Cleveland. Or buy us any time.

I was glad I didn't see him as Melody closed up the library. I didn't think I could look him in the eye at that moment.

"Let's go," she said, when we'd finished turning off the lights. "We'll think of something else tomorrow."

I'd let her drive me to my house. I didn't have my car.

But I didn't promise her I'd stay home.

I had one more idea, one last shot in the dark. I only hoped it would give us the answer we needed.

Chapter Five

Dawn broke as I pulled my ancient Cadillac into Holy Oak Cemetery. Neatly trimmed bushes surrounded the large memorial park. The iron gates stood open.

I drove past the caretaker's cottage and the landscaping shed, and straight down Resurrection Avenue. I knew the place well. I'd taken my Grandmother here many times to place flowers on the grave of both my Grandfather and my Father. Then I'd done the same next to her tombstone.

Instead of turning right toward the newer section, I made a left.

Rocks spit from under my tires as the older vaults loomed into view. Century old crypts clustered in the foggy haze of dawn.

I gasped and clutched the steering wheel as I saw spirits lingering among the tombs. This had happened once before without Frankie. Evidently, him showing me the other side had opened my mind to the possibility, and thus I could detect spirits strong enough to show themselves to me.

Knowing why didn't make it any less jarring. I slowed as a young woman, no more than eighteen, stood watching me from the door of her family vault. I shuddered and kept driving.

Deep breaths, I instructed myself, hoping I wouldn't see anything too unsettling. I headed straight back, past the vaults and monuments and grieving angel statues, to the right rear corner of Holy Oak, where soldiers from the Second World War lay buried.

As I drew closer, the sheer number of graves astonished me. It shouldn't have. I'd driven past this place before. I understood the price the men had paid. But after meeting Private Cleveland, after seeing his hopeful expression staring back at me from that yearbook, the acre-plus field of tombstones felt surreal.

He had been younger than me when he died.

Neat rows of white marker stones lined up like soldiers. I parked nearby and lingered near the car as a soldier in full paratrooper gear wandered down a row at the back.

Focus. He had every right to be here, just like I did.

I kept my keys in my hand as I approached the first row of graves.

I needed to stick to the plan.

Graves often held flowers. If someone had left a bouquet for Johnny, perhaps they'd included a note. I could look them up and drop by for a visit.

If that was too much to hope for, even a florist tag would allow me to learn who placed the flowers, who still remembered John Cleveland, and if they knew a girl who had ever gone by the name of Mary Bee Saks.

I was running out of options.

Row four, near the front, held the "C's." I walked it quietly, reverently, until I stood before his grave:

Jonathan Reeves Cleveland
Private
*US Army * World War II*
February 11, 1923
October 31, 1942

The headstone gleamed white. Immaculately trimmed grass crowded the base of the stone, and my heart sank. No evidence existed that anyone had come to visit.

It angered me for a moment, and then I reminded myself that maybe he didn't have any family left. His friends had likely died. Perhaps Maime was the last one who remained.

Which made me sad all over again.

I hoped John hadn't been able to follow me this far. He didn't need to see his final resting place abandoned.

"I'm sorry," I whispered. "I'm going to keep trying."

I bowed my head and said a quick prayer for him — or for hope, I wasn't sure which.

Slowly, regretfully, I retreated back toward the car.

Maybe I could find something more at the library. Perhaps Melody and I had missed a vital clue. My footsteps came slower, as if leaving this place meant admitting defeat.

Who was I kidding? It did.

The spirit of young woman sat kitting on a marble bench nestled under a tall oak tree near the road. Her fingers worked the needles deftly and I wondered how long she'd been at it. Her long skirt and high-necked white shirt appeared to be turn-of-the-century. Yet the sweater in her hands remained half-finished.

I joined her on the bench, resting my elbows on my knees. I'd taken this case, I'd said I would make a difference. I promised. And I had no idea how to make good on it.

I sighed and tried to clear my head. I focused on the green grass, the calls of the birds, the clicking of knitting needles. Stilling, I let the beauty of the morning wash over me. I liked this time of day. It was quiet. Peaceful. So unlike my routine lately.

I had the chance to help a brave soldier, and the sweet-looking Maime. I couldn't pass that up, even knowing what I did now, that it could be impossible.

The sun warmed my back as it burned off the morning dew.

I glanced next to me and saw the spirit had disappeared. Here one moment, gone the next. I supposed it was that way for all of us.

An old woman approached from my left. Pink blush topped her high cheekbones and set off her heart-shaped face. She wore a flowered skirt with tennis shoes, along with a light jacket. Her gait hitched, her pace slow. I scooted over a little on my bench, to let her know I'd welcome company if she needed a break before continuing.

She smiled gratefully as she neared. "Thank you," she said, taking the place the ghost had vacated. "My health's not so good lately." Her hands shook as she folded one over the other. "It's usually just me this early."

"I like it in the morning," I told her. "It's peaceful. I'll have to remember that next time I come see my dad and my grandma."

The wind blew at the scarf she'd tied over her hair. She brought a hand up, making sure it remained fastened. "I come here for my husband."

That had to be hard. "I'm sorry for your loss."

"Me, too," she said quietly. "My life would have been very different if he'd survived the war."

I had no doubt.

We sat in silence for a moment, facing the graves.

"He was everything to me," she said simply. "I never wanted anybody else."

"That's neat," I told her. It didn't lessen the loss, but it had to be comforting to enjoy that kind of certainty.

She gave a small smile. "It was hard. Especially back then. I raised our child alone." She shook her head. "He never knew his dad. He doesn't see the need to come back, just drops me off here on his way for coffee. But I like it here. It makes me feel close." She drew her hands to her body, as if she'd revealed too much. "Anyhow," she pushed up off the bench, "I'd best be on my way."

"Good talking to you," I said, meaning every word. She'd made an incredible sacrifice.

I watched as she made her way toward the field of tombstones, and wished I could have said something more to comfort her. She passed row one, rows two and three, and began a slow advance down row four.

It was a long shot, yet it still made my stomach tingle.

I stood, not eager to hamper her privacy at such a time. Yet she stopped very, very close to where I'd been. It could be a coincidence, or it could be more. I scarcely dared hope as quickly, quietly made my way toward her.

Head bowed, she placed a bottle cap on the grave of Private Jonathan Cleveland.

She knew him. Perhaps she'd been married to a friend of his. Or even...

I approached slowly as she stood, head bowed, before the grave. I waited until she finished her prayer. "Excuse me," I began, reaching into my bag, pulling out the ring box. "I don't want to bother you. But do you recognize this?" I opened the box. Inside nestled the pearl ring.

She gasped and brought a hand to her mouth. "How did you get that?"

I'd shocked her. Either I was a terrible person, or I'd just done a very good thing. "I'm looking for Mary Bee Saks," I said, throat tight. "Maime."

Tears welled in her eyes as she touched a finger to the pearl, much in the way Johnny had. "This belonged to his mother."

Johnny told me the same thing.

At the risk of sounding completely ridiculous, I forced the words out. "Are you...Maime?" She did look similar to the girl in the yearbook photo, that lightness about her, that heart-shaped face.

She nodded, tears streaming down her cheeks.

Oh my word. I felt the stinging behind my eyes. "Take it," I said, placing the box in her hand. "It's yours."

She opened her mouth. Closed it. "Thank you," she whispered, touching it as if she couldn't quite believe it were real. "I don't care how you got it."

I couldn't tell her. Not really. "I was asked to return it to you," I said. "Johnny would want you to have it."

She slid it onto her finger, a giggle bursting from her that turned into a hiccup. "I told him I'd wear it forever." It fit her perfectly. She fisted her hand. "My mother took it and said I couldn't have it back. I haven't seen it since that day." She held up her hand, watching in awe as it sparkled. "My sister must have kept it after mom passed. Neither one of them ever spoke to me again. Sissy passed last month. I had to see it in the paper."

"That's awful." I couldn't believe they'd be so harsh.

Her gaze darted back to his grave. "What I said before...about us being married. We intended to marry. We knew we would. Then he was called up earlier than we thought. He wasn't gone a month before I learned I was expecting. In those days...well, it just wasn't like it is now. My mother knew we hadn't married yet. She threw me out when I told her. I went to my uncle's in Memphis and changed my name to Cleveland. We told everyone I was his widow. I was you know."

"I know," I said. Without a doubt.

She squeezed her eyes tight as another tear slipped free. "They told me he didn't care. Or he wouldn't have done that to me."

"He cares." More than she'd ever know. Unless I could come out with it. How did I even begin to explain? She might not even believe me. But her hope, her eternal happiness may be at stake.

I had to try. My voice caught. "I have a friend —" That wouldn't do. I braced myself and came out with it. "I can communicate with spirits." *Damn it, damn it, damn it.* "Johnny asked me to find you, to give you the ring. He loves you with all his heart."

I wished I could take it back. At the same time, I yearned for something concrete to say to her, to prove

I wasn't blowing smoke. I supposed this is where psychics got labeled as frauds.

But she hung on my every word. Thank goodness. So I added, "he says you're his one true love." She deserved to know.

She simply nodded, swallowing hard. "He's mine as well."

CHAPTER SIX

"I thought you wanted a table," Melody said, as I flopped back onto the new-to-me purple couch in my parlor.

I leaned my head back. "This feels so much better," I said, running my hands over the velvet.

As soon as we'd removed Maime's ring from the display case and returned it to her, the disturbance stopped. I only hoped that meant Maime had begun believing again, that Private Cleveland had found her. I'd stopped by the next day and the day after that, but he hadn't returned to the bar.

I'd try again tonight.

In the meantime, Julie had given me a choice of any item from the store and I'd said, "couch" before I could change my mind.

I didn't regret it.

I could read here. Sleep here. I never needed to stand up again.

"Verity," Frankie called from the back door. "You need to see this."

"In a minute," I responded. Or perhaps never.

He shimmered into view next to me. "You have guests."

I didn't think he meant the physical kind.

"Okay," I said. It was the only thing that could have moved me. "Come on," I added to my sister as I lurched off the heavenly purple velvet.

"Just you," Frankie said. "You'll want to do this right."

I followed him through the kitchen and out to the back porch. Just past the apple tree, Johnny and Maime Cleveland stood by my lake. He shimmered in black and white. She appeared as the girl I'd seen in the yearbook photo.

Maime had passed.

She wore a simple blue dress, with her dark hair curled around her face. Pretty as a postcard. Her image appeared in transparent color, as newly deceased spirits did.

I couldn't help smiling as I approached.

"I hope we're not intruding," she said, clutching her hands to her chest, her ring sparkling with an ethereal brilliance.

The fact that she had it now meant she'd likely died wearing it. I was thankful all over again that I'd had the chance to return it to her, that she'd get to keep it with her forever.

"I was wondering what happened to you two," I said, stopping in front of him. Johnny had his arm wrapped around her waist and grinned like he'd won at life.

He had.

"It's hard for her to appear," he said, as the smiling Maime flickered. "She hasn't been here long."

I should have looked in the obits instead of the shop.

She gave him a shy, excited kiss on the cheek. "Thank you," she said.

"It was my pleasure," I told her. It truly was.

I watched as she shimmered away. He followed.

"We did good," Frankie said, as if he'd been behind this from the start.

I'd forgotten he was next to me. "Feels nice, doesn't it?" Maybe there was a lesson in this for him as well.

"Yeah," he said, "because now that I got you ghost hunting, we can get paid next time."

I sighed. It had been worth a try.

He drifted toward the porch. "Now come on. Melody is heating up the lasagna she made for you."

I headed back to the house with him. "You know she didn't really…"

"Yeah, yeah. I got it," the gangster said.

"Right," I smiled. I appreciated it all the same. "Let's go."

Maybe Frankie was right. Perhaps I could do this again. After all, I'd been given a lot of gifts in life, and I didn't intend to waste them.

Enjoy more of Verity and Frankie's adventures in the Southern Ghost Hunter mysteries by Angie Fox

GHOST OF A CHANCE

Chapter One

The smell of fresh-baked sugar cookies filled my kitchen, and the tinny sound of Frank Sinatra singing "White Christmas" echoed from my outdated iPhone. Behind me, the ghost of a 1920s gangster hovered while I pulled the last hot tray from the oven.

"Move. I don't want to burn you," I said automatically, realizing only afterward how ridiculous it sounded. Any object—hot or otherwise—would pass straight through the specter.

Frankie appeared in black and white, his image transparent enough that I could just make out the cooling trays on the kitchen island behind him. He wore a pin-striped suit coat with matching cuffed trousers and a fat tie.

He inhaled as if he could smell the crisp, warm cookies. "That's a killer batch, right there," he observed while I jockeyed around him, "but I gotta tell you, most of the gun barrels are crooked."

I winked, surprising him. "Everybody's a critic."

I'd given in to holiday cheer and let him tell me how to shape the last of the dough, and he'd chosen the things he loved most. Which meant I had a baking sheet full of revolvers, cigarettes, and booze bottles — all oddly shaped because, truly, who has cookie cutters for that sort of thing?

I placed the tray on a rack to start cooling, glad I'd included the surly gangster in my holiday festivities. He was technically a houseguest until I could find a way to free him. Although I had no clue what I was going to do with his contraband cookies.

I couldn't eat them all or explain them away to guests.

"What's next?" he asked before I'd even transferred one cookie off the baking tray, never mind the dough-flecked countertops or the dishes. The man obviously hadn't spent much time in the kitchen before.

"Why don't you go outside and look at the holiday lights?" I suggested. Perhaps that would get him into the spirit of the season.

My sister, Melody, had lent me a few strands of white ones in the shape of magnolia flowers. I'd foraged some lovely greenery from the woods and done up the front and back porches with pine garlands and homemade balsam wreaths. I'd been too broke to buy ready-made decorations, but these looked nicer anyway.

He snarled at the suggestion that he might be entertained by pretty decorations. "I'm Frankie the German," he clipped out, as if his words themselves should command respect. "Men fear me. Women want me."

"I'm very happy for you," I said, trying to straighten out a revolver barrel as I gently transferred the cookies to the cooling rack. "But this is the holiday season. It's the perfect time to take a break from inspiring fear. Try to live a little," I suggested, ignoring his scowl. "How about I finish cleaning the kitchen, and afterward you can challenge me to a game of chess."

Otherwise, he'd get bored and start making cold spots all over my kitchen. It felt nice in the summer, but right now, it would ruin the yeast bread I had rising.

He clenched and unclenched his hands a few times. "All right," he said, eyeing me as he glided through the stove and out to the back porch. His voice lingered in the air behind him. "You know I won't go far."

"Do I ever," I murmured. It was my fault he couldn't leave.

I'd tied him to my land when I accidentally emptied his funeral urn out onto my rosebushes. At the time, I'd believed my ex-fiancé had given me a dirty old vase in need of a good scrubbing or at least a rinse with the hose. But as it turns out, there's a reason why ashes are customarily scattered to the wind or at least spread out a bit. When I poured the entirety of Frankie's remains in one spot and then hosed him into the ground, the poor gangster had become my unwilling permanent housemate—at least until I could figure out how to set him free.

Only two people knew I had a ghost for a houseguest: my sister, Melody, and my sweet, strong almost-boyfriend, Ellis. I planned to keep it that way.

I transferred a cookie shaped like a bundle of dynamite that could have almost passed for a nice grouping of holiday candles, except for the "TnT" Frankie had made me etch into the side.

Frankie had opened up a whole new ghostly world

to me, and let's just say things had gotten a little crazy after that.

I left the tray on the stove to cool and brushed off the well-worn green and white checked gingham apron that had belonged to my grandmother. I tried not to sigh. I missed having a house full of people for the holidays. Of course, Melody had stopped by just this morning, and my mom was coming in town next week.

I began sudsing up the sink and placing my mixing bowls into the warm, soapy water.

If I were honest with myself, I missed Ellis. We'd become close enough that I felt his absence when we couldn't spend time together. He'd been booked solid with family events, and it's not like I could have joined him. Not after I'd broken my engagement to his brother and barely defended my livelihood and home from his vengeful mother.

He'd come by when he could.

And as if I'd summoned him out of thin air, I heard a knock at the door. It couldn't be. I dried my hands on my apron. Melody liked to knock and immediately walk inside. My friend Lauralee, too. I had an open-door policy at the cozy antebellum home I'd inherited from my grandmother. But when no one sauntered in, it made my heart skip a beat.

"Ellis?" I called, making sure I'd turned the oven off. And that my messy ponytail wasn't completely covered in flour. Oh, who cared if it was?

I hurried down the hallway to the foyer and dragged open my heavy front door.

"Matthew," I said, surprised.

The ghost of Major Matthew Jackson of the Union Army stood on my front porch, with his hands clasped in front of him, appearing almost shy. His image wavered and came into sharper focus. I could see the crisp lines of his uniform jacket, along with his high forehead and prominent cheekbones.

I'd met Matthew on my last adventure. Most of the time, I could only see ghosts when Frankie showed me the other side. But Matthew was one of the most powerful spirits I'd ever met, and he could appear to me on his own. He was also one of the more shy ones.

"Is everything all right?" I asked.

Major Jackson didn't get out much and I couldn't imagine what would bring him to my home.

He dipped his chin and glided straight through the glass storm door I'd neglected to open, his mind clearly elsewhere. I stepped back as he entered the foyer.

He stopped when he'd made it barely a few feet inside. "My sincerest apologies for intruding on your afternoon." He gave a formal bow, appearing somewhat awkward in his social skills, but clearly trying his best.

"It's quite all right," I assured him, gesturing him further inside as I closed the door. "My friends are always welcome. What can I do for you?" I didn't know the formalities involved in a late-nineteenth-century house call, and it's not like I could offer him a sherry, so we might as well cut to the chase. Still, I couldn't quite help myself from asking, "Would you like to sit in the back parlor?" just as my mother would have, and my grandmother before her.

Perhaps it was genetic.

He nodded and seemed more at ease with my formal response. I led him through my empty front room to the once-elegant sitting area in the back. The pink-

papered walls and polished wood accents appeared
so strange without the heirloom rugs and furniture
the room had once held. Unfortunately, there wasn't
much left besides a second-hand chessboard, a lopsid-
ed futon, and a purple couch I'd brought home after
solving a ghost-related issue for a local merchant.

Matthew opted for a place on the couch while I
tried to sit elegantly on the edge of the futon.

"I've come to ask a favor," he began earnestly.

Oh my. I crossed my legs at the ankles and sincerely
hoped his favor didn't involve me opening myself to
the spirit world. Yes, I'd been able to do a lot of good
in the few times I'd ventured forth, but it had been
scary and dangerous. Besides, I was a graphic designer, not a ghost whisperer.

As much as it pained me, I had to learn to start saying no.

Matthew cleared his throat. "I would like to locate a
Christmas gift for Josephine."

"How sweet of you." I felt my shoulders relax. That
didn't sound frightening or dangerous, and I was
glad to see a relationship developing between the two
ghosts. They'd reconnected during my last adventure.
He'd been hurt and so very alone. She'd been shy and
had suffered terrible luck with men — until that fateful
night in the haunted woods. It had been rather romantic. "I'm sure Josephine would love anything you
decide to give her, as long as it's from the heart."

Josephine cared about him for who he was, which
was a rarity in Matthew's life. His own family had
disowned him for joining the Union Army, and the local ghosts hadn't made him feel welcome in the afterlife for the same reason.

He glanced away before his gaze found mine. "She

means everything to me," he said, with an urgency most women only dreamed about. "That's why I want to give her my mother's opal necklace. Before the war—" he cleared his throat"—my mother said I could have the necklace when I found the girl I wish to marry."

"Oh, Matthew." I drew a hand to my chest. "You're going to propose?"

"At Christmas," he said simply.

I felt myself go a little teary eyed for them, for that perfect connection where you *just knew*. How wonderful for Josephine. She'd waited a hundred and fifty years to be loved like that.

"I just need you to get me the necklace," Matthew said.

I blinked back my tears. "What?"

He leaned forward, resting his elbows on his knees. "It's at my family estate, now occupied by the seventh generation of Jacksons."

Oh, I was familiar with the Jackson compound on the edge of the county, with its twenty sprawling acres and huge main house, occupied by his real, live descendants, none of whom would be pleased if I showed up and explained that the spirit of their great-great-great-uncle needed a family heirloom, a jeweled necklace for that matter, and I'd just be taking it…

"Why don't you go get it?" I suggested perkily. Most spirits couldn't interact with the living world, but Matthew's unusual strength made him an exception.

Like he hadn't thought of that.

Matthew's gaze dropped. "I can't," he said simply. "My mother told me I could never go home. Not after I signed my enlistment papers."

I wished I could hug him. "Oh, sweetie," I began. "Are you sure that's not all in your mind?" It had to be. I knew it was. But if he hadn't been able to get over it for more than one hundred and fifty years, I didn't see how I could make it happen tonight in my parlor.

He stood abruptly. "I'm not part of the family anymore." His shoulders heaved. "She said so." He took two paces away from me, as if he couldn't even face me as he added, "She'd never let me in the front door and I don't think I could handle even trying."

"I understand," I said, coming to my feet. I wanted to help. I did. But, "I don't know what I can do."

"We could steal it," Frankie said from above my left shoulder. I jumped as the ghost shimmered into view next to me. Sometimes I think he did it for fun. "I can have us in and out of there in two minutes," he reasoned. "Five if they try to foil us with a cannonball safe."

"I can't steal an antique necklace," I balked.

"Don't worry," Frankie said, opening his hands, as if this were old hat. "I'll teach you how."

Learning how was *not* the issue. "You don't even know why we're doing this," I pointed out.

"Fun?" the gangster guessed.

Matthew turned to face us, clearly vexed by Frankie's questionable morals.

He'd better get used to it.

"There's no need for stealing," the late soldier insisted. "The necklace is rightfully mine. And it's on the ghostly plane, so none of my living relatives would even know."

That meant someone had died with it. "Does your mother have it?" I asked, taking a wild guess.

Matthew gave a slow, sad nod.

Frankie crossed his arms over his chest, frowning. "That's a lot less fun," he said, eyeing the other ghost, as if he'd let Frankie down. "I see where this is going."

So did I. Matthew wanted me to borrow Frankie's powers to see the other side, something I'd promised I wouldn't do again.

It wasn't only that I put myself in danger every time I opened myself to the ghostly plane, but I had to use Frankie's spirit energy to do it. The unnatural energy flow temporarily weakened him to the point of making parts of him disappear. Plus I used the opportunity to do nice things for other people.

Let's just say Frankie wasn't a fan.

"I don't believe my mother is a vengeful ghost," Matthew assured me. "Although I haven't spoken to her since I left to enlist. Even though she's angry with me, I don't think she'd go back on her word," he added hopefully.

Frankie eyed him up and down. "Anything else in her stash? Something to make it worth our while?"

"Frankie!" I protested. "We don't blackmail our guests."

"Technically," he said, holding up a finger, "it's extortion."

Hmm. "What if Matthew lends me *his* powers?" I asked. Then Frankie would be off the hook.

My guest drew back. "Oh, I most definitely could not," he said, as if I'd shocked him. "Josephine would be so very jealous."

Frankie huffed. "So this guy gets to have both a girlfriend and his powers."

He needed our help. I turned to Matthew. "How

can we be sure your mother is still in her home?" She might have concluded her earthly business and gone to the light. And if that happened, she would have taken everything she'd died wearing with her, including the necklace.

Matthew strode to the old marble fireplace and rested a hand on the mantel next to Frankie's urn. "I still go home every Sunday. I watch my family from the yard. My mother still lives in that house."

Today was Sunday. "Did you check today?" Frankie pressed. He and I both knew ghosts weren't great at marking time.

Matthew turned to us. "I saw her through the window right before I came to you. She was upset. There were loud people pulling up in cars and vans. A party supply truck ran straight through me."

"That's right," I murmured. This was the last Sunday before Christmas. The Jackson family had been hosting their annual Christmas party on that same day every year for seven generations. "It's the day of the big party."

"It is." He lowered his eyes. "She was so busy with everyone else she didn't see me. She never sees me."

"I'll talk to her," I said quickly, and over Frankie's most inappropriate cursing. "Maybe I can get her to speak with you."

"No," Matthew said, clenching his hands at his sides, "I did the right thing. I'm not going to pretend otherwise or beg for her forgiveness. But I won't let her go back on her word about the necklace, either. Ask her for that. Please," he added, softening. "I have a new life now. That's all I want."

"Okay," I assured him. "I'll slip in tonight, during the party." Lord knew how, but I would.

"You think about asking me?" Frankie frowned.

"Yes, I did." I planted a hand on my hip. "Frankie, would you like to go to a legendary holiday party?" I could take him out of my house if I had his urn with me.

The gangster frowned. "It'll probably be full of stuffy society types."

"And ghostly ladies," I added cheerily. "I hear they love gangsters."

"I would be hard for them to resist," he agreed grudgingly.

"Then it's settled," I told him. We'd figure out a way into the Jackson's holiday party. We'd speak with the spirit of Matthew's mother.

I'd get the necklace for him and more. Somehow, I'd find a way to give the soldier an even better Christmas than he could imagine.

CHAPTER TWO

It turned out our way onto the Jackson property was through my best friend, Lauralee.

She shot me a grin as we rattled through the tall front gates in her husband's beater truck. "I always said you'd be a great server given the right opportunity." The cranked-up heater tousled her wild auburn hair. "I'm so glad you decided to try it again."

I drew my bag closer to me, the one with Frankie's urn inside. "I promise I won't be too friendly," I told her, only half kidding. She knew full well how I'd been fired from the steakhouse in college for talking to the customers too much.

"I just can't believe I got this job," Lauralee gushed. "The Jacksons have always used the big catering service from their country club for the annual holiday party. Lucky for me, the club backed out at the last minute." She appeared positively giddy at the idea of proving herself. "I'm so relieved you were available to help."

Me too. "I'll do good," I told her. "I promise."

I couldn't let Lauralee down. This job meant too much to her. Plus, she didn't know a thing about my ghost-hunting abilities. It wasn't the sort of thing I could easily explain—or count on her to believe. Besides, I'd promised myself I wouldn't do it again. Except for tonight.

She'd managed to slip me into a front-room server position, the kind I'd need if I were going to go looking for Matthew's long-dead mother. The money would be welcome as well. The least I could do was return the favor by being a bang-up worker bee when I wasn't ghost hunting.

"It'll be easy," she assured me. "I prep the appetizers in the back. You and the other servers put them on trays and give them out in the front."

I bit my lip. Before I started serving, I'd have to find a place to stash Frankie's urn. It's not like I could carry it on my appetizer tray.

Lauralee laughed. "Relax. You look almost scared."

"Concerned," I admitted as we traveled up the long driveway flanked by oak trees that had grown for generations. Their branches stretched over us, forming a canopy of naked, gnarled wood.

It must have been heartbreaking for Matthew to grow up in such a rustic, beautiful place and not be allowed back. If I'd lost my home like he did, I'd do anything for a chance to go home again. Especially for Christmas.

The house loomed ahead, a stately red brick manor with an elegant black iron two-story porch and a sharply curved circle drive clearly built for carriages instead of cars. This was nothing like the brand-new, faux-historic home of the Wydells, the other leading family in the county. I found it refreshing, if a bit dark and broody. If I recalled correctly, it had been built in the early 1800s, when the Jacksons began their iron-smelting dynasty. They'd added onto it over the years until it became this big, sprawling hulk of a building.

No telling how many ghosts lingered from seven-plus generations living and dying on the property. It would have been nice if Matthew had offered some guidance on where to look for his mother.

Frankie remained quiet and out of sight, hopefully saving his energy for our big night.

I reached down into my bag and rattled Frankie's urn a bit.

"Stop it," he groused. I turned and found him in the backseat of the cab. The corner of his mouth tipped up as he looked past me toward the house. "Get a load of that," he said, straightening. "Hot little number at five o'clock, rising up out of the ground and ready to party." He flashed me a grin. "This is her lucky night."

I raised my brows at him. *Focus.*

"Don't give me that look," he admonished, straightening his tie. "It has been far too long since I so much as danced with a dame." He pulled a flask out of his jacket pocket and gave it a small shake, as if to test how much booze he had left. Must have been enough because he grinned and took a long swig.

That was all fine and dandy, but, "I need to see the other side," I mouthed to him, twisting my features so he'd know I meant business.

"Relax," he snarled. "Geez-o-Pete. You got that same bug-eyed, grindy-mouth thing going that Suds's old lady used to give him when she'd catch us brewing gin in her washing machine. And you ain't my old lady." He slicked his hands through his hair, which never moved anyway. "You owe me this night out. And before you have puppies, I'll let you see my side of the fence. But that's all you get. After that, you're on your own. I'm going to party like it's 1929."

"Knock yourself out," I told him. Heaven knew Frankie wouldn't help if he didn't want to, so it wasn't a big loss to let him have an evening to himself.

Lauralee turned to me, her brow scrunched. "What?"

"Just psyching myself up," I told her, ignoring the ghost spit-shining his shoes in the backseat as she pulled the truck around the side drive.

Several cars lined the parking area to the rear of the house. Lauralee ground the truck to a stop and shoved it into park. "You'll do great, as long as you stay focused."

She had no idea.

I stepped out of the cab as an unearthly energy settled over me. It prickled against my skin. I closed the truck door and tried not to fight the dull throb that worked its way through my muscles and bones. Frankie's power felt forbidden, unsettling. Other ghosts had told us we shouldn't be bending natural laws like this. But at the moment, I didn't have a choice—not if I wanted to help Matthew.

A gray, shadowy form took shape directly in front of us, on the stairs leading to the back entrance of the house. It was too small to be Matthew.

I watched as the shadow formed into the figure of a corseted woman in black. She appeared to be in her early twenties and wore a Civil War-era dress with a lace veil, which floated behind her. She gave us a long look before she walked straight through the red brick wall of the mansion.

"You see her eyeing me?" Frankie asked, straightening his tie. "I think I need to give her daddy something to worry about." He didn't wait for my answer. Instead, the ghost of the gangster simply disappeared. Well, that solved one problem.

I headed to the back of the truck to help Lauralee unload the food. We carried it up the back steps and into the kitchen from the staff entrance.

"Wow." I whistled as we entered the large, modern kitchen. It was done in whites and grays with sleek granite countertops and appliances. The space bustled with activity and smelled like a high-end restaurant. "Nice office."

"I know, right?" Lauralee said as we unloaded our food trays on the huge kitchen island. "I could get used to this."

Tall polished wood cabinets stretched up to the high ceilings and into the narrow butler's pantry sandwiched between the kitchen and the dining room. A counter ran down the right side of the room, with cabinets above and below to store dishes and entertaining supplies. Living, breathing, black-clad bartenders counted glassware under the watchful eye of a ghostly butler who stood directly behind them.

At least they had no idea they were being judged.

One of Lauralee's friends from the diner stacked trays of savory meat pastry puffs beside a tall double oven while another made shrimp cocktails in mini martini glasses garnished with fresh dill.

"What took you so long?" asked the redhead making desserts. "We're almost done with our assignments."

"That's how I planned it." Lauralee winked. "You

both remember Verity."

We did a round of friendly greetings as the two women focused on their tasks. "Kim and Jen are serving after they finish with prep," Lauralee explained. "Mike and Steve work construction with my hubby, but both of them bartended in college."

The men in the butler's pantry grunted their hellos while hefting a large tub of ice out the swinging door and into the party area.

"You can put your purse under the table," Lauralee said, pointing to the personal items crowded underneath a dining table stacked with food service containers and serving trays. "And then help me unload the cold appetizers."

I left my purse with the heap of personal belongings under the table, but first I withdrew Frankie's urn. It was the only valuable thing in my simple hemp sack. If I lost it, well, I'd lose him. After a moment of consideration, I snuck it behind the trays on the table so no one would accidentally drop it.

One of the bartenders leaned in the door that separated the butler's pantry from the party. "Showtime," he said, rapping a hand on the edge of the door. The greetings and laughter of partygoers echoed behind him. "We've got guests arriving early."

"I got this," the redhead said, finished with her shrimp cocktail martini glasses. She grabbed a tray and began loading them up.

I took a tray from the table and moved to the center island to load deviled eggs with truffles, while the blonde handling the meat puff pastries took her hot-and-ready goodies over to the table and arranged her tray there.

All the while, I could hear the sounds from the

party growing louder. We were suddenly behind and we hadn't even started yet.

"I get why you didn't worry about me talking," I said to Lauralee, who slid a platter of bacon-wrapped shrimp out of the bottom oven. "There's no time."

My friend grinned. "It's like a dance," she said, watching her two friends bustle toward the door while I worked harder on my half-loaded tray.

I glanced at them enviously, my admiration ending when I saw what the blonde carried on the center of her tray. Frankie's squat, copper urn perched in the middle of a grouping of mini beef Wellingtons.

"Why did she take that?" I thrust out a finger, pointing as the door swung closed behind her.

Lauralee glanced over her shoulder too late to get a good look. "Centerpiece?" She was almost done with her tray. "Sometimes, clients leave things out for us to use."

"Not that." I gaped.

"Why?" Lauralee grinned. "Was it ugly?"

Not exactly. The green stones that circled the top were sort of pretty, but that wasn't the point. Although I couldn't quite figure out how to explain my shanghaied gangster and the dented copper urn to Lauralee.

"Keep moving," she reminded me gently.

"Right," I said. I needed to get out there before Frankie got a look at the blonde with the tray.

How did these people work so fast?

I loaded my deviled eggs as quickly as I could. I had to get out there and get Frankie's urn back. The last of his ashes—the only ones I hadn't rinsed away—were inside that urn. If they were spilled or lost, I'd never be able to take him out of my house again.

We'd both go bonkers.

When I had filled my tray, I plastered on my best, most waitress-worthy smile and hefted my holiday appetizers. "I'm going in."

With any luck, I'd locate Frankie's urn, speak to Matthew's mother, retrieve the necklace, and please all the party guests in one trip. Stranger things had happened, right?

Just then, a tray crashed to the floor outside and I heard something shatter.

Chapter Three

The ringing echo made us cringe.

Oh no.

Frankie! I rushed for the door, and when I reached it, I nearly ran smack into the redhead coming the other way.

The door swung closed behind her. "It's not my fault."

"You dropped your tray?" I demanded.

"Yes." The redhead touched a shaking hand to her forehead. "Some joker in the parlor hit me between the shoulder blades with an ice cube. Shocked the heck out of me."

At least it wasn't the blonde. I swung the door open with my hand and searched the dining room for the wayward waitress with the urn amid her appetizers, but I didn't spot her among the glittering society folk.

Meanwhile Lauralee took the ruined tray and placed an arm around her friend's shoulder. "What a jerk. Are you okay, Jen?"

"Yes," the redhead said, rallying. "I'm a pro. I'm fine." She reached for a tray of bacon-wrapped shrimp. "Mike is cleaning up," she said, heading past me out the door.

At least Frankie was okay for now.

As if he knew I was thinking about him, the gangster shimmered into view directly in front of me, blocking my path. He held his flask in one hand and a cigarette in the other. I would have hugged him if I could, even though he stood frowning. "This ain't no party. It's a funeral." He pointed the end of his cigarette at me. "You owe me the real McCoy."

Ah, he must have struck out with the young woman we'd seen earlier. I scooted around him and peered out through the swinging door. Only a few ghostly guests stood in the dining room, speaking in hushed tones. They did seem a bit older and stuffy, but that wasn't my fault. "I'm sorry this isn't your sort of crowd. But try to make the most of it, okay?" You could bring a gangster to a party, but you couldn't make him enjoy it.

Frankie followed me and my deviled eggs out into the large, ornate dining room. When I had Frankie's power, I could see things as the dominant ghost residing on the property did. This dining room appeared Victorian, with a fire blazing in the hearth, and the current generation of Sugarland's upper crust conversing in groups. An antique table stood at the center of the room, and over it hung a ghostly chandelier with dozens of blazing candles. It made the jewels worn by the real guests glitter.

These were the types of parties I used to attend with my ex, before the scandal that had left me an outsider in my own town.

I paused as an older man in a reindeer bowtie winked at me and took a deviled egg from my tray.

Frankie stood next to him. "I tried to work that cute skirt we saw before. Found her in the parlor," he said, as if I wasn't busy working. "She's got that whole Southern belle thing going on. But she only had eyes for some dead guy."

I hesitated to point out the obvious.

"Have you seen Matthew's mother?" I murmured, advancing through the crowd.

Frankie took a drag from his cigarette. "Yeah, and I knew it was her because she's wearing a name tag."

I heard another crash, this time from the direction of the front hall. I tried to keep my own tray balanced as I rushed to see what happened.

The redhead knelt at the entrance to the parlor, frantically scooping up bacon-wrapped shrimp. I hurried to help her.

The guests had shrunk back from the mess, but make no mistake, our fumbled trays were the talk of the party. At this point, I feared more food had ended up on the floor than with the guests.

"Somebody tripped me," she whispered frantically as I knelt down beside her. "I swear!"

Her friend walked out of the parlor, with Frankie's urn teetering at the center of her half-filled tray. The gangster glared at his last resting place, then at me as if I were responsible for him becoming a centerpiece. "That dame lifted my urn!"

"What do you expect me to do?" I hissed.

Frankie didn't hesitate. "Shoot her."

Luckily, the redhead and the blonde were too worried about the mess to notice me and my not-so-friendly ghost.

"I'll help you two in a second," Frankie's urn-napper said, maneuvering around the mess. She leaned down. "They're complaining that the food is cold," she said in a harsh whisper before heading for the kitchen.

"I'm on you like a tick, lady!" Frankie gnashed, following her.

Oh, heavens. He'd better not appear to her.

Quickly, I gave the redhead my deviled eggs and took the ruined shrimp tray. I hurried after the blonde and Frankie and the urn.

When I got to the kitchen, I found all three. And poor Lauralee. She stood wide-eyed, staring at her friend. "You didn't cook it all the way?"

"It was piping hot when I took it out of the oven," the blonde protested.

I touched the tray in her hand, ignoring the ghost directly behind her. "The whole thing is freezing."

She handed it to Lauralee and looked about ready to tear up. "I don't know how to explain it."

I could.

The cold sensation at the back, an accidental tripping, chilled appetizers. It all pointed to unhappy ghosts—ones with an even bigger beef than my gangster buddy—and I had a feeling I'd find them in the parlor.

"I'll keep serving, and try to calm any ruffled feathers," I told my friend. It's not like I could locate Matthew's mother or her necklace while standing in the kitchen.

Unfortunately, me being on the case didn't seem to reassure Lauralee. "Don't start talking to everyone," she warned.

"I won't." Not to everyone at least.

"Take this," Lauralee said, handing me a tray of artfully arranged holiday cookies on gold doilies.

"And this," I said, knocking a few beef Wellingtons loose as I freed Frankie's urn from Kim's tray and placed it squarely in the center of my own.

"Hey," Lauralee said, "isn't that…"

I hurried out of the kitchen, with Frankie on my heels.

"It's not a decoration," the gangster groused

Still, he seemed relieved that I had it. Me too. If we were taking on any more ghostly exploits, I'd have to find a better way to carry Frankie's urn. But for now, it was safe.

Guests snagged my cookies as I worked my way to the parlor. As far as I could tell, all of the disturbances had happened there. I couldn't imagine what I'd find.

"The Jacksons have terrible luck with catering," a woman in a clingy red dress said, waving away my tray as her well-built date grabbed two mini sugar bells and a chocolate chip. "The club could never get anything right, either. Last year, the entire buffet table went over. They said it had to be an uneven floor."

It was more than that. No wonder the club had dropped this event from their annual calendar.

I cringed as the woman's date dropped a handful of beef Wellington wrappers into Frankie's urn.

"Hey," the gangster hollered as the man walked away, "that ain't a trash can!"

I forced myself to smile at the finely dressed party-goers, thankful that none of them could hear Frankie's outburst. Although several did shiver from the chill.

"Focus," I whispered as we stepped past the giant, unlit Christmas tree and into the parlor.

The temperature plunged twenty degrees. Oh my.

"Welcome to the anti-party," Frankie murmured.

The country club crowd clustered in groups, sparser than in the other rooms, but still fairly thick. That probably had a lot to do with Mike and John serving drinks at the bar just inside the door. I gave them a small wave as I passed and soon realized that not everyone was celebrating.

A group of ghostly women huddled near the huge bay window overlooking the front yard, weeping. Heavy velvet curtains draped a good portion of the glass, making the room feel stifled and dark. In the light of the fading sun, I could see Matthew standing outside in the yard, looking in. He was counting on me.

Party guests walked straight through a grouping of empty overstuffed chairs at the center of the room and didn't notice the large black casket standing open near the wall opposite the window.

A casket. I halted for a moment, shocked.

"It really is a funeral in here," I murmured.

"That's what I've been trying to tell you," Frankie groused.

Wreathes of lavender and freesia draped the casket. Dozens of tightly massed floral monstrosities packed with roses, daisies, peonies, dahlias, and even pearls and fruit crowded the casket on either side. Not to mention the small mountains of ferns.

"Do you know who died?" I whispered to the gangster at my side.

Frankie perused the room half-filled with the living, half-filled with ghosts. "A lot of people from the looks of it."

As usual, my sidekick was no help.

Holding my tray aloft, my fingers shaking only slightly, I made my way to the casket.

Yards of tufted white silk lined the top and splayed

over the front edge. A pair of stuffed white doves clung to the rim. It seemed the deceased had been well loved.

If Matthew's mother lay inside, it would certainly make it easier to find the necklace, although I wasn't sure how I felt about taking such a thing from her coffin.

If it was even her. It could be a ghost with a different beef. I took a deep breath and tried to calm my racing pulse. If there was an angry ghost inside, we might as well introduce ourselves and get it over with.

I stared down into the casket and gasped.

Matthew.

He lay in state, his eyes closed, his face so waxy and formal it almost didn't look like him. He'd been stripped of his union officer's uniform and instead wore a severe black suit with a white shirt and collar. He looked so still. So *dead*.

I gathered my courage and leaned close.

"Matthew?"

The form in the casket didn't respond and I wondered if I was looking at my friend at all or merely an image of him. This may only be a memory, a view from the eyes of the most dominant ghost in the room.

He'd told me that he wasn't allowed back inside his house anymore, and I'd seen him alone in the yard. Which meant...

Just then, a handsome All-American guy I recognized from one of my ex-fiancé's golf foursomes brushed past me, laughing with another guy our age. I started as they strode right into the space where Matthew's body lay on the ghostly plane.

"Excuse me," I began, but before I could say anything else, a heavyset woman in black rushed him.

"Show some respect for the dead!" she hissed, slapping him on the cheek.

Her blow passed straight through him, but as it did, I saw his fingers loosen around his glass. "Hey," he said, staring down at his drink. "This hot toddy is freezing."

No kidding. I could see the beginnings of ice on the rim.

"Go get another one." His friend laughed, holding up his near-empty mixed drink. "And grab something for me, too."

The ghostly woman fumed under her black lace mourning veil. "This is a funeral, not a party." She tried to take Mr. All-American by the scruff of the neck.

He touched a hand between his shoulder blades. "Criminy. I think the air just kicked on. Are we under a vent?"

"Excuse me," I said again, this time trying to catch the ghost's attention.

The guy with the hot toddy shot me a winning smile. "I remember you, Verity." He drew closer, smelling faintly of cigars and scotch. "Does Beau know you're a waitress now?"

I didn't like his attitude. My ex had nothing to do with this. And besides, "Are you saying there's something wrong with being a waitress?"

He shot me a cocky grin. "I just didn't know if I was allowed to talk to the help."

"Actually, you're not," I said, pretending to regret it, glad when he barked out a laugh and resumed the conversation with his friend.

I drew closer to the ghost woman, who had begun

to weep, and resisted the urge to offer her a comforting touch. She didn't seem to be wearing a necklace, although I couldn't tell from her high collar. I pitched my voice low, for her ears only. "Are you Matthew's mother, by chance?"

She turned her head and stared at me, tears shimmering on her cheeks. The blank look in her cold and lifeless eyes sent a chill straight down to my toes. "Matthew is dead."

Chapter Four

I had to cut the ghost some slack. She was in pain. Even if her mere presence sent chills up my spine and made my fingers numb with cold, I had a job to do.

Courage.

This ghost was powerful, just like her son. I couldn't afford to upset her. We didn't need any more incidents like last year's overturned buffet table. But if I could get her to listen to me, I might be able to make things right for her, for Matthew, and even for poor Lauralee back in the kitchen.

Mrs. Jackson stood over Matthew's coffin, keeping vigil.

There was no good thing to say, nothing that would make it better, so I said what I felt in my heart. "Mrs. Jackson, ma'am, I'm so sorry for your loss."

I couldn't imagine how it might feel to lose a child, even if he did consider himself a man. Matthew couldn't have been more than twenty-two or twenty-three when he died. He'd had so much to look forward to in life.

A portion of the anger drained from her as she turned back to the coffin that held her son. "He's right here," she murmured, stroking his cheek. "For as long as I stay with him."

Matthew's mother had been reliving his funeral and loving him for more than 150 years. And all that time, Matthew had been locked away in the basement of the library, thinking nobody cared. It didn't have to be that way.

"Can I show you something outside?" I asked her.

"No," she said quickly. "I don't even look outside. My life is in here now. With my boy."

Then he'd have to come to her. "Your son was very brave," I said softly, as his mother nodded.

But would he have the courage to come home?

I had to try.

"Will you excuse me?" I asked the ghost.

Matthew's mother nodded graciously, and I hurried to the front door.

Matthew had believed his mother no longer wanted him after she threw him out of the house. Even now, he stood on the lawn, convinced he wasn't welcome, when she'd mourned him since the day he died. And likely even before that.

I hurried out onto the porch, tucking my empty tray under one arm and Frankie's urn under the other. "Matthew!" I called, trying to spot the ghost on the darkening lawn. His image strengthened, glowing in the moonlight, and I rushed to where he stood.

"Do you have the necklace?" he asked, looking me over as if he expected me to produce it.

"I didn't get it yet," I said, watching him deflate. "But I spoke with your mother. She misses you, Matthew," I said, even as he pressed his lips together and shook his head no. "Please. Go inside and you'll see."

"Shame on you, Verity," he uttered before he disappeared.

Oh, darn it. "Matthew?" I searched frantically for any sign of the ghost.

His voice hit me like a punch to the stomach. "Do not meddle in my affairs," he boomed, sounding like a dangerous stranger instead of my friend.

"I'm sorry," I told him. "I realize I overstepped. Badly. But you deserve so much more."

He didn't appreciate the effort. "Bring me the necklace. That's all I ask."

"Matthew —"

"The necklace." His energy washed over me, forcing me a step back, making me cringe at the malice and the anger I hadn't felt from him since the first time we'd met, back in the haunted library.

"Okay," I said softly.

We'd find another way.

Quickly, quietly, with my heart nearly beating out of my chest, I returned to the chaos of the house. The noise assaulted me as soon as I opened the front door.

The redhead spotted me from the dining room and rushed toward me, carrying a tray. "We're backed up in the kitchen. Take these." She handed over a serving plate of mini beef Wellingtons.

"Déjà vu," the gangster muttered as I cleared a space for his urn.

"I'll be in the parlor," I told her.

I knew Frankie would follow if for no other reason than to make sure I didn't drop his urn.

"I don't know what to do," I whispered to him. "Matthew's mother hasn't so much as glanced outside in a century and a half, and he won't come in. How do I get them together?"

"Don't bother. Just do what he asked and get him the necklace," Frankie muttered.

"That won't solve his problem," I said as the gangster rolled his eyes. "There's way more at stake here than a necklace."

We needed to do more.

Matthew needed to know his mother loved him, and I was going to make that clear to him even if it was the last thing I did, even if I had to drag her outside to do it.

Wait. That wasn't a half-bad idea. Without the dragging part.

"Whatever you do, make it fast," the gangster warned.

His left foot had disappeared. Dang.

"Follow my lead and I'll take you to a real party," I said to the poor gangster, pausing to allow a guest to snag three mini beef Wellingtons.

We approached the entrance to the parlor and saw Matthew's mother stalking a man who was about to kiss his date under the mistletoe.

I breezed past them in the doorway, knocking them apart before the ghost could do anything worse.

"Mrs. Jackson," I said, inwardly cringing when two live women turned to me. It seemed to be a common enough name around here. And both living Mrs. Jacksons would think I was nuts.

"Did you see that couple?" Matthew's mother fumed, her black veil askew. "Kissing at a funeral!"

"Terrible," I agreed, hoping to calm her down.

The live Mrs. Jacksons raised their brows and moved away from me, whispering over their wineglasses.

Lovely.

The dead Mrs. Jackson made a sign of the cross.

We needed some privacy. Soon.

I approached the live Mrs. Jacksons and hoped one of them was the matriarch. If I wasn't mistaken, it was the sixty-year-old blonde with the large diamond earrings. "Isn't it about time for the annual tree lighting?" I asked her, trying to keep the desperation out of my voice.

She seemed surprised at the question, most likely because it was a waitress asking it. But she did think it over. "Is it dusk already?" she asked, looking past me toward the bay window. "We usually do it when night falls."

Close enough. I cleared my throat. "Ladies and gentlemen," I called out, addressing the partygoers in the parlor. The live ones. "Now that it's getting dark, Mrs. Jackson has requested that you please proceed to the foyer for the annual tree lighting!"

"Thank you," she said, still a little taken aback.

Anything to keep everyone happy.

As the crowd chatted and filtered out, I approached the bartenders. "You guys, too. Mrs. Jackson needs this room cleared." The dead Mrs. Jackson, at least. "She's very adamant about it."

The taller one gave a shrug. "Come on," he said to his coworker, "let's take a smoke and then start restocking." He gave me a wink. "These people are drinking scotch like it's water."

I pasted on a smile and hustled them out, closing the pocket doors to the parlor.

The ghost kept up her vigil at her son's coffin. The room had quieted, save for the roar of the party crowd outside.

Slowly, delicately I approached her. I was careful to keep my voice low and my hot hors d'oeuvres at arm's length. "Mrs. Jackson," I said gently, "I have some news for you and it may be quite shocking." I paused, giving her time to adjust. "Matthew died, but he's not gone, not in the way you think. I can arrange for you to see him."

She seemed pained by the news. "I know I'm dead," she said slowly. "It doesn't make a difference. We'll never be together again."

That surprised me. The way she'd been grieving, I'd expected her to think death still separated them.

She lowered her gaze. "I still can't see him, no matter how long I stay. He's never coming back," she said simply.

"What would you do if he did?" I asked her gently.

She gave a small smile. "I'd tell him how sorry I am. For everything I said." She shook her head. "For all the things I didn't do. For how unhappy I made him."

"He's at peace now," I told her.

"He's gone," she corrected me softly.

"Listen, Mrs. Jackson," I said, drawing as close as I dared. "You've spent the last hundred and fifty years in mourning because you believe the son you loved is truly gone. I'm here to tell you, you can believe in something else."

Matthew's mother kept her head lowered, her veil shielding her expression.

"Please," I added gently. "Let yourself believe that your son still loves you. I've spoken with him, and I know it's true. He would give anything to be with you again, but he needs to know you feel the same way." I moved slowly to the window, and to my immense relief, she drew to my side.

"Matthew is right outside. Look," I said, directing her gaze at her son.

With shaking fingers, she lifted the veil from her eyes. And for the first time, she saw.

* * *

"Matthew!" She burst straight through the window and out into the yard.

He appeared startled as she threw her arms around him and let him feel her love for the first time in more than a century. It took only a moment's hesitation for him to return her embrace.

I cracked a window, glad for the scene unfolding in front of me.

When Mrs. Jackson finally let go, he stepped back, bewildered. "I…I haven't changed my mind about who I am or what I believe."

She took his hands in hers. "I always loved you, son, even when I was angry. I'm sorry I didn't know how to show it, and that we left things the way we did."

His face crumpled. "Me too, Mom."

They hugged each other tight once again.

Frankie materialized beside me. "I see what you did there."

"Yes," I said, feeling a little wistful. Matthew had just taken a big step to being welcomed back to his old place among the dearly departed of Sugarland. I knew how hard it had been on him to be excluded. After all, I was going through a bit of the same.

"Let's let them be," I said to my gangster buddy as I closed the window once more.

Was it me, or had the air in the parlor warmed a bit, even with the cracked window?

I stood next to Frankie and watched as the casket and the ghostly image of a lifeless body began to disappear.

"Keep the flowers. I have use for them," Matthew said, passing through the closed pocket doors, escorting his mother. With the weight of their separation off her shoulders, she appeared at least ten years younger than before.

I could feel the difference in the atmosphere beyond the parlor as well. It felt lighter inside the house, more festive.

His mother ran a hand down his arm, as if she still couldn't quite believe she had him back. "You never liked flowers before."

"No." He grinned, motioning me over. "But there's someone I'd like you to meet, and she positively adores roses."

He plucked a bloom from a standing wreath as Josephine stepped in through the window, her hair done up in an elaborate braid, her white gown trailing behind her. She looked stunning, yet confused. She brought a hand to her chest, glancing around her. "Matthew, I never would have thought to look for you inside."

"Josephine," he said, taking her hand, "I'd like you to meet my mother." The women exchanged a formal curtsey, and I saw Josephine stifle a gasp. "Mother," he said, still holding Josephine's hand, "this is the girl I love with all my heart. She's everything to me." Josephine blushed at his bold words, but that didn't slow him down a bit. He motioned me forward, including me in the moment as he turned to Josephine. "I can't find your father to ask his blessing, so I'll ask you directly. Will you do me the honor of becoming my wife?"

Tears welled in her eyes as she brought her hands to her mouth. "Yes! Oh, goodness, Matthew. Yes!"

He took her hands in his, beaming, as his mother reached behind her neck and unhooked her necklace. She drew it out from under the high neckline of her mourning gown, a stunning opal necklace set in silver, and presented it to Matthew.

He held it as if it were the queen's jewels. "I thought you might have forgotten."

"It's as much a part of this family as we are." She gave a small smile. "And as Josephine will be."

Matthew placed the heirloom jewel around Josephine's neck while she glowed with excitement and love.

His mother drew a black lace handkerchief from the pocket of her dress. "I can't believe I have you back at last. And now a daughter as well." She dabbed at her eyes. "Although look at this dress," she added, gazing down at her mourning gown. "It's so somber."

The heavy black gown began to shimmer until it changed into a gorgeous silver ball gown, with ribbons on the sleeves. The mourning veil faded, and in its place, Matthew's mother wore a sparkling rhinestone comb in her hair.

"Much better for a holiday party. Or rather, an engagement party." She leaned close to him. "You should wear your dress uniform, dear."

Matthew's face crumpled at her acceptance and he nodded, his uniform shimmering from basic blue to a double-buttoned formal blue coat with a silk sash around his waist and the epaulettes of a major in the

Union Army.

Josephine just about swooned and I didn't blame the girl. With tears in her eyes and quite a bit of determination, the white nightgown she'd worn since I'd known her began to morph into a beautiful gown the same color as Matthew's uniform, as if she wished to honor him. Or perhaps simply let everyone know who belonged with the handsome Yankee.

A cheer echoed from the foyer. The live partygoers must have lit the tree.

The air had warmed; the holiday music sounded brighter.

The pocket doors slid open and I watched as guests—both alive and ghostly—began to filter back into the room.

Matthew's friends and relatives greeted him warmly, patting him on the back and shaking his hand, while the women made a fuss over Josephine and her engagement.

Laughter erupted from a group of live guests at the bar and warmth bubbled up inside me. Everything was going to be okay.

"Merry Christmas," I said to Frankie.

"This might actually turn into a real party after all," he mused.

I couldn't fight back a grin. "I think so."

I held up my tray and left the ghosts to their celebration. It was time to focus on the party for the living.

"Now that's a good beef Wellington," said a man in a red suit jacket as he left a crumpled wrapper on my tray and reached for another appetizer. "Warm and flaky."

"Thanks," I said, brightening. "I'll pass your compliments to our caterer, Lauralee Clementine. She loves to do big parties like this."

He nodded as he downed another appetizer. "Good. Because every other year has been a disaster."

"But not this year?" I prodded.

"I wasn't sure at first," he said, "but it seems our new catering company has saved the day."

I nodded and offered a delicious appetizer to his companion, and the woman beside her, and the next grouping, until I'd collected a few more compliments for Lauralee and her amazing food.

Soon the blonde and the redheaded server followed the crowd into the parlor, and we served the rest of Lauralee's delicious treats until every Mrs. Jackson in the place declared the party a success.

Later that evening, Lauralee handed me a glass of leftover wine as I helped her clean the kitchen and pack up her supplies.

"This turned out to be one nice party," she mused, taking a sip as the ghost butler tried in vain to hand her a linen cocktail napkin. "I was really worried for a while there."

"You have the touch," I said, holding up my glass to her.

"A toast, then," she countered. "To Christmas and to friendship."

"And to love," I said, clinking our glasses together, knowing that friendship and family, love in all its forms, was something to be celebrated — in this life and the next.

Enjoy more of Verity and Frankie's adventures in the Southern Ghost Hunter mysteries by Angie Fox

GENTLEMEN PREFER
VOODOO

CHAPTER ONE

Amie could barely see her customer as the woman lurched toward the counter, arms loaded with a voodoo love spell kit, fat pink altar candles, a well-endowed Love Doll, a twelve-pack of Fire of Love incense, and "breath mints," the woman huffed. She dumped everything on the mosaic countertop and reached for the Altoids display, a nervous smile tickling her lips. "Not that I expect all of this to work right away."

Amie couldn't help laughing as she caught a super-size bottle of Heat Up the Bedroom linen mist before it rolled under an arrangement of Good Fortune charms. "You never know."

Her customer couldn't have been more than forty, with gorgeous green eyes, a warm, well-rounded face, and a lonely heart. Amie could see it as clearly as the glow-in-the-dark Find Your Lover charm at the top of the heap.

Well, Amie had just the thing.

She closed her eyes, blocking out the pink and

green painted walls and loaded display tables.

Wind chimes at the back of the shop swung in circles. Their limbs, carved from bayou swamp trees, clacked together.

She let her magic well up inside her, vibrant and sweet. "Now." She reached across the counter and found the woman's hands. She eased up, let it come as the power flowed through her. "You'll find what you need."

She squeezed once and let go. Once was all it took.

That's when the growling started.

It began as a low rumbling at the back of the shop and continued until a thin line of smoke seeped from behind the Voodoo Wash Yourself Clean soap display.

"It's a faulty heater," Amie said, well aware that it was July. "Ignore it."

"Sure," the woman said, watching Amie pack her purchases into two overflowing bags. "Some of this is bound to work, right?"

"Voodoo can be very powerful," Amie said, "if you believe."

Amie smiled to herself as the door swung shut against the sweltering New Orleans heat.

Flower petals and grave dust sprinkled down from the spell bundle she'd hung from the vintage tin ceiling. Made from an old family recipe and wrapped in her lucky green scarf, it warded off evil spirits and helped cut down on shoplifting.

Amie scooted around the counter, her bracelets jangling as she smoothed back her thick black hair.

"Okay, you big, bad beast, you can come out now."

A red leathery creature the size of a swamp cat burst out from behind a display of bath fizzies. He resembled a small flying dinosaur. "By thunder and

lightning and Papa Limba," he said with a thick
Congo accent, blowing out a breath as pink and white
begonias threatened to land on the tip of his beak.
"You are giving your magic away to people off the
street?"

Isoke was small for a Kongamato. His wingspan
was only about three feet. He had leathery skin, gorgeous blue eyelashes, and all the tact of a battering
ram.

"You need to stay on your perch." At least while
customers were in the store. "What if that poor woman had gone back for another Mango Mamma bath
melt?"

"Go dunk your head in the Jiundu swamp. I am
not here to be a ceiling decoration." He sniffed at his
usual place, where he hung upside down near a display of rainbow-colored wind socks.

His eyes glowed yellow. "I am here to protect you,"
he said, flaunting two rows of razor-sharp teeth.
"Maybe next time I will bite the woman. That will
keep her from robbing you."

"My magic is freely given," Amie insisted, straightening the bath fizzie display. She might not mind
grave dust on her floor—that had a purpose. But the
rest of her shop was immaculate.

The dragon watched her with a guarded expression. "Amiele Fanchon D'Honore Baptiste, you waste
your magic. It's bad juju. First, your mother and now
you."

Amie's back stiffened at the insinuation. Her mother had lived fast, died young—and left Amie very
much alone. Well, with one rather obnoxious exception.

"Your mother wasted her love magic on a legion of

worthless men. You give yours away to strangers. In three hundred and eighty-six years, I have never seen anything like it."

"You're being unfair." She refused to look at him. Instead, she busied herself rearranging a sagging display of gris-gris bags near the front of the shop. The bright red and yellow bundles contrasted against the hot pink walls and silver posters of Erzulie, the spirit of love, and Papa Ghede, lord of the erotic. "Mom gave her love magic away to men who didn't appreciate it," she said, with more than a twinge of regret. There had been many, many men.

"And she received none of it back," he replied, his voice low in his throat. "I watched her waste away. I'm not going to watch you too."

Amie fingered a Fall in Love bag before stuffing it back down with the rest. "Ah, but there is a difference. I am getting bits of magic back. You don't think I'm going to feel that woman's happiness? She might not know what I did, but every time someone is grateful, it filters home."

"Crumbs," Isoke declared. "You need a man, someone who will take your love magic and give his to you tenfold."

Amie's stomach dropped as she tidied an already perfect row of voodoo history books. "I've tried that."

She'd dated. None of the men fit the bill. New Orleans was a wild city, and she wasn't going to lash herself to some beer-guzzling party boy just to save a little magic.

"When? When did you last see a man?" the Kongamato prodded.

Amie opened her mouth to answer.

"A man you trusted with your love magic?"

Her smart answer died on her lips.

"Nine years." Her stomach twisted at the realization. *Nine years* since her last boyfriend. And, no, he hadn't returned her love magic. If her mother was any indication, men never did.

Isoke cocked his head. She felt his hot breath against her leg, even through her gauzy yellow skirt.

"Look, I'm fine the way I am. I don't want to worry about when some guy is going to call or how to act on a date or whether he's going to turn into a cretin if I let him get too far."

"Eeking out a life is not fine." Isoke huffed like a blast furnace.

"Stop it," Amie admonished, "you're going to singe the floor again." She couldn't keep throwing rugs everywhere. Her landlord was suspicious enough when he found the hot tub in her back storage room full of muddy water, sticks, and Spanish moss. You could take the Kongamato out of the swamp, but you couldn't take the swamp out of the Kongamato.

Just then, a group of giggling teenagers burst through the door. Isoke froze mid-snarl while Amie went to help them. After they'd left, loaded down with passion fruit incense, Amie returned to her display. Isoke resumed his grumbling, his tail dragging along the floor.

"Stop it. You're messing up the grave dirt."

"Even your dirt is organized?"

"Yes." It had to lay where it fell. "What kind of Kongamato are you?"

"One who is about to lose his tail."

"Excuse me?"

"For three hundred and eighty-six years, I serve. I help the women of your family fulfill their destinies as women of voodoo. But with you? I get stressed. You do everything wrong. And when I stress, I molt."

She planted a hand on her hip. "So your tail is going to fall off if I don't go out with some rum-swilling boozehound?"

"Yes. I mean, no." His wide nostrils quivered. "You do not go out with a boozehound...you go out with a man!"

Amie rubbed her fingers along the bridge of her nose to tamp down the dull ache forming there.

Did she really have to discuss her dating life with her dead mother's mythical monster?

No. She didn't owe the Kongamato anything. Not after he blew flames out the upstairs window last week. Sure, he'd managed to lure a half dozen firemen into Amie's bedroom, but she'd had a devil of a time explaining how seven 911 callers had been mistaken about the fire.

Too bad for Amie, Kongamatos were as stubborn as they were loyal. "I worry about you," Isoke said, following her. "This is not natural. The women in your line—they are passionate."

"I am passionate," she said, fighting the urge to stuff him in a doggie carrier and mail him back to Zambia. "Look at this store. This is my passion." Couldn't he see what she'd done here?

She was darned proud of it.

Every detail was perfect. Everything was in its place.

His yellow eyes drilled into her. "The women in your line are women of action."

What did he want from her? "You know what? The women in my line are gone. Mom is gone. You have me now. This is how I am and I like it."

He studied her for a moment. "No. You are unhappy."

"I am happy!" she shouted.

"That's better," he said, utterly delighted as Amie
clapped a hand over her mouth. She never yelled.

Amie waited to make sure nothing bad was going to come out before she spoke. There was nothing
wrong with being in control. "Okay, it's not that I
wouldn't like a man in my life." Who wouldn't, right?
"I'm just not going to settle for anything less than
perfect."

Isoke growled.

"And no more firemen."

He rolled his eyes. *Drama queen.*

Amie selected a Love and Happiness candle from
the shelf next to the organic bath oils and lit it. "See?
Look. I'm starting already."

Isoke landed on the multicolored countertop next
to the candle, clipping a wing on the cash register.
"Eyak. This store was not made for Kongamato."

Amie managed a weak smile. "I didn't know I'd
inherit you so soon."

"I could not save your mother, which means I will
try doubly hard with you." He folded his wings like a
bat. "Please, for the sake of my tail, you must consider
it."

Amie ruffled the three stiff feathers on the top of his
head. "For you, Isoke. I will try."

* * *

Nine years. The shop had been busy all afternoon
and still she couldn't get it out of her mind.

She hadn't had a date in nine years. Amie closed her

cash register and said good-bye to the young couple who had just purchased a fertility doll and an extra large bottle of sandalwood massage oil.

She had to think of something else. Her eyes settled on the poster of Papa Ghede, laughing and cavorting with his latest conquest. Yeah, that didn't help.

Okay, so it had been a long time—too long—but Amie had been busy. She'd graduated college, opened her own shop, fixed up the apartment upstairs. The second floor had needed a lot of work. Her landlord had used it as storage. It still had the French-style mirrors on the ceiling from its glory days as a bordello. Okay, so Amie had left the mirrors. But she had done a lot of other things to the place.

It's not like many people held down jobs and decorated their apartments *and* dated, right?

Hmm… Maybe she did have a problem.

She glanced at the Kongamato settling in on his perch. He hung from the ceiling, folding his wings around him like a giant bat.

She hoped Isoke wasn't the type to gloat when he got his way.

True, she would never be able to bring herself to go out with any of the men she saw up and down Bourbon Street at all hours of the day and night. And she definitely didn't want a man like the kind her mother had dated. They might appear nice at first, but all of them were drunks, gamblers, or cheaters in the end.

Luckily for Amie, she knew another way.

She fingered her blue and silver beaded necklace, a Do Good charm she'd fashioned years ago. *My power is both a gift and an obligation. Let good works flow through me.* She'd been using her spells to help her customers find love. So why hadn't she used it on herself? Because men were brash and unpredictable; and often dishonest.

But what if she could eliminate the risk?

She'd tried that once, with her last boyfriend. He'd been nice and safe, soft and accommodating, with an average build and eyes that focused on ESPN more than her. He'd never surprised her, never challenged her, and when he left, she hadn't cared.

While she was quite pleased that she hadn't been hurt like her mother, Amie also knew she'd wasted her time.

But if she went about this smart, perhaps she could welcome some passion into her life—without the pain. She could actually let herself feel, dream, give her love with absolutely no fear that he'd break her heart.

She could summon Mr. Right!

He'd know how to act, know how to dress, and know how to please her. He wouldn't complicate her life.

At last she'd have someone to spend her evenings with, to walk the French Quarter with, someone who might want to eventually try out the mirrors over the bed. The mere thought of it sent a skitter of anticipation down her spine. Yes, the Kongamato had a point. Perhaps it was time to voodoo herself a valentine.

* * *

Amie locked the shop early that night, feeling nervous, as if she were heading out on a date. Ideally, the spell should be performed at sunset. Of course Amie knew better than anyone that love spells took time, and they only worked if a girl was ready to accept love into her life.

Was she ready?

Amie already loved her shop, and her life. But, still…there had to be something more.

She turned off the metal, industrial-style VooDoo Works sign outside and punched in the alarm code. With the waning sun and soft security lights to guide her way, she gathered a single sheet of thick white paper and two quartz crystals from her private stash. Then she ducked under the counter to find her odds-and-ends box.

She'd put together a selection of colorful jewelry-making kits a while back and had kept the extra weaving thread…"Here," she said as her fingers located the red and black strands.

Amie swallowed her excitement as Isoke, bathed in shadows, stirred on his perch.

She hoped she could finish before he woke up to go hunting. If she was smart, she'd wait until after her Kongamato was gone for the evening. But Amie didn't know how long her courage would last.

Isoke sank back into his slumber, a bit of drool sizzling down onto the floor. She was never going to get her security deposit back at this rate. She slid a copper incense burner under him and fought the urge to straighten the three rumpled feathers that stuck out from the top of his head.

She eased into the back room of the shop, closing the Employees Only door behind her.

The cloying incense was stronger back here, mixed with the heady scent of beeswax altar candles. Isoke's hot tub hummed in the center. On two sides of the room, wooden shelves held boxes of merchandise while drying herbs hung along the third wall. In the very back, under a small stained-glass window, stood a humble wooden altar that had been her great-grandmother's. Amie touched the battered surface reverently as she laid out her spell ingredients and closed her eyes.

The air was thick and warm. She inhaled deeply, letting peace wash over her. To anyone else, this might have looked like a highly organized, if unusual, storage room, but to her, it was a special place. Here, she was surrounded by the things she loved.

Crickets had begun to chirp outside. Paired with the earthy bubbling of Isoke's hot tub swamp, Amie almost felt like she was back in her grandmother's old stilted house on the bayou.

Amie focused on the affection she felt for her mother, her grandmother, and all her ancestors. These women had passed along their power, their strength, their passion—their love.

Love.

Amie lit the fat red altar candles.

She relaxed, letting her mind take her where she needed to be. She saw her perfect man—cultured and refined. He was lean, yet strong. He was passionate, determined. He wouldn't drink to excess, like her mother's men had. He wouldn't lie, cheat, steal. He wouldn't leave. No, he would wrap his strong arms around her and keep her safe. She could almost see him in her mind. Almost. It was as though he was barely out of reach.

Amie cracked open one eye. The spell would work better if she were naked. Amie wasn't particularly fond of stripping in her storage room. But if she was serious about finding the right kind of love—and she was...

She adjusted the altar candles, tested the weight of her crystals, her stomach twisting with indecision. She was stalling and she knew it.

Slowly, her fingers trailed down her sides and found the edge of her cami top. Her breath hitched as she drew it over her head. The bra soon followed, along with her flowing yellow skirt and her hot pink panties.

Amie ignored the cool breeze along her back as she ripped the paper, shredding it into two rough hearts. She placed them together and, her voice hoarse, chanted, "I call on Erzulie, loa of the heart; Papa Ghede, loa of passion; my ancestors, women whose blood boiled strong with the love of their men."

She now saw her ideal man clearly in her mind's eye. He had a small scar above one arched brow, dark brown hair clipped short and tight, and the most arresting blue eyes. Strange that she should see him so clearly. Sharp recognition wound through Amie.

She gasped. He seemed to be looking right at her.

She drew the crystal against her bare chest, the roughened stone teasing her smooth skin, sending shivers down the length of her body. She could feel the vibrations in the gemstone as she lowered it over the paper hearts.

"Send to me…" She paused. *The man I just saw.* In her haste, she hadn't quite decided how to word her request.

She knew the more specific the better, but really, she didn't care if he had that square jaw or that rugged look about him.

She wanted someone she could love.

How hard was that?

Amie swallowed. "Send to me," she said, her voice

husky, "the *perfect man* for me." She needed someone kind, loving, *hers*.

A man she could give her love magic to without being afraid.

Her stomach tingled at the thought.

Slowly, she wove the black and red threads into a homemade ring. All the while, she filled her mind with thoughts of love in its purest form — passion, giving, acceptance.

"The perfect man for me," she repeated, tying off the ring and slipping it onto her right ring finger. She was careful to blow out the candle in a single breath before gathering up the hearts.

The room was nearly dark, which meant the sun had almost slipped under the horizon. Good. Because Amie was naked and she still had to bury the torn hearts.

She hesitated at the back door. This was the French Quarter, but still, what would the neighbors think?

Do it fast.

Amie double-checked the key in the pocket of her skirt before throwing the whole thing over her shoulder. She slipped out into the back alley, squinching her nose at the smell of old beer and garbage.

Never mind. The spell was complete. The burial only sealed it.

Luckily she kept a flowerpot filled with consecrated earth for that very purpose. Now if she could only keep Mrs. Fontane down the way from filling it with geraniums. Amie reached past the roots of the plant and buried the torn hearts deep.

"Earth to earth. Dust to dust."

Now all she had to do was wait.

Chapter Two

Amie took a long, hot shower and changed into a simple white nightgown. She traded her contacts for glasses and eased onto the edge of her wide four-poster bed to comb out her hair. Amie loved her bedroom, with its gauzy white drapes and comfortable furnishings. Everything in here was well-used and loved.

She'd chosen the smallest of the three upstairs rooms as hers because it was the only one that faced the back of the house. She liked to forget she lived smack dab in the middle of Royale Street, in the heart of party central.

The old bordello's main boudoir had become Amie's living room — or given the bookshelves that lined every wall, her library. She'd converted the rest of the space into an efficient kitchen and eating area.

Amie smiled to herself as she slipped into bed. Perhaps before long, she'd have to set another place at her bright yellow kitchen table.

She'd just about drifted off to sleep with the latest Charlaine Harris novel when three distinct knocks echoed through the house.

"What the—?" She scrambled upright and managed to bump her glasses off the end of her nose and onto the floor.

The knocks sounded again.

"Isoke?" Amie scooted out of bed, using her toes to locate her glasses on the hardwood. Leave it to the dragon to be dramatic. It's not like she hadn't taught him how to disable the alarm.

Bam. Bam. Bam.

"Coming!" She shoved on her glasses and hurried for the back stairs. No telling what mythical monster fists could do to her back door.

Isoke claimed Kongamatos were bad with numbers. Well, if he couldn't memorize a simple alarm code, she had a good mind to install a perch outside.

Bam. Bam. Bam.

"Hold your tail," she said, flicking on the lights and punching the alarm code on the back door. "If you can't remember how to let yourself in the house or to stop leaving muddy Kongamato tracks on my floor or dead mice in my shoes or—"

Amie flung open the door and gasped.

A man stood on the slab of concrete that was her back porch. Not just any man, either. Broad shoulders, tousled dark hair, a small scar above his left brow—he was the man from her vision.

His lips quirked in a smile and he gave her a heated look that would have melted her into a puddle on the floor, if she'd been susceptible to that sort of thing—which she was not.

He strode straight for her, cupped her face in his hands, and kissed her.

The rush of sensation shocked her, and making her

utterly incapable of thought. At least that was her excuse for not pulling away.

Perhaps just one moment more…

His touch stirred something deep inside of her, an urge she hadn't even known was there. So this was what sheer desire felt like.

She couldn't talk, could barely think as he wound his fingers through her hair. Her body collided flush with his. Her skin tingled.

He groaned deep, his hands sliding down the exposed skin of her arms, leaving goose bumps in their wake. He smelled earthy and elemental. Real. And she was a powerful, sexy voodoo mambo. Wild pleasure shot through her as she wound her arms around his shoulders.

She wanted to feel him, connect with him. No man had ever affected her in such an intense and immediate way. She'd never let one get close enough.

But now here he was, the man from her vision, and he was just as mind-blowingly real as she'd imagined. He slid his hands down to the small of her back, tempting her closer, until she could feel him—every bit of him—against her.

It was the craziest thing she'd ever done. He was a complete stranger and yet he made her want to do things that she hadn't let herself think about in years.

He nipped at the sweet spot behind her ear.

He must have just gotten up in the middle of the night and come straight to her. It was insane.

"What are we doing?" she gasped.

His hands circled her waist as his lips touched her collarbone. "Finding each other," he said, his voice husky, his Spanish accent pronounced as he turned his impossibly blue eyes up to her.

Amie traced her fingers over the solid line of his jaw. Deep down inside, she wanted this.

"My one true love," he murmured, drawing her in for a slow, sensual kiss.

Mmm…it was crazy talk, of course. These kinds of things didn't happen, especially not to Amie. But she wouldn't argue. Not at that moment. She could pretend, for maybe a little bit more.

She melted a little with every touch of his lips. She wound her fingers through his short dark hair. She gripped his muscled shoulders. She slid her hands down his back, past the sweat-slicked skin at his waist, to where his pants should have been.

If he'd been wearing pants. Amie gasped as her hands closed around his bare butt.

By Kalfu's gate! This Adonis of a man was as naked as the day he was born.

Amie broke the kiss, her eyes darting over his wide shoulders, down his well-built chest, past the narrow stretch of hair that began just below his belly button, to where she should not have been looking at all.

Heat shot through her. "I'm sorry," Amie said quickly.

Great juju, the door was still open. She slammed it behind him, averting her eyes a little too late as he strolled past her into the storage room. The space suddenly seemed quite a bit smaller.

He didn't seem to be bothered at all by his complete lack of clothing. Why should he be? The man had a lot to be proud of.

Don't think about it.

Amie shoved her hair out of her eyes and adjusted her glasses. He was going to turn around again. She had to at least pretend to have it together.

She scanned his handsome face, strong chest, flat abs—dang. Her eyes just had to go there.

"Forgive me," he said, noticing her completely inappropriate stare. "I've never appeared naked at a woman's door." He ran a hand down his chest. "Or naked anywhere, for that matter."

"Believe me, it's all right." No doubt the spell had hastened him to her doorstep at a most inconvenient moment.

She felt the color rise to her face. "How about we find you something to wear?" she said, reaching for the first thing she could get her hands around—a silk wall hanging of le grand zombie, a very powerful snake spirit.

Who said the voodoo gods didn't have a sense of humor?

Her mystery man wrapped the green and gold cloth around his waist like a towel. Amie wished she could close her eyes. If anything, the fabric accented him in some very interesting places.

"Much better," he said, double-checking the knot.

If he only knew.

She'd asked for moonlight walks through the French Quarter, not this.

"Why on earth were you—"

"Naked?" he asked. "Not the best circumstances, I admit." He reached for her, and frowned when she dodged him. "Still, when you think about it logically, you cannot expect clothes to survive almost two hundred years."

She didn't get it right away. Perhaps it was his startling presence or the heat in her cheeks or the fact that he'd said, "two hundred years?" Amie stammered.

He tilted his head. "Are you all right?"

She took two steps back, thought about it, and took two more. "By Ghede." She wiped at the cold sweat on her brow. Her mouth felt dry. Amie took a deep breath and asked the question she really, really didn't want the answer to. "Where did you come from?"

"You called me," he said, as if that explained everything.

Dread hung heavy over her. She'd asked for her perfect man. She didn't call anyone from anywhere. In fact, she was hoping she'd meet a cute guy in church or maybe over a beignet at Café Du Monde.

"I'll ask you one more time," she said, as calmly as she could manage. "Where did you come from?"

He took a step toward her. "St. Louis Cemetery Number One."

She froze on the spot. "Oh no." She blinked hard. "You're," she forced herself to say it, "dead."

He stood inches away from her, dark, brooding, and sexy as sin. "Not anymore."

Her heart sped up. By Papa Legba, what had she done?

This was unnatural. This was wrong. She'd misused her magic in the worst possible way. How could she be so irresponsible?

"Thank you," he said, touching her cheek. "You do not know how long I have waited for a second chance."

Amie realized she was gawking, but she couldn't help it.

She'd spent her life promising herself she'd never repeat her mother's mistakes. She'd never date men who gambled her money away, who lied, who cheated. No. Her man would be different.

And he was.

She'd called him from the grave.

Chapter Three

He brushed her hair out of her eyes. "It's okay, Amie. It's not every day you meet your ideal partner. This is overwhelming for me too." He leaned down to kiss her.

"Stop it," she croaked. He wasn't her better half. He was a mistake. And how did he know her name? Of course. She'd called him. She'd asked for him. She'd practically given him her cosmic Social Security number.

Think. She needed to think.

He stepped back, giving her space. "I could use a bath." He brushed at his muscled arms. "Grave dust." He caught her gaze and held it. "Or once you calm down, perhaps we can take a bath together."

"Oh no," Amie stammered, "out of the question." She wasn't letting this man take one more step into her shop or her house, much less into her bathtub.

He gave her a hungry look. "Of course I will marry you before I bed you."

Amie crossed her arms over her chest. He had to be

kidding. This man wasn't going to walk her down the aisle. He was going back to the earth.

Then she was going to take a long, cold shower and never date again.

While she was mentally reprogramming her life, he slipped past her into the shop.

"Stop," she ordered as he clanged into the bowl she'd set down to catch Isoke's drool.

Amie flipped on the lights to find her Spanish love god inspecting her colorful display of gris-gris bags.

"Hands off," Amie said.

"Of course." He nodded, looking at her as if she was the one in the towel.

Amie wrinkled her nose at the smell of singed... floor. The Kongamato drool!

With one eye on her man, she rushed to the counter for a rag.

"Can you wait in the storage room?" she asked, her rag smoking as she sopped up the mess he'd made.

"There's no need. I'm much more comfortable in here," he said, touching off a set of wind chimes. "I find your store utterly fascinating. Very well done, mi corazon. Beautiful and colorful, just like you." His fingers closed around a glass bottle with a bejeweled skeleton label. "Florida water," he said, turning the bottle sideways and watching the shaved orange rinds—her family's special ingredient—float through the liquid.

"Give me that." She dropped the rag and shoved the bottle under her arm. "And I'm not your love," she said, retrieving the rag with two fingers and depositing it in the trash. "This is a big mistake."

Huge.

Her grandmother had told stories of voodoo mambos calling zombies, mostly to work in the fields at harvest. One particularly powerful voodoo queen asked for a bodyguard and gained a mobster with a price on his head. Little Mickey was killed (again) as soon as he set foot in New Orleans. It was considered gutsy to call a man from the grave. Rarer if one came, and even though the undead looked — and acted — like their human selves, to her knowledge no one had ever tried to date one.

The zombies lingered until they'd completed their task, and then they returned to their graves.

Well, she didn't want this love zombie to do anything for her — or to her. She had to put him back and end this mess.

What she needed was a neutralizing spell.

She'd have to look one up, but right off the bat, she knew she needed Florida water. She glanced at the bottle under her arm. Check. She'd need a pair of black candles...

Amie took two candles from the display next to the counter. While he browsed the books for sale, she grabbed a pink and yellow striped bag off the hook behind the counter, tossing the ingredients inside.

She'd need grave dust. She looked her zombie up and down, from his strong jaw to his wide toes. "I think we have that covered."

"Ah, The Complete Illustrated Kama Sutra." The blue of his eyes deepened as he gave her a smoky look.

Amie stomped up to him with her hand out. "Give it back."

He grinned. "The spine is creased." He flipped through the pages. "Right here. Do you look at this book sometimes?"

"It's available for the customers," she insisted.

The next time Isoke had any great ideas about finding her a man, she'd tie his beak shut with a fire hose.

He examined the Moon position. "Now that looks interesting," he said, his fingers splayed wide over a couple having a lot more fun that Amie ever had. She felt the heat rise to her cheeks.

"Stop it. We're not doing Kama Sutra. We're not going to fall in love. I don't even know you."

"I wouldn't be here if we weren't meant to be together," he said, as if he was informing her of the weather or how the Hornets had played the night before. "Would you like me to prove it?"

"Only if you can do it without any more kissing," Amie said flippantly.

He closed the book and placed it back on the shelf, seeming to forget about the Moon, the Lotus, and the rest of the positions she couldn't quite get out of her head. "Come. You will go with me back to my grave." He took her hands in his and kissed them.

"You know what?" Amie said, removing her hands from his grip. A plan of her own had begun to take shape. "You have a good idea. Let's go see where you were buried." She really didn't want to put him back to earth right here in the storage room. There was the matter of the body. Or his bones. Or whatever would be left of him. She couldn't just carry him down Canal Street and back to the cemetery. But if she could follow him back to his grave, it would be like zombie express delivery.

His face lit up. "Excellent. No one has visited my grave since the Cleveland administration."

"You have to wait right here while I get ready, okay?"

"Absolutely." He resumed his assault on her bookcase, one hand at his waist holding his silk wrapper closed.

She paused on the bottom step. "I'll also find you something to wear."

Amie almost asked him what he wanted to show her at his grave, but stopped herself. She didn't want to be any more involved in his undead life than she had to be. Besides, she'd put him down as soon as they arrived. "Be back soon," she said, taking the steep stairs as fast as she could manage.

"During that time, do you mind if I remove a few geraniums from the pot outside? We'll be passing my grandmother's crypt on the way in."

"Knock yourself out," Amie called. She'd prefer her zombie outside anyway.

Amie dashed into the library and found her spell book. She flopped it on the kitchen table. "Zombie... zombie care, zombie feeding, zombie summoning...

On rare occasions, the dead can be called with a spell in order to assist with a task.

Ah, so that's what her love life had come down to. A task. Evidently, his job had been to kiss her silly.

A zombie will deteriorate and die again once it has fulfilled its purpose or once the voodoo mambo no longer requires its services.

Well, Amie didn't require his services. And she certainly wasn't going to let him fulfill his purpose — not if he thought it meant becoming her one and only. Or marrying her.

She flipped through the book again and pressed her finger to a final entry, "zombie termination." She made a mental list of the ingredients she needed before shoving the book in her bag. Digging through her kitchen drawers, she found a flashlight and a box of matches.

Amie caught her reflection in the hand decorated mirror above her kitchen sink. Her black hair frizzed about her face and her eyes were wide with shock.

"If I get out of this," she told herself, "I will never wish for another date. Because this is what happens." Men were trouble every time.

And undead men were worse.

Amie blew out a breath. She didn't have time to be feeling sorry for herself.

In less than a minute, she'd changed into a long orange skirt and a yellow top. She pulled on her barely used tennis shoes, grabbed him a pair of sweat pants, and headed down for the shop.

"Hi."

"Ga!" She clutched her chest and pitched forward. She fell the last three steps and directly into his arms. He was warm, strong.

She lurched away. "What are you doing? You were supposed to be outside." He didn't feel dead. She remembered what it felt like to have his arms wrapped around her. And his kiss had been downright electrifying. Didn't matter. He was dead.

He eased a lock of hair behind her ear. "Here I am, bursting into your home, ready to marry you tomorrow." He raised a brow. "Or tonight if you know a priest." When she couldn't quite move her mouth to respond, he continued. "Then it occurred to me that we haven't been properly introduced."

Every cell in her body screamed for her to close the distance between them. Feeling his arms around her reminded her too much of how it had felt when he kissed her. That's what she got for making him her first kiss in nine years. Damn the man.

He was clearly wrong in more ways than one. She refused to marry a dead man, or kiss him again. She didn't even want to talk to him.

Amie took a deep breath. *Patience.* She'd made a mistake and she'd fix it.

"I don't need to know your name," she said, inching past his massive form and plucking an extra cleaning rag from under the counter. She'd be glad to have it if things got messy.

"I am Dante Montenegro," he said, bowing slightly, his accent even more pronounced.

Okay, well good. At least she knew what grave they needed to find.

"Put these on." She handed him a pair of her largest sweatpants, the kind with the string tie.

He held them up. "Canary yellow?"

"Beggars can't be choosers."

He ignored her sarcasm like the gentleman he was. "Actually, I used to own a pair of breeches in this very shade."

His civility was making her uncomfortable. "Okay, well just put them on," she said, turning away. She did not need to see his sexy, muscled rear end again. Or anything else for that matter. Plus, she needed one more thing from the shop.

She had to find something of hers that she could burn, dust to dust, ashes to ashes. It should be small, so she could carry it. It had to have been in the presence of magic. "Preferably something I've owned for years," she said to herself, as the perfect sacrifice came to mind. She hated to lose the Lisa Simpson keychain she had looped over the corner of her register, but desperate times called for desperate measures.

Amie stuffed the keychain into her bag.

Let's see, she had candles, Florida water, Lisa Simpson, grave dust, a zombie. She glanced back at the stud behind her. She'd give him one thing — he was the Don Juan of the zombie world.

She shook her head. It didn't matter. He didn't belong here.

"After you," he said, as she led them out into the night.

Chapter Four

Laughter and conversation from the party crowd erupted in waves on the other side of the wall of buildings as Amie and Dante hurried down the alley that led to Canal Street. For the first time in her life, Amie wished she could be one of them, instead of running side-by-side with a hot, dead Romeo through the back streets of New Orleans.

How had she gotten herself into this?

He actually believed he was going to marry her.

If he thought he was going to convince her based on something they'd find in a cemetery at one in the morning, he was even crazier than she'd imagined. No true love of hers would act this way.

This little trip through la-la land was her penance for thinking, believing, dreaming she could step out of her normal life and expect more than she had any right to have. Hadn't her mother taught her that? Her grandmother? The women of her line were destined to be alone. She had to stop listening to bossy red monsters and start behaving like a proper voodoo mambo.

Sweat trickled down her back. There was no escaping the humid heat of New Orleans, even after midnight.

Amie felt a familiar tug as the white stone walls of the graveyard came into view. Her calling as a voodoo mambo gave her a certain kinship with the dead. It was part of the job. Still, she didn't like the way the ingredients in her bag began to stir.

St. Louis Cemetery Number One used to be located at the outskirts of the city, which now meant the edge of the French Quarter. The cemetery closed at dusk to keep vandals and criminals at bay. Visitors were often robbed in broad daylight. Drug deals went down day and night. Tourists were always encouraged to visit in groups.

More than one hundred thousand former New Orleans residents rested inside the aged, whitewashed walls. Most had been buried in the eighteenth and nineteenth centuries. Entire extended families shared mausoleums separated by narrow pathways. Many of the dead had practiced voodoo, and now their power called to her. She'd have to put her zombie down quietly and get the heck out.

Amie kept a hand on her bag as she followed the zombie down the deserted sidewalk past the front entrance, with its tall gate topped by a simple wrought-iron cross. She stiffened as they passed the crumbling tombs inside. A red spiral of energy curled from one of the graves closest to her, the filmy tendril reaching for her.

She'd never seen a red apparition before. Her breath hitched. She really didn't want to learn anything new tonight.

"This way," he said, leading her to an area at the

north edge where the streetlights were widely spaced
and foot traffic was nonexistent. He mounted the
thick white stone wall like a Marine and reached
down for her.

"Oh no," she said, refusing his outstretched hand.
While Amie was all for getting inside, she was even
more interested in having a way out. "Can't we find a
back gate or something?"

"Trust me, my love," he said, his face obscured by
shadows as he reached for her again.

"I'm not your love." She took a step backward.
"And you can't possibly expect me to—eek!" He
caught her by the wrists and vaulted her up onto the
top of the wall.

She pushed against his chest, but it was like fighting with a boulder. "Listen, Tarzan. I don't know what
century you're from, but—"

"Quickly, now." He wrapped an arm around her
waist as they thundered to the ground. She felt the
impact vibrate through his body as her toes scraped
the rocky path on the other side of the wall.

She shoved away from him. This time, he let her.
"You could have killed me!" she hissed. She could
have broken her neck or smashed her head in or—

He shot her a glare. "Death is not something to
speak of lightly," he said in a coarse whisper. "Now
come. We are not alone."

Lovely, just lovely.

Amie glanced back at the eight-foot-high wall. Last
night, she'd been snuggled in bed with a book. Tonight, she was in a haunted cemetery with no way out
and a dead guy telling her what to do.

As they left the shadows of the trees, the moon lit
their path. She followed him, cursing at his firm back-

side as he wound through mausoleums of all shapes
and sizes. The place smelled like mold and concrete
and New Orleans heat. Wrought-iron gates with thick
spikes hugged some of the white stone vaults, while
others lay neglected, their plaster falling away to ex-
pose redbrick skeletons. Still others had sunk into the
ground, their inscriptions worn and barely visible as
the earth swallowed them whole.

Amie paused as she heard men's voices a few rows
away. They sounded tense and angry. Wonderful.
Amie cringed. She just hoped they were grave robbers
instead of muggers. Either way, she didn't want to
run into them.

Dante touched a hand to her shoulder and silently
bid her to continue. Amie nodded. They needed to
keep moving.

The cemetery was alive. She caught another wisp
spiraling skyward, like a paranormal spotlight. It was
a fine time to be trapped.

She held her bag to her side, wishing she was haul-
ing around a ferret instead of restless spell ingredients. The zombie moved silently ahead of her, like a
bloodhound on a scent.

That was another problem. After she put him back
to ground, what was she going to do? Avoid the muggers and the apparitions until the gates opened in the
morning? She certainly couldn't scale the wall.

"Stop," he whispered, reaching back to steady her.

"What?" she rasped, trying to keep her Maglite
from clanking against the bottle of Florida water.

"Dominga Deloroso El Montenegro," he said, bowing his head before a squat white vault. The plaster
had crumbled away around the arched top, revealing
brick and a small cropping of weeds.

Right, his grandmother.

He placed the geraniums on the uneven pavement at the front of the tomb. The moonlight played off his handsome features as he bowed his head. "Que oró por mi segunda oportunidad," he said, "y ahora está aquí."

Amie fidgeted. He'd said something about second chances. Written Spanish she could do. Hearing it out loud could be tough to translate. And she didn't like to think of him having a grandma—or a life.

She studied the other names etched into the gray stone and stiffened as she read the curling inscription dedicated to the memory of *Dante Montenegro 1779–1811. El hombre adoro demasiado.*

He loved too much?

He'd also died too young. Well, she'd known that already. Her stomach quivered. Seeing it in stone made it so real.

His arm brushed hers. "Now I will show you," he said. "You see?" He touched a circular area on the front of his tomb where some of the rock had been chipped away. "It is a symbol of the sun. Placed here when I decided to wait for voodoo to bring me back. You etched it deeper when you brought me back tonight."

She'd never heard of anything like it. Of course, she didn't know any zombie raisers. Amie squinted at the crude carving. It looked more like a squashed bug than a sun. "You think I'm going to fall in love with you because of a defaced piece of rock?"

He flinched as if he'd been slapped. "This is proof."

"Not in my world."

She hated to burst his bubble. Or hurt him, but, she wasn't going to lie, either.

Anger rolled off him. "You want more proof?" He turned back to the tomb and placed his hands on either side of the stone marker. "Fine. I will go get it."

Amie's stomach twisted and her jaw slackened as he lifted the stone away, opening the grave. She wasn't going to ask. She just stared at the gaping hole that led into the crypt.

She wrapped her arms around her as an unwelcome chill seeped through her. She'd called up a man from the dead. Now she was hurting him in ways she'd never imagined. The shocks just kept coming. And the guilt.

On top of that, she was scared to death.

If her ancestors could only see her now.

Amie's fingernails dug into her arms. Please help me fix this.

A cloud moved over the moon and the cemetery plunged into even deeper darkness. She fought to ignore the churning in her stomach, almost glad for the shadows as the zombie crawled back inside his grave.

Scraping sounds echoed from inside the vault as Amie set her bag on the concrete path and unloaded her supplies. This will all be over soon.

Please let this be over soon.

Everything was too dark and too scary and too… dead.

She had to make this right.

Amie quickly lit the black candles and rubbed their sides with the grave dust he'd left on her arms when he touched her. She sprinkled Florida water over everything.

"How's it going?" she asked in a rough whisper, forcing her voice to remain even. She needed to focus her power, but she'd have a hard time concentrating knowing Dante could pop out of his grave at any moment.

A frustrated sigh echoed from the tomb. "I'm having trouble finding it. It's dark. There are many fragile things on all sides."

Yeah, like bones.

He grumbled under his breath. "I am too large. I feel like a clumsy ox."

Amie adjusted her candles, one in front of her and one behind. Their flames created twin oases of orange light. If she did this right, he'd be just another pile of bones.

She closed her eyes and focused her power.

Earth to earth. Dust to dust.

She felt her life force well up inside of her. Amie took her Lisa Simpson keychain and held it over the flame in front of her, watching the plastic smoke and curl.

"I give of my magic," she whispered. "I give of myself. To let this man go back to ground."

Please, let me fix this.

Amie removed the ring she'd woven and dug her fingers into it, separating the black and red strands.

"We are not connected. We are not bound. As it began, so does it end."

She felt the power stir inside her.

She stood slowly.

She almost had him.

Amie approached him from behind, her fingers burrowing into the pocket of her skirt for the two dirty paper hearts she had unearthed from the planter outside her door. She ripped them in half and sprinkled them over the only part of him she could see—a muscular calf and a very large foot. The magic shot off orange sparks where it touched him.

Such a waste, she thought as she willed him back down, into the ground, to the earth.

"Ow!" He banged against something inside the tomb and came out rubbing his head. He brushed the torn hearts away like they were fireplace embers.

"What is this?" He saw her supplies and his eyes went narrow. "Are you trying to kill me?"

Amie's breath hitched. She really didn't want to watch this—watch him turn from a fine man to dust and bones. Her heart tugged.

In his own deluded way, the creature had loved her.

She held her breath. Waiting for the collapse. This was her doing. Her mistake. She owed it to him to watch him go back to ground. As if forcing her to witness what she'd done, the moon chose that moment to emerge from behind the cloud. It shone full once more on the man Amie had condemned.

Amie waited for the end.

And waited…

And waited.

Instead of crumbling to powder, he straightened and stood over her, looking gorgeous and unkempt with a smudge of dirt along his cheek.

Amie stared at him.

Damn the man. He should have been dead. She couldn't mess this up too. She chewed her lip as she ran through her spell in her mind. She'd done it correctly.

So why was he still here?

"I ask you again"—he took a powerful step toward her—"my love." He ground out each word as she took three steps back, scattering her candles across the pavement, "Are you trying to kill me?"

Amie froze. She dug her fingernails into her palms as dread blanketed her. She was trapped. In a cemetery. With the undead. A second later, she snapped.

It was too overwhelming, too intimidating, and frankly—too absurd. "Of course I'm trying to kill you," she said, her voice an octave higher than it should have been. "What am I saying? I'm not killing you. You're already dead! You see your name on that tombstone? I do. Dante Montenegro. Dead."

He gave a mirthless laugh. "What does that have to do with anything?"

He had to be kidding. "It has everything to do with—everything. I can't be with a dead man."

"Ah!" he said, the twinkle back in his eye. "Every couple has issues they need to work out."

"Work out?" Amie stammered. "This isn't a question of whose parents we see on Thanksgiving or what side of the bed you sleep on or…"

"Left," he said.

She rubbed at her temples. "What?"

"I like the left side of the bed." He leaned against his tombstone, clearly amused.

Anger rocketed through her. "Oh is this fun for you? Well, this is not fun. This is wrong. This is unnatural. I don't know how I got this kind of power, or how I called you up, but you are going back into the ground!"

The zombie hitched his thumbs under the waistband of his borrowed pants. "All evidence to the contrary."

Of all the cocky… "You think I can't do it?"

"Your bag is on fire."

"Ohhh!" Amie rushed to where one of the scattered candles had ignited her mother's pink striped sack.

She stomped out the blaze.

If he thought this was the end of their conversation, then maybe he'd been reanimated without a brain.

"Don't you understand?" she said, refusing to even spare a glance at the smoldering remains of the bag. "This is one giant horrible mistake. I'm not kissing you. I'm not picturing you naked." Where had that come from? Never mind. Amie plowed forward. "I'm not marrying you, so you might as well admit that your usefulness has ended and you can rest in peace."

He towered over her, angry now. "You called me," he said, as the night breeze scattered the torn hearts down the narrow path. "You burned a resurrection symbol into my grave."

"I didn't know," she said, her hope for an easy answer spinning into oblivion with those hearts. Even if she chased them down, she'd never be able to recover enough pieces to perform the spell again.

What would it matter anyway? It hadn't worked. Everything in her tidy little world was hopelessly, horribly out of control. And here he stood, all gorgeous and…dead, expecting her to accept that. She just couldn't do it. She raised her chin. "I thought I wanted you, but obviously not you."

He cupped the back of her head, his fingers threading through her hair, drawing her close enough to kiss. "Listen, sweetheart. It's not my problem that you don't know what you want."

Her lips parted. Abruptly, he let her go. He strode past her and took the last lit candle.

"Hey! Give that back!"

"Come and get it, darling," he said, ducking back into the tomb.

Amie wanted to bang her own head against the

nearest vault. What kind of a zombie-killer was she if the zombie started taking her spell ingredients? And she couldn't imagine what she was going to do now that her spell hadn't worked. Now that he knew she wanted to end him. She'd have to find another way to put him down and, frankly, that might be tough.

He eased back out of the grave, looking triumphant, a gold wedding ring in hand.

"You're married?" she gaped. Well, that solved everything, didn't it?

"I was." He placed the candle on the ground and made a move to slip the ring onto his finger. "Now look. It will not fit anymore."

The ring seemed to resist as he drew it over his finger. It stopped less than an inch down, refusing to go farther.

What did that have to do with it? "Maybe your knuckles swelled."

Anger flashed across his face. "No. I can no longer wear this because I have found my one true love," he said, gripping the ring between two fingers, holding the shimmering gold band between them. "That is you. Why do you find this so hard to accept?"

"Oh, I don't know. Because it's impossible?"

He looked mad enough to spit. "It is true!"

"So you say."

"So I know! I feel this with every breath in my body and I will not stop until you understand what it is you mean to me."

Amie's gaze drifted down the path. She had asked for a guy who would stick around. "How did I get into this?"

"Quiet." He stiffened, his eyes fixed out into the night. "Do you hear it?"

Amie strained her ears. Yes. She heard a definite crunching coming from the graves to the left. This was too much. She'd better not have called up a whole army of lovers. How would she explain a harem to poor Isoke? He'd lose his tail and his top feathers too.

Amie crouched closer to Dante's grave. Her breath quickened as she saw two scarlet shadows fall across the path in front of her.

Oh no.

She'd heard of this — residual ghosts called up by voodoo magic. But she'd kept her magic contained.

Until it had escaped down the path.

Holy hoodoo.

How could she have been so careless?

"This is my fault," she said under her breath, warning him. She didn't know what was coming, but it couldn't be good.

He stood next to his grave, waiting. "Quiet. I've got this."

She glanced at the long, dark path behind her. It would feel so good to run. The kicker was, there was nowhere to go. Besides, she had to fix her mistakes. She glanced at Dante. Okay, she'd fix the most recent mistake.

Gripping her bottle of Florida water, she crouched low. One hand curled around the moldering brick tomb. Her heart beating low in her chest as the red shadows grew longer.

They were going to find her. She stiffened, unscrewing the bottle with shaking fingers.

By Papa Ghede! She gasped as a pair of thugs stepped out onto the path in front of them. Their eyes glowed red with possession.

A chill ran though Amie. She's seen the dead possess the living during voodoo rituals. The chwals she knew only allowed themselves to be taken by clean spirits. These men hadn't done as well.

"I believe these are the men we heard before," Dante said under his breath. "Only...changed."

They moved like predators, and they were armed.

"What do they want?" Amie stammered.

Dante hesitated. "You."

As they drew closer, she could see their gang colors and the fiery burning of their eyes. The one on the left snarled, his face a mass of anger and hate.

This was her fault. She'd never dared practice death magic. She didn't know what could happen if it escaped. She'd been too rash in coming here.

Amie's fingers tightened around her blessed water. They were looking straight at her.

She could exorcise the spirits if only she had a bottle of 151 proof rum and a live chicken. Without those key ingredients? She'd have to do the best she could. Amie poured her Florida water onto a patch of dirt, rubbing her fingers frantically into the mud.

"I command you to the earth," she said, low in her throat. She focused her power and dug harder. "I command you to the earth."

The one on the right laughed. It was a hollow, menacing sound. He turned the barrel of his gun toward her. As if the world had slowed to contain only that moment, she watched the thug's trigger finger squeeze tight.

Dante slammed into her as the shot cracked the night air, ringing in her ears. Her cheek hit the ground as she watched blood splash onto the white gravel in front of her.

"Oh my god." She landed hard.

Dante leapt for the first possessed man, knocking the gun from his hand.

Amie scrambled for the gun as her zombie barreled for the second man. Dante kicked the gun out of his hands and crashed into a crumbling brick vault. The second gun skittered into the night as Amie closed her hands around the first.

"Freeze," Amie commanded, aiming the weapon at the men. "Leave now or I'm going to send you straight to hell."

The thugs spasmed as the spirits shoved their way out of the human hosts. Their eyes rolled up into their heads. Two red masses shot into the night before the men crumpled to the ground.

Dante climbed to his feet and put his fingers to the neck of the closest man. "He's not dead, just out cold."

Heart hammering, Amie hunched next to the other man and lifted his eyelid. The pupils were clear. He'd have a massive headache, but he should be awake by the time the first tour group rolled through in the morning.

"Come." Dante reached a hand down to her. His wide shoulders shook with tension and his left arm was a bloody mess.

"Oh my goodness."

He ignored her. "We have to go."

Amie laid the gun on the path next to her and grasped the neck of the Florida water bottle. It was mostly rubbing alcohol anyway. But it had been smashed on the ground. She used the broken edge to rip a strip of cloth from the bottom of her skirt. She closed her eyes for a moment, fighting the fabric.

When she had enough, she wadded it into a bandage and touched it to his arm.

"Ow!" He jerked back.

"Calm down," she said, her own pulse racing as she wiped the blood. "Hold this on there. We can clean it out at my house."

He gave her a long look. "As long as you promise not to try to kill me."

She rolled her eyes as if she hadn't been attempting that very thing a few moments ago.

Only before, he wasn't quite human. Now, she didn't know.

By Gedhe, this was such a mess.

Amie watched Dante seal the guns in his vault and grab the ring. Who was this man who had burst into her life, kissed her silly, and brought her here?

Is that what he was?

A man?

She didn't quite believe it. In fact, this entire night had been one big surprise after another.

"Dante," she said, watching him startle as she called him by name for the first time, "let's get out of here."

Chapter Five

Pain seared his upper arm, but Dante didn't care. Pain meant he was alive. As for her attempt to kill him, he'd deal with that soon enough.

Amie moved with liquid grace, strong yet undeniably feminine as she dialed in the alarm code at the back of her building. She was all curves and substance, with large almond-shaped eyes, gorgeous caramel skin, and a lush mouth. But what he really liked was her squared-off chin. It was bold, defiant. Too bad she'd grown from delectable to downright infuriating. She seemed to sense his anger as she opened the door to the storage room.

"Hell-o!" A Kongamato lounged in what looked to be a pit of mud and sticks.

Amie cringed. "Dante, this is Isoke."

If she was counting on the creature to save her, she was sadly mistaken.

Dante bowed toward the Kongamato. The beast sat up, positively beaming.

"Isoke, this is Dante."

He showed a double row of teeth. "Charmed, *rafiki*. She is quite a catch, no?"

She would be, once she understood what was happening. Dante ran a hand down Amie's back, pleased at the way she stiffened. She might not accept him, but she still wanted him.

Isoke launched himself out of the tub, sending sticks and pieces of moss flying. "Would you care for a soak? I was just going to go for a cool-down swim in the Mississippi." He waggled his brows at them like a proud uncle as he shook a wet leaf from between his toes. "This mud is good for your pores, no? And very romantic."

"We have to go," Amie said, leading Dante through the door to the shop.

"Have fun, kids!" Isoke called. "And just so you know, I will not be leaving gifts in your shoes if you are busy making love!"

She seemed embarrassed. "I'm sorry. He's just..."

"A Kongamato." Dante had seen voodoo mambos in the cemetery.

"Right," Amie said, avoiding his gaze. They were back to being polite. It would not do.

"This way," she said, leading him upstairs to her apartment.

Her living space was as colorful as her shop and stacked with books and various homemade oddities. Yet instinct told him there was more to this woman than she'd revealed.

He would get to the bottom of it.

She led him into a small bathroom off of the library and flipped on the bright overhead light.

Amie gasped when she saw his injury clearly for the first time. "I'm so sorry."

The wound was ugly, his olive skin ripped and torn.

He shrugged and immediately regretted the move as hot fire shot down his arm.

There didn't seem to be any major damage, but he bled quite a bit. Her fault, but he wouldn't get into that right now. Her knee bumped against his leg. This was the closest she stood to him — voluntarily — since she'd kissed him.

"I'll fix it," she said, earnestly.

Dante's anger eased as he watched Amie wrestle with an impossible number of tubes and jars in a miniscule cabinet over the pedestal sink. That's not to say anything was out of place. If he wasn't mistaken, the items were actually lined up by size. He just didn't understand why a woman would need that many.

Some things never changed.

He turned her to face him. "Forget the bandages. We need to talk."

She seemed wary, afraid. It was ridiculous.

He'd proved to her tonight that she was his one true love. He'd shown her the mark on his tomb. He'd been unable to wear the wedding ring his former wife had given him. Despite that, Amie had rejected him outright.

She might have reacted with shock at first, as any woman would. He had not expected her to progress to joy and absolute glee right away. But outright denial? He never would have imagined it.

Why fight a chance at true happiness?

What more proof did this modern woman need?

Her gaze fell on his arm. "We *do* need to talk. But not with you looking like that."

"Amie," he warned.

She turned back to the medicine cabinet.

His fists clenched and his shoulder burned. He wanted to be a gentleman, but, at the same time, he needed to get through to her. "I'm finished with excuses."

Amie was supposed to be his one true love—a once-in-a-lifetime connection—a woman who could call him back from the grave and give him a second chance at love and at life.

She was passionate. Her kiss at the door had proven that. His body tightened just thinking about it.

So why was she fighting?

It was insulting as hell. "Why did you call me?" Why put him through this for nothing?

She didn't answer. Her lips pursed as she selected bandages and clanked through the bottles in the medicine cabinet—as if that was the most important thing they had to deal with.

Damn it, he wouldn't be cast aside.

He reached for her, ignoring her squeak of surprise as he took her by the waist and set her down on the edge of the sink.

"Ow!" she protested.

"It does not hurt." He brushed his fingertips along the trembling at her collarbone. *"Mi corazon."*

Her breath quickened. She tried to avoid him, her thick hair falling over one eye. "Don't you manhandle me."

Hands on her hips, he pulled her up against him so that she was forced to see him. "Don't play games with me."

She drew a careful breath, her fingers absently tracing the velvety soft skin he'd just touched.

He'd have a conversation with her if it killed him.

What he hadn't counted on was the hot lick of desire that slid down his spine.

He pushed closer, just to test her and watched the rosy flush creep up her cheeks. "Tell me. Be truthful," he ground out. "Why did you call me?"

She touched her lips together nervously.

Madre de dios. His whole future hung in the balance and this woman, this savior of his couldn't even answer a simple question.

She chewed at her delectable lower lip, her eyes wide, her hair damp around her face. "Look," she said, "I made a mistake."

No. "That kind of power doesn't come from accident. You did this on purpose."

At first he had been amused that her need for his love could be so powerful that she could call him and not understand what it meant. But if she didn't want him anymore, that was downright terrifying.

"Why do you need to know?" she demanded.

He fought the urge to touch her hair. "Because it's not supposed to be this way. Not for me."

Dante had never been an overly patient man, but he'd haunted the cemetery for two hundred years. The only thing that had kept him going was the one in a million shot that his ideal girl would call him back and give him another chance.

Tears filled her eyes. "Just let me fix you."

He stepped back. "I am afraid that is impossible."

Dante sat on the edge of her tub, his head in his hands. He had to make her understand.

She leaned over him, her yellow sleeve brushing his cheek, her nose red. "This won't hurt a bit," she said, right before she poured what felt like molten lava down his arm. He cringed.

She sniffed and wiped at her eyes. "It's iodine," she explained, dabbing at him again with the cotton ball. "It'll help, I promise." She swallowed. "I was actually hoping you'd be healed by now."

"And why is that?" He asked, teeth gritted.

"Well, you're…" She paused, obviously trying to think of a polite way to say what he probably didn't want to hear. "Supernatural. Or should I say reanimated?"

He planted his hands on his knees and felt a drop of sweat slide down his back as she resumed her assault. "I regret to inform you that while I may be reconstituted, as it may. I have always been, and I remain, a mortal man."

She winced. "Right. Sorry. I suppose I was thinking about vampires."

"I'm not a vampire," he rubbed a hand over his eyes. "I can age and I can certainly die."

Her lips parted slightly.

The hollow feeling in his gut grew.

Dante didn't know how much time he had, but if Amie didn't offer him more of her magic, freely and completely, their bond would wear away. Then he'd be truly and forever dead.

He couldn't let that happen.

"Put it down," he said, taking the cotton and the iodine from her and placing them behind him in the tub. "Now," he said, standing, purposely keeping his distance, "I will show you just how alive I am." He held out his hand to her.

Amie hesitated. He could see the wild pulse at her neck, hear her shallow breathing. The air in the small room had grown quite warm. Slowly, he reached for her hand. She swallowed hard as he drew her closer and placed her hand over his beating heart.

She exhaled as they both felt his heart pound against his chest.

He took her other hand and touched it to his lips. "I am human. Just like you."

She blinked once, twice. Confusion trickled across her features. "But back in the cemetery, you went after those possessed men unarmed."

"Yes," he said. He'd do it again.

She lingered on his arm. "You mean, if the bullet had hit you in the chest, you would have died?" Realization dawned in her. "You almost died for me? Why?"

He felt the corners of his mouth tug as he returned his tired and battered body to the edge of the tub. "I am a gentleman. And I didn't want to watch you die."

She sat down next to him. "Nobody's ever risked themselves for me like that."

He closed his hand over hers. "I'm sorry to hear it," he said. And he meant it.

She deserved that kind of love, that kind of respect.

He'd be that kind of man for her if she'd only let him.

Why today's women did everything on their own was beyond him. In his time, most came from large, extended families. Husbands protected their wives. Families spent lifetimes building large networks of friends. People helped one another.

It was one of the things he'd missed most of all, haunting the cemetery alone after his own family had passed on.

"The bleeding isn't stopping," she said, worried.

"No," he said. He couldn't fully heal himself. Not until she could open herself up and give him a little of the magic she'd used to call him, the magic he needed to survive.

The kicker was, he couldn't ask. It had to be freely given.

Still, she was wary of him. He'd have to proceed carefully.

He watched as she wound a thick white bandage around his arm.

What had his grandmother always said? Patience. Small steps. He'd never been good at that. Dante drew his fingers slowly over Amie's as she secured the bandage with medical tape. Perhaps he'd learned to temper himself over the past two centuries. He'd gotten her talking, which was no small thing.

And perhaps she understood him a little better too.

Life was precious. He knew that now.

Now all he had to do was convince her.

Tomorrow, he thought, as he moved to her library and sank into a soft recliner. He'd do it. Somehow, he'd convince her he deserved a second chance at life.

And perhaps he'd show her a thing or two about living as well.

Chapter Six

For the first time, Amie regretted the mirrors on her ceiling. They used to be fun and funky. Now all she could do was stare at herself lying in bed amid an immense pile of books she'd dragged in from her library.

Past the sleeping Dante.

At least someone could get some rest. It was five in the morning—nearly dawn. Amie stared at her reflection. Her hair frizzed at odd angles, her eyelids had puffed to twice the normal size, and she had a line down the side of her face from falling asleep on top of a hardback collector's edition of *Out of the Darkness: The Ethnobiology of the Modern Zombie.*

She looked like hell. And why not? She'd certainly put herself through it in the last five hours. Five hours? Is that all it took to ruin a life?

The past night had been a disaster.

Well, except for those scorching kisses. And the strong beat of his heart on the palm of her hand. The gesture had been oddly comforting. It made her feel safe, which was ridiculous.

Dante was dangerous, unpredictable. She shouldn't like it. Men like him were nothing but trouble.

She wriggled at the memory of Dante—all of him—as he pulled her flush against him and kissed her senseless. Well, there was nothing wrong with having a moment or two. She couldn't deny that she enjoyed his touch. She just needed to keep things in perspective. The only difference between this and her mother's failed attempts at love was that Amie *knew* Dante was going to leave.

A zombie will deteriorate and die again once it has fulfilled its purpose or once the voodoo mambo no longer requires its services.

She refused to let him hurt her on the way out.

Amie rubbed her eyes, red and gritty from lack of sleep. Why hadn't she gotten a zombie who would clean her shop? Or keep Isoke from chasing alligators? But no. She'd called up a man who wanted to make her fall in love with him. Amie tensed as she heard him moan in his sleep. She could almost see him stretched out shirtless on her green La-Z-Boy. Part of her couldn't believe a man like that wanted her. Voodoo zombies wouldn't come unless they were called to do something they wanted to do.

She rolled over into the pillow. Bosou! What was she thinking?

This time yesterday, she'd been totally in control. Oh for the days of all work and no play, when men were boring and life made sense.

What she'd discovered reading through her research books, well, she still couldn't believe it. Amie rolled to her side and reached for a thick red book with a broken spine—a magical tome that had been her grandmother's. Her mother had sworn it only contained the absolute truth.

Amie had snapped the binding when she threw it off the bed earlier this morning. She brushed through its crushed opening pages. Her fault, when she'd fisted them out of shock. She opened the book to the place she didn't really want to see again. Still, she had to look. It was like a car wreck—she couldn't look away.

A love spell can only be used to call a zombie if said zombie is the voodoo practitioner's one true love.

Ridiculous.

Laughable.

If she didn't have the niggling suspicion that it could be true.

"Oh god, oh god, oh god..." She shoved the book off the bed and watched it land in a heap on the floor. The pages crackled as they began fixing themselves.

He couldn't be. He just couldn't. Dante was temporary. He was leaving. He was all wrong.

And Amie was always right.

* * *

Dante needed another cup of coffee. Hell, he needed another pot. His head swam as he braced one hand on Amie's living room window sill and watched the sun rise over Royale Street.

He was not going back into that kitchen.

The Good Girl's Guide to Love Magik lay open on the flowered tablecloth, right where he'd left it. The thick tome was pink, which made it worse.

Besides, he didn't need to look at the starred, underlined entry to know what it said.

A love spell will bind for a maximum of three days and

nights. If love magic is not exchanged during that time, the spell will be broken.

She'd made it clear she didn't want him. She had no desire to fall in love with him. Now he had three days to convince her. It wasn't enough time. Hell, he'd been engaged to his late wife for six months and he hadn't known she didn't care until he found her in bed with the arrogant ass that owned the estate next door.

Maybe he just hadn't wanted to see the truth.

Dante swiped at the blood trickling down his arm. He'd need to find a new bandage. The wound throbbed, refusing to heal.

It wouldn't get better without her love magic. He didn't have the ability to heal himself. Not until the spell was permanent.

Did he even want that anymore?

He watched a few industrious shopkeepers hose off the streets in front of their stores. His former wife, Sophia, had married him out of duty. Their fathers ran a shipping business together. Sure, she'd been attracted to him. At least, she had been at first. But like the feathered hats she collected, Dante was one more object to be had, one more conquest. At least she'd admitted it.

While she'd been pleading with him not to shoot her lover.

He felt the stab in his gut as if it were yesterday.

The kicker was—he'd loved her. Now she was dead and he might be—again—sooner rather than later.

Dante rubbed his chin, feeling the start of a beard and gave a small chuckle. He hadn't had to shave in one hundred and ninety-eight years.

Now he had another chance at life. Dante opened

the window and let morning filter into the room—
birds chirping, the smell of sunshine and fresh cut
grass, shopkeepers laughing and calling to one another. He stood for a moment and just listened. He'd
enjoy the little things while they lasted.

Dante glanced behind him at Amie's closed door.
He'd take one day at a time, because right now, his
one true love didn't seem to know what she wanted
and he was running out of time.

He sighed.

Well, he'd rather be dead than have another woman pledge herself to him out of obligation. His feet
moved on their own until he stood outside her orange
painted door. He detected a trace of her honeysuckle
perfume and placed a hand on the smooth wood. If
Amie didn't want him, he'd leave. But first, he'd do
his damnedest to show her why she'd brought him
back.

* * *

Amie rolled over and stretched. Mmm…something
was baking. She detected the heavenly aroma of cinnamon and bananas, along with fresh brewed coffee.
Her house never smelled like this. She certainly didn't
cook.

She cracked her eyes open. She couldn't believe
she'd actually fallen asleep. Sunlight streamed in from
her window. Delivery trucks rumbled down the alley.
Then she heard Dante singing, low and deep.

Yawning, she extricated a book out from under her
cheek and rubbed at her face.

She'd give it to him. The man had an amazing
voice. She sat up slowly as the cobwebs cleared from

her head.

For a moment, she thought she recognized the song. "I Can't Help Falling in Love with You," only different.

Plaisir d'amour ne dure qu'un moment.

A haunting melody.

Chagrin d'amour dure toute la vie.

He sounded like a Spanish Elvis. And from the sound of lapping water, he was in her tub.

She pushed her way through the books, to where her bedside clock lay facedown. She lifted it enough to look at the big, red numbers. It was only nine in the morning. She let go of the clock and it tumbled down, face-first again. According to her books, zombies had to sleep at least twelve hours a night. Just who did he think he was?

J'ai tout quitté pour l'ingrate Celeste.
Elle me quitte et prend un autre aimant.

Water splashed in her tub as he hit a low note. She lurched out of bed and made her way to the kitchen.

Coffee gurgled on the stove. He'd used her grandma's ancient pot instead of the plug-in KitchenAid on her counter. To each his own. She opened the oven and peeked at the bubbling dough inside. He could cook too. It figured.

Wouldn't it be nice if her life was really like this? Waking up to a hot breakfast and a hot man.

It was such a tease.

Amie pulled a *Doctor Who* mug from above the sink and poured herself a hot, steaming cup of coffee. She closed her eyes at the rich flavor with just a hint of vanilla.

She scanned her countertops for the package he'd used. She hadn't bought any vanilla coffee.

Her fingers tightened on her cup when she saw one of her spell books open on the kitchen table. He'd been doing some research of his own.

It was the pink love magic book, one of her mother's. Amie groaned. She hadn't had time to go through all of her mom's books yet. This one was well used. It figured her mom would resort to voodoo.

And now Amie had too.

Terrific. Just like Mom.

She sighed. Well, at least she wasn't taking any strange men to bed. She dragged a hand across her face. She was just letting them in her tub.

Water splashed as he got out. She heard the towel bar clank. As if she needed him in her kitchen too. She topped off her coffee.

Fingers shaking, Amie rubbed at her temples and told herself she had about two minutes to get it together.

She was wrong.

The bathroom door swung open. "Ah! You are awake."

Water droplets beaded at his shoulders as he strolled through her front room with a towel wrapped around his waist and a fresh bandage white against his skin. His short black hair stood at spiky angles, which only accented the sharp planes of his face.

Amie straightened, felt her toes curl.

She took a quick swallow of coffee, just to do something—anything—and singed her throat. "Of course I'm awake," she croaked, telling herself the heat in her belly was, in fact, from the coffee. She cleared her throat. "The real question is why are you up and about?"

"Community Coffee Dark Roast," he said, as he

pulled a House of Blues mug from the sink and poured himself another helping. "I find myself acting like a complete zombie before my first cup."

"That's not funny," she said, momentarily distracted by a water droplet that slid down his perfect back and settled under the towel.

"Breakfast?" he asked, using one of her grandma's woven pot holders to pull a tray of banana fritters out of the oven.

They looked like a cross between a doughnut and a pancake. "You made these?"

He sprinkled the fritters with powdered sugar and grabbed them each a plate. "I watched Cook do it many times. Then I merely dreamed about them for twenty decades," he added wistfully, as he served her a portion. "I admit the stove was a bit of a trick."

Amie bit into a warm, doughy fritter and almost had an orgasm.

He joined her, and they ate in silence. It was almost too domestic. Amie squirmed in her seat. She had no business wanting this.

She welcomed the distraction of gathering up the plates and insisting he take the last cup of coffee.

"Now that we have eaten, there is something we need to discuss." He leaned against her yellow countertop and took a long sip from his mug, eyeing her as he did it. "You used a love spell to call me from the grave."

"Yes," she said, stacking the plates in the sink, "but I didn't call *you* necessarily."

Amie fought back a sliver of guilt. Who was she kidding? She did call him. She saw him in her mind's eye, scar and all. He'd responded voluntarily because he could love her back. Now, here he was, her perfect man.

And if he could somehow touch her that deep, then having him and losing him would be worse than all of her mom's heartbreak put together.

She just wasn't ready.

She didn't think she'd ever be ready.

"Give me three days," he said.

She nearly knocked her cup off the counter. "Excuse me?" He couldn't be serious. She didn't know if she could ever open herself up to the kind of hurt she might find in a real relationship, but, rushing certainly wouldn't help. "Three days? I can't decide anything in three days." It had taken her longer than that to pick out her kitchen curtains. "Besides, I have a life. I have a shop to run."

Dante set his mug on the table behind him. "Yes, but is this the life you want?" he asked pointedly.

"Yes." Mostly. How could he look confident and inviting when what he was asking was absurd? "You don't understand."

He walked to her and took her hands in his. They were warm and strong. It felt both exciting and nerve wracking. She wanted to run, but she knew it would kill her to destroy this moment. So she didn't. She waited. He leaned down to her, his face inches from hers.

Was he going to kiss her again?

She hesitated. Would she let him?

"Let me court you," he said, a breath from her ear.

"For real?" she asked, warmth settling in a place she'd rather not think about. She liked it when men opened doors for her, but to be courted? By a ravishingly handsome eighteenth-century gentleman? In a towel?

His hands traveled up her arms, burning a path to her shoulders. "*Sí.* If it is right, three days will have to be enough," he said, his expression intense, earnest. "If it is not, I will accept that."

She searched his face, his blue eyes so electric and sincere. "Will you really?" She was suddenly disappointed that it could be over so soon.

"I will leave," he said solemnly.

"Knowing that it took me more than three days to decide if I even wanted to go out with my last boyfriend?" she said, giving fair warning.

The lines around his eyes crinkled as he gave her a tight smile. "Yes."

Interesting. She hadn't him pegged as the type to give up in less than a week. "What's the catch?"

He touched his fingers to her chin, rubbing his thumb back and forth on the soft patch of skin below her lips. Heat curled through her. "No catch, *querida.* I have waited two hundred years for you." He brushed his lips against her forehead, "You called me back. Now I will show you why." His lips brushed her cheek.

"I already know why." She'd been weak. She'd been lonely, and only too human.

If she wasn't careful, it was going to hurt something terrible when he left.

She forced herself to stand tall, ignoring the insane desire to touch him back.

"You will enjoy my attentions, I assure you," he murmured.

She broke away from him. "Look, I'm not an eighteenth-century miss. I don't expect love poems and flattery. I know better than to think flowers cure everything. I'd think you were crazy if you threw your

jacket over a puddle or expected me to simper around
while you do manly things. I have a mind of my own,
a successful business, a *life*, for goodness sake, and
I'm not going to fall in love and make a lifetime com-
mitment because somebody says I should."

"Are you finished?" he asked.

She lifted her chin. "Yes."

His head dipped toward hers. "Three days," he
whispered in her ear.

She knew she shouldn't want it, but she did.

Amie wet her lips. What harm could come in three
days? If she knew she couldn't have him past that,
then she wouldn't expect more. He would be fulfilling
his purpose, hopefully with more fritters and coffee,
and then she'd be free of him. Better yet, she could relax and have fun, with no strings attached. This could
be safe, if she watched herself.

It would certainly be exciting.

"Okay." She shivered. "Three days."

Heaven help her.

CHAPTER SEVEN

Amie stuffed her feet into her white Keds, thankful that Isoke hadn't left her any gifts last night.

She hoped the Kongamato hadn't given Dante too much trouble. She'd sent the creature downstairs with directions to her friend Oliver's store, and asked him to find something for Dante to wear. She hoped that something included a shirt. She didn't need to be drooling over the hot Spaniard all day. Control was key.

Besides, Oliver owed her. She'd used her magic to find him a man, and a decent three-year lease on a building near Jackson Square.

When Amie hopped out into her living room, tugging on the back of her sneaker, she realized both her friend and her monster had failed her in the worst possible way. Dante sat at her kitchen table with the newspaper spread out in front of him, sipping coffee and looking better than he did half-naked.

He wore a black T-shirt that should have been modest. Instead, it hugged his chest and arms in all the right places. And if that wasn't bad, he wore a pair of tan cargo shorts that made him look relaxed and sexy as hell. A pair of black flip-flops completed the outfit.

Damn Oliver.

"Are you ready?" Dante said, easing back from the table.

Would she ever be?

He'd even cleaned her kitchen.

Enjoy it while it lasts.

"What's the plan?" she asked just to have something to say. He was looking at her as if he'd like a repeat of what they'd done when they'd met.

Amie straightened. *Get it together.* She'd be in trouble if she couldn't maintain her focus.

He approached her, completely relaxed and sexy as hell. "No plan," he said, easing an arm around her as he led them to the door.

"That's right," she said. "You're probably not familiar with the city anymore." He smelled like Ivory soap and pure man. *Three days,* she reminded herself. One foot in front of the other. Shoulders back. And no drooling.

Of course Isoke had left them love and fertility presents on the stairs.

"Your dragon works fast," Dante said, navigating her past a series of mud-coated rocks and hairballs. "I had these cleaned up a half hour ago."

"You should have seen what he did for my birthday."

Amie tamped down the urge to clean before they left. It wouldn't help, not if the Kongamato was determined to bring them his brand of luck.

But love charms didn't work on the unwilling, and Amie knew her limits. Whatever she had going on with Dante would end in three days.

She leaned against her man as he lifted her over a particularly tricky spot.

Isoke would say she was settling for crumbs again, but he wasn't the one who had to bear responsibility when things got out of control—and they would if she wasn't careful.

Lasting love didn't happen to the women in her family. Wishing for it would only make her end up like her mom.

Much to Amie's relief, she and Dante escaped Voo-Doo Works without Isoke trying to help them further. She kept the *Closed* sign in the front window of the store, feeling strange and, for the first time in a long time, free.

The sunshine warmed her face as they strolled past the people and shops that crowded Royale Street. Two- and three-story buildings lined the way, topped with wrought-iron balconies and rich with flowering plants and vines. Amie breathed deep. Mmm...jasmine and roasted almonds.

And dead rat?

The acrid odor touched Amie's nose a second before she spotted a red Kongamato tail disappear into The New Orleans House of Wax.

A muddy brown rat flew out of the door behind him, very dead and sporting a necklace of white Life Savers breath mints.

"Isoke!" she hissed, as the rat slid across the pavement.

She zigzagged around the festooned rodent as she barreled through the door.

What was he thinking?

No Kongamato went out during the day. Isoke

would be seen. She didn't want him hunted, hounded...or worse.

Amie closed the door of the wax museum and almost tripped over the stack of free tabloid newspapers and coupon books at the front. She breathed a sigh of relief as she spied Isoke in the front entryway, posed next to a life-sized statue of voodoo queen Marie Laveau. The Kongamato's teeth shone in rows of white and his face and body contorted into a giant snarl.

"What are you doing?" Amie hissed, glancing around the small front room.

Isoke dropped the pose. "I am helping you fall in love. Did you get my rat?"

Amie squinched her nose. "Yes," she said, peeking out the door. "Dante is cleaning it up right now."

Isoke brightened. "Good. Lots of love magic in that one. And breath mints! You know, for before you kiss."

"Stop it. Go home now. You know this is against the rules."

A teenager in a House of Wax polo shirt stepped out from the main lobby. "Can I help you?"

Amie jumped. "Err..." She eyed Isoke, who had fallen down dead dragon-style at Marie Laveau's feet.

"Ticket sales are this way," the girl continued.

Isoke refused to budge, except the edges of his mouth seemed to tip into the start of a smile.

Amie hesitated. What was she supposed to say? I can't leave without my bullheaded-pain-in-the-neck-better-go-home-if-he-knows-what-is-good-for-him Kongamato?

And now she couldn't even look at him because she sure as heck didn't want the ticket girl noticing anything.

"You behave," she said to the Marie Laveau statue before turning on her heel and leaving the Kongamato to obey — or not.

Outside, the dead rat had vanished and Dante leaned against a streetlamp as if nothing had happened.

"I told him to go home," Amie said.

He raised a brow. "You think he will?"

"No," she said, glancing back, "but he's going to keep hiding in plain sight until we leave."

"Then come," Dante said, offering his arm, "let's oblige the little monster. Isoke has to handle things his own way."

That's what worried her.

Amie fought the urge to glance backward as she and Dante continued down Royale Street.

She wished she knew more about her own city. Truth was, she didn't leave the neighborhood much. "I can suggest a few things to do," she said, enjoying the tingle of excitement as she leaned against his hard frame. They did need a plan.

"No," he said, his fingers lingering at the top of her pink silk skirt. She sucked in a breath as he found the warm skin just above her waist.

"We could go to the information office," she said quickly.

"No." His fingers drew lazy circles on her skin.

"Tour guide?" she suggested, ending in a squeak.

Rat or no rat — in a minute, she was going to have to drag him behind Ed's Oyster Stand or run straight home.

He laughed at that, delighted. "No." He took her hand in his, not bothered at all by the people who had to walk around them. It was as if he was carving out a little piece of New Orleans just for them. "I think we will do quite well on our own." He nudged her. "Relax."

"I'm relaxed," she said too quickly.

He wrapped an arm around her and they began walking again. "Why is it so hard for you to simply let good things come to you?"

"I like to know what to expect." She trailed one hand over a sculpted guitar outside Manny's Jazz Club.

They wandered past vendors and street musicians and mimes. Soon they came upon St. Louis Cathedral, where his youngest sister had married. He steered Amie over to the spot just to the right of the church, where his sister's wedding party had fled after guests pelted a beehive with rice meant for the bride and groom.

He smiled as he told her the story. "You have to understand the dresses back then," Dante said, holding his hands wide.

"I have some idea," Amie said, trying not to laugh.

"For a moment, we believed a bee had gotten up there. I certainly wasn't going to check. And my sister's attendants were scattered everywhere. I told Antonio it was his job," he said.

"Another brother?" she asked.

"The groom," he corrected.

Amie gasped. "He didn't."

"He escorted her directly behind that wide oak for a quick inspection."

Amie gave an exaggerated gasp. "The morals of the eighteenth century."

"Scandalous," Dante agreed.

He leaned in to kiss her and Amie was about to close her eyes when the tree above them shook. A giant black rat hit every branch on the way down and thwumped at their feet.

"Isoke!" she shrieked.

Then she noticed the gold band tied to the rodent's tail.

"My apologies." The Kongamato flapped his wings as he settled on a high branch. "I saw you heading for the church and wanted you to be ready!"

Amie opened her mouth for the lecture of the century when Dante touched her arm. "Don't."

A crowd had begun to gather, murmuring questions.

Two boys rushed up. "It's a rat!" they yelled, to a chorus of *eeews*!

Amie kicked the rat's tail until the ring came loose and Dante—bless him—pocketed it. No telling where Isoke had found the gold band, but he *would* return it.

"Come with me." Dante took her hand and led her over to Café du Monde.

"The little beast is going to get himself captured," she muttered. Or killed. And dang it, she really would have enjoyed that kiss.

"Let him be," Dante said, pulling back a chair for her. "Maybe he'll give up."

He didn't know Isoke.

At least the crowd hadn't noticed the red Kongamato waving to Amie and Dante from the high branches of the ancient oak.

Amie introduced Dante to caffe lattes as they watched the small mob disperse.

"I swear that monster has nine lives."

Dante's gaze slid over her, warm and sensuous.

"Let's just hope I only need two."

Afterward, they kept an eye out for rats bearing gifts as they wandered to the Farmers Market. There, Dante completely lost his mind over the variety and flavors of hot sauce. Amie bought a bottle of Gib's Bottled Hell and he rewarded her with an utterly blissful shrimp jambalaya upon their return home.

She pushed back from the yellow table, unable to eat another bite. "Amazing."

Dante leaned over her to take her bowl. "Don't thank *me*." He nodded to a book open on the countertop. Smiling crawdads holding forks and knives danced over the cover of *The Rajun Cajun: Recipes from New Orleans*. It had been a gift from Oliver. Naturally, she'd never cracked it open.

Dante rinsed the bowls and poured himself another cup of coffee—his third since they'd returned. Then he leaned against the counter and smiled for no reason at all.

It made no sense, but she found herself smiling too.

She could almost excuse the last twenty-four hours as something that had been done to her. He'd showed up at her door. He'd suggested a date. He'd asked permission to court her. She flushed, remembering the purple cone flower he'd picked for her from a planter box along the way. She'd tucked it behind her ear and felt every inch the lady.

Maybe it was time for her to treat him back. She'd been thinking about kissing him all day and now was her chance. Amie stood.

"*Querida?*" he asked, setting aside his coffee mug.

Amie drew close to him. Their first kiss had been mind-numbingly intense. She'd waited, expected him to kiss her again today. He'd held her hand, touched her side, laughed close. But aside from the near kiss under the tree, he'd never taken the next step. She couldn't believe she was actually going to be the one to make a move.

He was so beautiful, so alive. After her dull dating history and nine dry years, she'd earned this. Amie practically sighed in anticipation. She knew just what she needed—and just how much she was willing to give.

Amie slid her arms around Dante's neck, warm and strong. "Thank you," she said. "This has been a wonderful day."

She raised her lips to the long column of his throat and was delighted when he let out a soft groan. She licked his ear and he shuddered. She touched her lips to his and he pulled away.

"Amie, wait," he whispered against her.

"It's just a kiss," she said, nuzzling him. A small thing, really.

They'd done it before. They'd almost done it this afternoon. Nothing had changed.

"You don't mean it," he said quietly.

"Yes, I do," she coaxed, nibbling at his lower lip.

He gathered her into his arms. "No," he said, touching his forehead to hers. "You don't."

She could feel him—all of him—pressed full against her. He wanted this.

Dante rubbed his hand along her back. She could feel the tension in him, and the longing. "It has to be real," he said simply, quietly. "This either means you want me, that you're willing to at least try to love me. Or it doesn't." His eyes flicked to hers and held. "You tell me which."

"Dante," she protested. This was a big step for her.

Besides, what did he expect? He was leaving soon. "I'm out on a limb here as it is."

He caressed her cheek, ran his thumb along her chin. "I don't want you out on a branch. I need you to jump."

She drew back, hurt. "You know I can't do that." This was her first date in nine years. She'd closed her shop. She'd shared the whole day with him. She'd dodged rats bearing gifts. She'd told him what to expect from the start. This had to be enough.

Amie saw the pain in his eyes. "I can't settle for less than the real thing," he said. "Not this time."

"You've got to be kidding." She'd just tried to give him more than she'd given anybody and he somehow needed more? "What do you want from me?"

He gave her a penetrating look as his hands snaked up her back, leaving ribbons of pleasure in their wake. "You know."

Love magic. Amie closed her eyes. She couldn't imagine what it would be like to share love magic with a man like him. It would be passionate, explosive. It could eat her alive and leave her with nothing.

She shook her head. "I'm sorry." She couldn't do it. She couldn't risk it. Not in a million years.

Chapter Eight

Dante was still hard as a rock when he woke up twelve hours later. His shoulder throbbed. Well, what else was new? He pushed the thought aside and shoved his way out of the La-Z-Boy.

He heard Amie in the kitchen and smelled a fresh pot of coffee, French roast if he wasn't mistaken. The cargo shorts dug into his waist. They'd been uncomfortable as hell to sleep in, but he'd been too tired take them off.

The fatigue had come on quickly last night, and he'd slept in today. The spell was wearing off. He'd better make today count.

He could hear Amie in there talking to herself. The woman was trouble — more so than he'd imagined.

Dante ran a hand through his hair. It had all seemed so simple. A powerful woman, truly meant for him would seek him out. He'd have a new life and a new love at the same time.

At last — someone who could love him back.

Amie could be that woman if she gave herself half

a chance. Instead, she wanted to give him scraps of herself. Well, he wouldn't do it.

Dante tucked his shirt into his shorts, his gaze settling on the wedding ring he'd left on the top shelf of her bookcase. Amie needed to decide what she wanted. He'd already married one woman who didn't care enough. He'd rather die than go through that again.

"Latte?" she asked, as he made his way into the kitchen. Amie wore an orange sheath dress that accented her curves. For a moment, his focus lingered only on her. Then he saw she'd been busy while he slept.

The woman had not only bought a cappuccino maker, she'd laid out jeans and a dark green button-down shirt over one of the kitchen chairs.

"Thanks," he said. He would have been embarrassed if he'd let himself think on it too long. He couldn't remember anyone, save his mother, buying gifts for him.

He leaned against the counter and watched her make foam.

She gave him a sideways glance. "Four cups a day keeps the zombie away."

"Then you'd better stick to three," he said, as Amie handed him a fresh latte.

He took a long sip, savoring the sweet warmth. He took her delicate hand in his and squeezed it.

If he did die again and if he had to go away for good this time, he'd know he had this moment.

"Come on," she said, "let's try to get out before Isoke wakes up."

Dante showered and dressed before they headed downstairs.

Amie's shoulders dropped slightly when they spied

the empty perch at the back of the store.

Dante touched the top of her arm. "I'm sure Isoke is fine."

Amie sighed. "I just wish we knew where he was."

Dante opened the door for her, as had become their habit, and Amie hadn't even hesitated today when she left the *Closed* sign on the door of the shop.

"Why VooDoo Works?" he asked, admiring the display of love charms in the window.

She glanced at the industrial sign that she'd commissioned. "Because it does." She laughed. "Sure the spirits can be unpredictable, but the everyday practice of voodoo is quite practical."

"You don't have to convince me," he said as grave dust wafted down on the other side of the door.

"You can't always determine exactly what results you're going to get," she clarified, slipping her hand into his, "but you usually get what you truly need."

Indeed.

Amie got her wish when they boarded the St. Charles Streetcar and spotted a Kongamato roof ornament. Dante could hear the beast's claws clattering against the tin roof the entire way from Canal Street and into the Garden District.

Dante pointed to a corner of Audubon, which was packed with neat, modern homes. "I used to live right about there."

She leaned against him. "Do you miss it?"

"No," he said, surprised. Rather, Dante found the new houses most intriguing with their wraparound porches and big yards, perfect for raising a family. His old life was a thing of the past. Amie was his future. "Although," he said, leaning close and breathing in her honeysuckle perfume, "I do miss the crawfish."

Amie wrinkled her nose. "I never cared for them. Too ugly."

He leaned back, his arm slung over the seatback behind her. "Well, you would have loved our crawfish. We used to catch them in the freshwater stream out back. The most handsome crustaceans you'd ever meet."

"I am a sucker for a handsome face," she said, leaning into him.

They reached the end of the line—twice. Each time, the streetcar tracks ended, the driver would flip the shiny wood bench seats in the opposite direction. They'd pay a dollar twenty-five and continue on their way.

Dante laughed out loud when she described the young girl who'd bought a love potion for her two turtles.

"I didn't have the heart to tell her she had two boy turtles."

"Well what's wrong with that?" he asked.

"She wanted babies."

"Ah," he said, delighting in it. "I can see where that could be a challenge."

She grinned up at him, radiant.

For the first time, Amie understood just why her mother could want a relationship like this. She couldn't remember a time when she felt so good. Dante brought out the best in her. It was invigorating and electrifying, and addicting if she wasn't careful. Luckily, Amie was always careful.

He toyed with a curl of hair at her shoulder. "Speaking of creatures, tell me about Isoke."

She gave him a sideways glance. "He's a pain in the rear, that's for sure."

"Watch it," she heard a faint voice from the roof.

"And he has supersonic Kongamato hearing."

His claws dug through the metal roof. "Aye mambo! They have spotted me!"

Amie clutched the edge of the window as Isoke shot up into the sky.

"By Ghede's ghost!"

"At least he's gotten away," Dante said, as a confused group of tourists ranted to a nearby police officer and pointed toward the empty blue sky.

Amie leaned back against the bench. "He'd better behave." She'd grown more accustomed to that Kongamato than she'd like to admit. He was, in essence, the last of her family. "I've only had him since the holidays," she said. "He came to live with me after my mother passed."

"Is your father still with you?" Dante asked.

Amie gave a brittle laugh. "My mom didn't even know who my dad was. She wasn't what you'd call picky." She paused, swaying against him as the streetcar rattled over the tracks. He waited, as if he understood she needed time to gather her thoughts. He really was a gentleman.

She took a deep breath and let it out. "Mom dated. A lot." Amie frowned hard, remembering. "If she didn't go for a loser, she went for a drunk. If they weren't stealing our grocery money, they were cheating on her. Every one of them crushed her on the way out the door."

It had hurt so bad to watch it happen, over and over again. Every time her mother wept, Amie had lost a piece of herself too.

She stared at the window, focusing on the breeze. It was a welcome relief from the heat of the day.

Dante watched her carefully. "You are afraid of dating men like that."

"Of course not," she said, shaking off his concern. "I'd never do that to myself." She let out a small sigh. "If you'd have seen how she looked when one of them left — like he'd stolen a part of her."

Dante drew her into the crook of his arm. "Love can tear us apart."

"I know," she said, letting her head rest against his shoulder. She had watched her mom give until she had nothing left. "I still can't believe she's gone."

Dante nodded and held her closer. Here he'd been trying to get her to understand him, when what he'd really needed to do was listen.

He kissed Amie on top of the head. A small gesture, meant for comfort and nothing more. Still, she pulled away from him, her eyes red around the edges.

"I'm certainly not going to go through that."

He fought the urge to close the distance between them. "I know."

She shook her head. "I'm sorry, Dante. I know you think you love me and that we're supposed to be together, but I'm not the kind of girl who falls in love. It's just not in me." She wiped at her eyes, but not before he saw the start of a tear. "I'm sorry."

He felt it then, the weight of her resolve — and her despair.

"I'm sorry too," he said, letting the full measure of her declaration settle around him.

He should have been angry. He wanted to be the kind of man to take that love from her. But he wasn't.

She'd called him. She owed it to him. Still, Dante would not demand what she couldn't give, what she couldn't understand.

"You'll meet someone else. You'll have another chance," she said, her back against the hard bench, looking out the window as he settled his arm on the seat back behind her.

He didn't respond. It would do no good to explain. He didn't want her pity, or any half-hearted attempts at love.

They rattled down Carrollton, past the restaurants, old houses, and a small cemetery. It was nearing the dinner hour, and most of the tourists had abandoned the trolley for the restaurants. And still, they rode.

He drew into himself, to the point where it startled him when she spoke. "You were a ghost for two hundred years."

Dante nodded, knowing it would be personal. They were beyond the polite stage.

She watched him for a few seconds. "Why did you stay? Did you have a bad life?"

He spied an older couple cuddling on one of the balconies overlooking the street. "Bad? No. Just incomplete."

She tilted her head toward him. "How so?"

Dante looked away from her, out into traffic. Perhaps sharing secrets wasn't such a wise idea.

"What was your wife's name?" She touched his arm.

He didn't respond. After two hundred years, it still hurt to think about it. This was going to be harder than he'd thought.

"Did she have something to do with your death?"

"No," he said much too quickly.

"I think she did," Amie said quietly.

The kicker was, she was right. He'd eat his eyeballs before he'd admit it to her, but still he couldn't help but remember.

Sophia. Beautiful, treacherous Sophia.

Everyone in his large family had found someone to love them—his five sisters, his parents, his grandparents. Going to a family gathering could be downright depressing.

You'll find someone.

She's out there.

Yes, Sophia had been out there. But she never loved him back.

He followed Amie's gaze to where he'd been absently stroking his ring finger. Damn.

"Did you get shot for her too?" Her expression darkened, "You did." She gasped. "I can see the blue in your aura."

He felt the insane urge to cover up his aura, which was as useless as it was impossible. "I didn't know voodoo mambos believed in that."

She hadn't taken her eyes off him. "I do."

Well hadn't he hit the jackpot? "Yes, I was shot," he ground out.

She closed her hand over his. "Why?"

If she really wanted to hear, he'd tell her. Maybe then she'd be sorry she'd asked.

He took a deep breath and let it out. "I loved my wife with all my heart," he said. Why did Amie have to look at him like that? Like she cared? He swallowed down his pride and admitted the ugly truth. "Sophia did not feel the same."

"You can't possibly know—"

"I found her in bed with another man."

"Oh."

Dante gritted his teeth at the reminder. "I challenged that man, as we did back then. He shot me here," he said, running his finger over the puckered scar above his right eye. "I was dead. She married him."

"I'm sorry," Amie said on an exhale.

He didn't want her sympathy.

The past was the past. Sophie had moved on a long time ago. She'd joined her lover in the afterlife.

Dante looked down at Amie, glad to see the sympathy gone from her eyes.

"And you never left."

"No." It would be hard to spend eternity as the odd man out. He'd met Marie Laveau in the cemetery. She understood him. He told her how he wanted, *needed* a second chance. That's when she told him about that rare kind of voodoo. She'd said he had to be chosen to come back. That there would be much love behind that calling.

He had to believe that.

He'd appeared in dreams to his aunt, a believer. She'd had the resurrection symbol etched onto his tomb.

"You waited all that time?" He could see Amie's surprise. Strange.

"Who wouldn't wait for real love?" There was no choice in that, no doubt or deciding. "I couldn't leave if there was a chance," he ran his fingers along her arm, tangled his hand in hers. "I still can't."

He leaned down and touched his lips to hers. A soft taste, simple and pure. A kiss worthy of her. She sighed against him and deepened their kiss. He touched the back of her neck and drew her closer. She was trembling as he pulled away.

"I don't know what to say," she whispered.

"Mi corazon." He wrapped his uninjured arm

around her, holding her close as the streetcar rattled down the tracks.

He supposed neither of them had a reason to trust. But since when was love reasonable?

Dante smiled down at her. She felt good against him, solid. "My family would have loved you."

A shy smile teased her lips. "You really think so?"

"Without a doubt." He certainly did. Dante let his gaze linger on the gates of Tulane University.

He loved her. She was smart. She was funny. She was *good*.

There was no sense fighting it. It was only natural. Love magic had called him to her.

His chest tightened. He only hoped he hadn't fallen for another woman who couldn't love him back. At least this time, he didn't have to stay.

"Dante?" She looked up at him with those big brown eyes.

"Yes," he said, careful to mask his emotions.

She snuggled against him. "Let's ride again."

* * *

That evening, as they reached the bluffs overlooking the Mississippi River, Dante let himself tumble to the soft ground. He could feel himself tiring quicker than before. The spell had worn thin.

He lay in the grass with his arm around her, watching the endless flow of the river. He knew she feared loss. He did too. There was nothing so awful as to lose the one you love. But that did not mean she should stop feeling. If she did that, she would be as dead as he once was.

Dante refused to let her hide.

If he couldn't be with her, then maybe he could teach her this at least.

He touched her at the waist, his lips skimming hers. "I'm glad you let yourself have fun with me."

She drew back, her fingers tracing the outline of his face. "Me, too."

"Remember that feeling," he urged.

She looked at him imploringly, as if she wanted to say something more. But she held back.

He felt his hand twitch against her waist.

More than anything, love had to be a choice.

He kissed her and drew her to her feet in the soft grass. The night had cooled somewhat and a slight breeze had found her hair. He closed his eyes at the sensation of her pressed up against him. "Let's go home."

"Mmmm...yes," she said, hands trailing down his back. "And this time, don't worry."

A riverboat horn sounded in the distance.

"No?" he asked, nipping her lips.

She gave him one last kiss and then leaned her cheek against his chest. "I won't lead you on," she said. "I promise."

He nodded, even though a part of him had just split in half.

Hadn't he said he wanted all of her or nothing at all?

Fatigue crept up on him with bone-wearying tendrils.

At least he had her for one more day.

Chapter Nine

He'd grown worse by the time they arrived home. She'd seen signs of it all day. His hand would shake slightly as he held her. His eye would twitch, but then be fine. Dante had ignored it, or maybe he didn't realize what was happening. It worried her.

"I think I can help you," she said, reaching for her voodoo reference guides as he sank, bone weary, into the La-Z-Boy.

He leaned back, his profile clean and strong, even as he began to lose his grip on life. "What I need isn't in a book," he said, his eyes widening slightly as he held his hand out in front of him. His pinkie and the two fingers next to it had begun to twitch.

"Um hmm, and who's the voodoo mamb—" She stopped short. His left foot had begun to jerk uncontrollably. Amie gripped the book tightly. This was worse than she thought.

Dante followed her gaze before leaning his head back, spent.

He was being far too calm about this. "What aren't

you telling me? Have you seen this happen before?"

"Once," he said, not looking at her, "about seventy years ago."

"And?" She didn't have time for him to hold back on this.

"It didn't end well."

Her stomach tightened.

"I'm not going to lose you," she told him, and herself.

She grabbed two more books off the shelf and plopped down on the floor. The answer had to be here...somewhere. She scrambled through the index of the first book, her mind racing until she forced herself to take a step back and focus. *Think.* So the spell was wearing off. Well, she'd cast it and she could fix it.

Amie reached back to the bookshelf. Heart pounding, she dumped all of her zombie books on the floor around her. The answer had to be in one of them.

Seven books later, her head pounded. Worse, she wasn't any closer to a solution. None of her spell books talked about reanimating an already animated zombie. It was as if she had missed a crucial step.

"Where's the pink book?" she asked. The entire left half of his body twitched uncontrollably. Could he even hear her anymore? She forced her voice to remain even. "You know. The one you had out on the table yesterday. My mom's pink book."

"With the cookbooks," he mumbled, not even opening his eyes.

Well, no wonder she hadn't seen it. She hurried into the kitchen and found it next to her mother's old *Betty Crocker Homemaker's Guide.*

She turned back to find him trying to stand.

"Dante!" She rushed to him.

He reached out to her for a moment, before his entire arm dropped lifelessly to his side.

"Just...hang on." She helped him back into the chair. Blood soaked through the bandage on his arm. "You need another one," she said, thankful to focus on something as mundane as a gunshot wound.

As for the rest, Amie didn't know what she was going to do.

She'd just gotten Dante back into the chair when she heard the alarm beep downstairs.

Isoke!

The alarm gave a low *bong* sound as it rejected whatever code he'd dialed in. Typical. Still, her heart lightened. She'd welcome Isoke and a dozen dead rats if he could just tell her what had gone wrong with Dante. The Kongamato may not know how to string a set of numbers together, but he had eight generations' worth of practical voodoo.

Amie rushed downstairs, dashed through her shop and threw open the storage room door.

"Yak!" Isoke jumped backward and stumbled into a flowerpot. His beak flew open and he dropped the large black rat he'd been carrying. "*Kipofu!* You have ruined the surprise."

Amie let out a shriek as the live rodent ran straight for her. "Get it out of here!" Luckily, the rat turned on a dime. It dashed under the Kongamato's spread feet and out into the night.

"Quickly," Amie said, ushering him inside.

The Kongamato flapped his wings as he maneuvered sideways through the door. "What's the rush?" Isoke grumbled, folding his wings and waddling past Amie. "I'm ignoring all of my instincts letting that resplendent creature go."

She closed the door behind him. "It's not important right now. I need your help."

Worry clouded his features as he read the look on her face. "What have you done?"

Amie chewed her lip. Would he even want her with Dante if he knew the truth? She'd hate to see Isoke if he was trying to *discourage* a romance. "I summoned a zombie," she admitted.

There. She said it. She was a failure as a voodoo mambo and as a human being. She'd called a man from the dead and if she wasn't careful, she was going to kill him again.

Isoke's mouth dropped open, showing a double row of razor sharp teeth. In the strangled silence, two red scales pinged to the floor.

Oh no. "Are you alright?"

The feathers on the top of his head shook, along with the rest of him. "Have you been smoking *mlima* leaves?" he barked. "Of course I am not alright. I leave you with a nice healthy man and you call up a zombie."

Amie took a breath. "The nice man is the zombie," she confessed.

The Kongamato looked puzzled for a moment, then broke into a grin. "Ah! Well, why didn't you say so? This is fine." He puffed out his chest. "This is wonderful!"

"No, it's not," she said, leading Isoke toward the stairs. "He's sick. The spell is wearing off."

"I've never heard of such a thing," he said, following. "Then again, your line does not have the best luck with men."

Yeah, well it was worse than that.

"Hurry." She urged Isoke through the door upstairs.

Dante lay on the recliner. He looked like death. His eyes were sunken behind dark circles. His skin had gone pasty and his entire left hand twitched uncontrollably.

"It was an accident," she insisted, crouching close and taking his hand. "I woke him as part of a love spell." But now? She'd never touch him again if that's what it took to save him.

Isoke landed on the arm of the recliner and leaned forward to inspect Dante. He was shaking badly. Blood trickled from under his bandage.

She'd thought she wanted love, but she didn't. Not this way.

Isoke looked at Amie as if he blamed her too. "Something is very wrong. I have seen soul mates raised. It is a beautiful thing. This is not."

"I know." Amie touched her hand to Dante's forehead. It was cold. He shivered, and she wanted to curl up in his lap and cry.

He was going to be taken from her forever. There would be no one else. She couldn't handle it. Besides, she knew there would never be another man like him.

Isoke leaned his head against her. "It is powerful magic to bring back the dead. You must need him very much."

Needing was one thing. Having was quite another. "I'll leave him alone forever if you can help me fix him."

She swore she'd never follow in her mother's footsteps and she wouldn't. It was going to be safe and boring from here on out.

Isoke drew away from her. "I'm sorry," he said,

"there is no spell for reanimating a zombie. And if he dies again, he is truly and forever dead."

Her heart stuttered. "We have to do something." She couldn't lose him. Not yet.

"I will leave you alone," Isoke said, waddling across the room. "Follow your heart, *bembe*." He closed the door softly behind him. "This is something you must do on your own."

He'd said Dante was her soul mate.

"Amie," Dante murmured, his lips barely parting.

Not here. Not now. The tears welled in her eyes as she squeezed in next to him. He was cold. She wrapped herself around him, trying to keep him warm. "We have another day," she said, embarrassed at how her voice cracked.

"We don't," he said.

"Dante. Please." There was so much to say and she had no idea where to start. He'd shown her so many things about herself in such a short time. She needed more of him. She needed to know if she was truly meant to be with him. It couldn't end this way. "I don't want you to die."

"That's not enough," he said, on what might have been his last breath.

Her throat constricted. "But I don't want you to leave."

Dante's eyes cracked open, dazed. "That's not enough."

Her tears flowed freely as he closed his eyes once more.

He wasn't moving anymore. He was barely breathing.

He was leaving.

"I love you," she whispered. Heaven help her, she

loved him. And it was awful. She already felt the
loss, the dread. Amie took his face in her hands and
kissed his cold lips, his cheek, his chin. She felt her
magic build inside her as she opened herself to him,
in honor of him.

Amie touched her forehead to his and closed her
eyes, savoring the moment, her last time with him.
She focused on the beauty and the happiness she'd
found as the magic thrummed through her. Maybe
she'd never get it back. Maybe she was a damned
crazy fool to feel this way, but she loved him. And she
needed him to know.

She needed him to feel the goodness and light and
strength he gave to her, just by being with her.

It built so sweet and strong that she wept with it.
Her tears fell against his cheeks as she touched her
lips to his and released her love magic in one glorious
wave.

It poured into him, stunning and whole. The air
around them shimmered as pure love glowed between them. She held nothing back. For the first time
in her life, she gave everything. She had to think that
he felt it, that he understood.

Amie knew she would never be the same.

This magic would never come back and she didn't
care. She gave it to him, brilliant and true, because of
who he was...how he made her feel. It was the most
natural gift she could give. It was her love spun out
like silk. She needed him to have it before he died.

Amie laid her head on his cold hard chest, drained,
yet more at peace than she'd ever been.

Her heart fluttered as traces of her love magic
sizzled between them. Her breath caught. She didn't
know exactly what that meant, only that her magic

had slowly begun to grow instead of diminish.

The traces weren't flowing to him, but from him and through her and back to him. She could see it like golden cords between them. She raised her head and discovered him watching her. "Dante?" she asked breathlessly.

She was almost afraid to hope, worried it would be snatched away.

He cocked a weak grin. Amie wet her lips. His face had regained some color. He still appeared tired, but..."What's happening?" she asked.

"You love me." She went weak as he reached for her, his arms holding her tight. "You care. It was all I needed."

She buried herself against the warmth of his chest. "Yes," she sobbed against him.

"And I love you." He leaned forward and kissed her lightly, tasting the salt of her tears.

She felt the power this time, a soul-deep tug as it spiraled through her. It warmed her, fulfilled her and..."Please tell me it's going to be okay."

"It is." The corner of his mouth tipped up as he looked at her with a love that humbled her. "You saved me, Amie," he whispered. She followed his gaze to the empty place on her bookshelf. His wedding ring had disappeared.

"I can't believe it," she said, and yet she could. For once in her life, she'd been willing to give herself, fully and completely.

She'd been given a second chance.

And so had he.

Her heart squeezed. "You're really going to be fine?"

"More than fine," he said against her lips. His arms

slipped around her and he demonstrated exactly how he had recovered.

It was beautiful and intense and — confusing. "Wait. How?"

He drew her back down to him. "Because you were brave enough to love me."

Meet Amie and Dante again in Night of the Living Demon Slayer, *part of the Accidental Demon Slayer series by Angie Fox*

I Brake for Biker Witches

Author's Note: This short story takes place two weeks after the events in *The Last of the Demon Slayers,* and refers indirectly to the events in *What Slays in Vegas* (from the *So I Married a Demon Slayer* anthology). It's not necessary to read any of the other demon slayer stories, though, in order to enjoy this one. As the biker witches would say: No worries. It's all good. Now where did I put that bottle of Jack?...

Chapter One

It was a dark and lonely night. No, seriously — it was. You wouldn't believe the pitch black you get in the middle of the desert in California. No lights. No people. Nothing. We hadn't even seen another vehicle in almost an hour.

I gunned my Harley and heard the answering roar of two dozen biker witches on my tail.

We were one-hundred-and-fifty miles into the Mojave desert, on our way back from Las Vegas to L.A. Some over-zealous jerk had reported a demon infestation in Sin City, but when we'd gotten there, we'd only found a half-succubus running a pampered pet salon.

We let her be. I couldn't smite a dog person, especially after she had my Jack Russell Terrier smelling like Paws-4-Patchouli. Besides, the girl with the demonic bent was more good than bad. My demon slayer powers had told me that much.

The headset inside my silver helmet buzzed with static and then clicked. "Where the hell are we?"

My biker witch grandma's voice tickled my ear. "Zzyzx."

I didn't quite catch that. "You cut out."

"Zzyzx." Grandma said, "It's the name of the town."

Frankly, I didn't see anything but a straight dark road and acres of scrub. Still, there was something here that wasn't quite right. I'd felt it at back of my neck for the last fifty miles, the prickling unease that signaled trouble.

It had gotten worse in the last minute. Way worse. "Does anyone else feel that?"

"You mean like low in my stomach?" Ant Eater asked.

"Yes." And tingling up my spine. It wasn't necessarily demonic—I knew exactly what that felt like. But it was something *else*. Something I'd never felt before.

The radio crackled. "Maybe we need to stop and get some snacks," my Jack Russell terrier suggested.

"No," everyone said at once.

In his defense, Pirate was a dog with a one-track mind, usually trained on food. Because of our powers, we could hear him talk, and talk...and talk. We should never have given him a head set.

At least the sweet-smelling troublemaker was riding shotgun with Bob. I didn't want Pirate up here with me if we ran into trouble.

Our headlights reflected off a lone green highway sign up ahead. "Well would you look at that," I said under my breath. In big, white letters it read: Zzyzx.

Pirate gave a yip. "I just won the alphabet game."

"Wait." Ant Eater's voice sharpened. She was the scariest biker I knew. That's why she always rode shotgun. "You see that? Dead ahead."

"I see it." My pulse thrummed with anticipation. A figure of a man stood under the sign. We wouldn't have seen him so far out, except he was glowing.

Jesus, Mary, Joseph and the mule. We couldn't even take one ride through the desert without trouble.

I could almost hear the witches going for their spell jars.

We slowed as we approached, our headlights trained on a bald man with a thick, braided beard. I strained for a better look as recognition wound through me.

"Holy hell," Frieda whispered.

I remembered where I'd seen him before. Frieda had been carrying his picture for as long as I'd known her. She'd post it over her bed, clip it on her spell books, have it handy wherever we happened to be. She'd rub him on the forehead and hum the same tune every time.

This was Mister *Love in an Elevator.*

He'd been dead for as long as I'd known her.

I ground my bike to a halt about ten feet back from him. Close enough to talk, far enough to throw a switch star if it came to that.

Frieda would tan my hide. I said a silent prayer for him to behave.

One by one, the Red Skull witches cut their engines. I took my helmet off and hung it over a handle bar.

Frieda had already scrambled out from behind one of the bikers toward the front. She approached the phantom slowly, all the while holding a spell jar behind her back. It swirled with a brackish, blue and gold liquid.

Grandma stood next to me as I dismounted, one hand on my weapons belt. I tilted my head toward her. "What's she got?"

"Ghost zapper," she said, her voice gritty from years of hard riding and semi-truck exhaust, "It blasts their energy field. Damned thing better not be expired."

Good point. We didn't get too many ghosts.

This one wore leather chaps, a black leather jacket and a Texas bikers t-shirt.

I pulled a switch star from my belt, just in case. It was flat and round. Five blades curled around the edge.

The white from Frieda's zebra print leather pants glowed in our headlights as she tottered forward on four-inch red wedge sandals. "Carl? Is that you, baby?"

Sweat tickled the back of my neck. Frieda was a sitting duck if this didn't work.

Amusement sparked from the ghost's heavy lidded eyes. "Well don't you look pretty?"

She stopped a few feet in front of him, her red dice earrings swaying as she shook. "Are you...alive?"

He wound his thumbs under his black leather belt. "Aw, now you know I'da come back for you if I was." He glanced past Frieda, his bottomless blue eyes locking on me. "I wouldn't be back now. Except we need your help."

Dread pooled in my stomach. This couldn't be good "Who's *we*?"

The ghost eyed me. "We got a new gang going, for those of us who have passed on."

Oh lordy.

"Shouldn't you be in heaven or something?" Frieda asked.

"Not yet, baby." He touched her fluffy blonde

hair. It ruffled slightly as his fingers moved straight through it. "You still need us, whether you realize it or not. But we've gotten into a little trouble in the mean time."

He had to be kidding. I was a demon slayer, not a ghost whisperer. I couldn't babysit a bunch of undead bikers. "What exactly do you want me to do?"

He turned his back on us as a chrome and black Harley appeared on the side of the road. Neat trick.

"Come on," he said, heading for his bike, "I'll show you."

Chapter Two

"Oh sure," I muttered as we trailed after him through the darkness, sharp rocks sounding like fireworks under our tires. "Go off road. Follow an undead biker through the middle of the Mojave desert." I could feel the dirt in my eyes. I could taste it in my mouth. Our Harley's weren't built for this.

"No worries, demon slayer," Ant Eater's voice sounded behind my ear, "I know where we are."

My bike was vibrating so bad my arms were going numb. "What? With magic?"

"GPS."

Okay. Well there was that.

Ant Eater chuckled low in her throat.

We'd been following the former Carl for at least twenty miles. I stared out into the night sky, the stars impossibly bright now that we were truly in the middle of nowhere. And about due for a breakdown.

We gunned our engines up and over a small rise.

I stopped so hard my bike skid sideways.

"What the hell is that?" Grandma choked.

Lights shone from a building below. Only it wasn't a building exactly. It was a shell of a foundation, half buried in the dirt. Phantom walls surrounded it and I could see glowing figures moving inside.

The building shimmered and in that moment, I could make out a distinct, two-story Wild West tavern. Cracked paint announced the Tanglefoot Saloon. The rough wood front looked gray from the weather and age. At the horse hitch outside, I saw a line of ghostly gray horses. And motorcycles.

The image shifted and I saw the faint outline of a two-story stucco building with neon bar signs in the window. Then it shifted back to the saloon. Iron Maiden's *Twilight Zone* thumped out into the parking lot, mixed with the faint tinkling of a piano.

What the—? I glanced at Grandma, who just shook her head.

We pulled closer. Weeds sprouted around the front of the saloon and a prickly pear cactus grew straight through the sign for the Paradise Bar and Grill.

Our tires nudged the edge of a cracked parking lot. The desert stretched for miles in every direction.

"It's not real," I said, almost convinced.

"Damn straight," Ant Eater said, agreeing with me for once.

We could deny it until gypsies grew wings, but there it was, as if it had sprung from the desert floor itself.

"I smell pickled eggs," Pirate said, scrambling through the maze of Red Skull bikers, heading for the front door.

"Wait," I scooped him up. I was detecting something else.

"Demonic?" Grandma asked.

I opened my senses. "Maybe."

There was a raw energy to this place, like nothing I'd ever felt before. There was also a wrong-ness that I couldn't quite put my finger on. I tucked my dog under my arm. "Stick close, buddy," I said, not giving him a choice.

"Aw now, Lizzie. Why don't you let me have any fun?" His legs dangled as he tried to push off me and jump down. "I'll be careful."

Like a bulldozer.

Grandma studied the phantom bar. "Okay," she said, rubbing at her mouth. "I want half of you to stay outside and make a perimeter," she said to the witches. "Get your spells out and be ready to use them." She eyed Carl, who had already walked up to the front door and stood beckoning us. She raised her voice. "The rest of us will follow Carl."

Ant Eater leaned in close, as she pried off her leather riding gloves. "You sure that's a good plan?"

"Best one we got," Grandma muttered.

I was with Ant Eater on this one. A demon could take on many forms. Of course I wasn't naïve enough to think we were safe outside, or anywhere for that matter. "I'll go first," I said, setting my dog down on the ground. "You," I said, pointing at him, "are on backup patrol." Maybe I could at least keep him out of trouble.

"Now that's just crazy." He said, circling before he sat. "Who ever heard of a watch dog going last?"

I gave him a quick rub on the head before Grandma, Ant Eater and I led the way across the parking lot.

The ghost paused at a shimmering wooden door. Clusters of cinnamon sticks wrapped in sage faded in and out of the wood and a rusty red substance streamed down the frame.

It was all too familiar — and stinky. Okay, so maybe I was starting to believe that Carl really was the ghost of a Red Skull biker witch.

He opened the door and music poured out, along with a great deal of bar noise.

I stepped inside and nearly fell sideways.

The Tanglefoot/Paradise looked like a saloon, straight out of a Wild West movie. The large high-ceiling room featured a scattering of rounded tables under gas-lit chandeliers. The walls were rough wood. A long carved bar stretched along the back, with a mirror behind it. Along one side, a standing piano hunkered next to a modern sound system.

Biker witches crowded the tables, playing poker with outlaws and cowhands. Saloon girls weaved between the tables. Cheers erupted over a minor fistfight next to some kind of big, round gambling wheel.

Sadly, this wasn't the strangest thing I'd ever seen.

And then I saw them.

"There's Hog Wild Harriet," I gasped, "dealing poker." And cheating from the look of the cards stuffed in her bra. I could see them every time she faded out.

And there was Easy Edna, Lucinda the Lush and a half dozen other dead witches. They'd been killed helping us, sacrificing for us.

Grandma drew up short. "Son of a bitch."

"Heyyy!" Betty Two Sticks staggered up to us, a bottle of 1800 whiskey in hand. "This stuff is good. Now I'm seeing demon slayers." She poked me with a finger, only it went straight through. "Damn it all, it is a demon slayer. I was hoping you'd make it."

I turned to Grandma. "She's smashing drunk."

Betty screwed up her face like she had to think about that one. "I know you are, but what am I?"

"They're all here," Grandma muttered. "I know every god damned one of them."

Unbelievable. I stared at drunkard next to me, from her tie-dyed bandana to her steel toed boots. "What is this place?"

Betty stuck her face inches from mine. She smelled like the inside of a Jack Daniels bottle. "Hey," she tried to whisper, only she was on full volume, "you gotta meet this guy. He shot seven people. He's the fastest gun in," she turned around, "what are you the fastest gun in?" she yelled to a table of outlaws behind her.

This was too much. "Where's Carl?" I leaned to see past Betty. "Oh. Great." He was over by the juke box, making out with Frieda. That was a big help.

The bar flashed to modern and then back west again. And Betty had clearly forgotten the meaning of personal space. I took a step back. "Why are you here?"

She screwed up her face like it was a tough question, not even flinching as one ghostly cowboy clocked another over the head with a whiskey bottle. "I'm socializing," she concluded. "Had my eye on a few of them hotties from the Lazy K Ranch."

Oh geez. "No, I meant—" How could I explain?

It was like reasoning with Pirate, only way worse. I didn't want to think of these dead bikers stuck here. They deserved to be in a better place.

"You can move on, Betty," I said, ducking as a chair flew past my head. It didn't matter. The chair crashed straight through Grandma and skittered across the hard wood floor. "Why didn't you go to the light?"

I wasn't sure how one went to the light, or got out of this place for that matter, but I hoped somebody around here could give her a few hints. Then again, it could be a spiritually sticky place. Clearly the Wild West show had been playing for awhile.

She clutched the neck of her whiskey bottle, eyeing me intently. "Scarlet went to the light."

At least that was one.

"She was a real pussy about it too. The rest of us are waiting," she said proudly.

My head was starting to hurt. "For what?"

She flipped her long grey braid behind her back. "For you."

Okay that was creepy. My heart thudded in my chest. This had better not be a trap.

"You see this?" Grandma clapped a hand on my shoulder. "Battina, Easy Edna," she said as the ghosts of biker witches ambled up behind her.

I gave a half wave, not getting this at all. Grandma merely grinned, watching as the biker witches, live and dead re-united. Some tried hugs, but their arms went straight through their friends, so they'd settled on clinking whiskey glasses and gathering around the rough, wooden tables and along dusty barstools.

"Damn it's good to see everyone. I wouldn't mind spending a century or two holed up here," Grandma said, her gaze traveling over the bar. "Except for that," she added, fixing on a rickety wooden staircase near the back bar. A thick yellow fog tumbled from the top. I could feel malice at the top of those stairs.

I focused my demon slayer senses and saw it like a dot in the back of my mind — latent evil waiting to strike.

And then I saw someone else and my heart instantly lightened. "Uncle Phil!"

I'd lost my fairy grandfather almost a year before. He'd died saving me.

Leave it to Phil. He wasn't partying or goofing around. He was busy working some kind of a spell at the bottom of the stairway. Well, at least that was the only thing I could figure from the way he waved his short, thick arms.

He stood in a cloud of silver sparkles, his bushy eyebrows fixed in concentration and his bulbous nose as red as it had ever been. I could almost smell his familiar bubblegum scent.

"Watch my back," I said to Grandma as I made a path straight for him.

Phil didn't see me until I was almost up on him. When he did, his mouth broke into a wide grin. "Lizzie! I knew you'd come. I just knew it." His voice shot through me like sunshine. "I'd hug you, but I'd go right through you."

Didn't I know it. "What are you doing here?"

Fairy dust settled over his pointy ears, which looked like they'd been crammed on as an afterthought. "I told you I'd always watch out for you."

Sure, but, "here?"

A frigid wind whipped from the top of the stairs, startling us both.

"Just a second," Phil said, replacing pennies that had tumbled down. It was then I noticed the coins littering the stairs.

"What are you doing?"

"Basic fairy protection," he said, hurrying. "We use coins for good wishes, but the positive energy can also work against evil spirits, or any basic malicious entity."

Another dose of cold power blasted the stairs and more pennies scattered down the steps.

"Cripes. We're down seven," he said, lobbing them back up. He glanced over his shoulder. "You wouldn't happen to have any extra change, would you?"

I hitched my switch star and began digging in my pockets. "Two quarters and a dime."

His eyes lit up. "Oh yes. That's good. We like the big spenders."

I'd never been accused of that. "What is this?"

"Wish magic," he said, carefully arranging the coins on the bottom steps. "Only this is a lot more powerful that what you humans do when you throw pennies in the fountain at the park."

No kidding. "Is that where we got it?"

"Of course. Now aim for the top. As you throw it, wish for the darkness to fade. I want to get as many up there as I can."

"Okay," I said, stepping onto the bottom stair.

"Wait. No!" He grabbed for my arm and his fingers went straight through. "You'll be incinerated!"

"How?" I froze, one foot on the stairway, scattering change as I drew a switch star.

Phil's eyes had gone wide with shock. They darted to me, then down to my foot, then back up at me. "By stepping on the stair," he said slowly.

He gawked at me like I was the crazy part of this equation.

"Yes, well I suppose that's one advantage of being a demon slayer," I said, suddenly embarrassed. Of course there were a whole lot of disadvantages as well, one being whatever was waiting for me on the second floor.

"Keep up the magic down here," I said, double checking my switch stars, "I'm going to go see what's eating your quarters."

Phil's nostrils flared. I could see he was torn. "I can't protect you, Lizzie. Not up there."

"I know," I said, my hand hovering above his arm, wishing I could give him a little reassurance. "Maybe I can protect you."

Chapter Three

I took one step at a time, trying not to disturb the change, more for Phil's sake than my own. If I failed up here, he'd need the protection.

The coins were slick under my feet as I made my way upward.

The evil at the top of the stairs pulsed with energy. It called to me as the air temperature plummeted.

I blew out a breath and watched it cloud. Ice meant evil.

My fingers tightened in the handle of my switch star.

Focus.

This wasn't about me. It was about what needed to be done up here. I braced myself on the second to last step.

It was pitch black beyond the doorway. I could almost feel whatever-it-was breathing in the darkness. Adrenaline slammed through my veins.

I reached into the front left pocket of my weapons belt and drew out a Lamp Spell, a little something special Grandma had brewed up for me. It skittered across the floor and light burst from the broken gas lights along the walls of the second floor hallway.

It illuminated a narrow hallway and a portal unlike any I'd ever seen before.

H-e-double-hockey-sticks. It was as large as two people and glowed with an unearthly blue fire. Sparks scattered from it, charring the walls and floor. It thrummed, as if it were trying to grow.

My mouth went dry. I gripped the entry way as it slowly began to advance on me.

Could I switch star a portal?

I didn't know.

Portals thrived on energy. For all I knew, my switch star would be like hitting it with a power boost.

Hell.

"Grandma?" I called down the stairs. There was no response. Either she couldn't hear me or she couldn't get close. I wasn't about to turn my back on this thing to find out.

"Oh frick." I didn't have much of a choice here. I drew back, ready to fire.

"Wait!" A red headed witch stepped from behind the pulsing blue mass.

It hit me like a rock to the stomach. "Scarlet?"

She was supposed to have gone to the light. I wanted that for her, needed it. She'd died saving me. She deserved some peace.

But there she stood, in black leather pants and an emerald bustier. She flipped her long red hair behind her shoulder as she gathered her composure. I think she was as surprised to see me as I was to see her.

"They told me you'd moved on," I said.

"Not yet," she said, worry creasing her brow. "I

can't leave everyone else here. They refuse to go," she said, as if she couldn't quite believe it.

"They need to leave," I said, thinking of the trashed Betty. "But you can't make that decision for them."

"Oh so you want me to abandon them here forever?" She crossed her arms over her chest. "Typical, coming from you. Always the individual. You never thought about the group."

That wasn't true, but I wasn't about to get into it with her. I flinched as the portal spit a blue spark way too close to my arm. "Whatever you're working on here has gone bad." Besides, "I don't think our friends want to go." At least, not yet.

"Doesn't matter," she said, as if it were fact. "I'm going to save them whether they like it or not." She smiled, a sweet turn of the lips laced with venom. "So kindly keep your switch stars away from my portal."

I shook my head. "You're messing with free will, Scarlet." No wonder evil had seeped in. "This is a portal to a bad realm."

"Impossible," she said, her eyes widening as I drew back to fire. She rushed to stand in front of the pulsing blue mass, blocking me.

"Move aside," I ordered.

"No." She was frantic now. "It will go to the light. I'll make sure it does."

The portal was growing behind her. "You can't choose that for anyone but yourself, Scarlet." My fingers whitened on the grips of the switch star. "Now back away." I didn't want to take a chance on her getting hit, but I wasn't about to let this thing get any more out of hand than it was.

"Don't fuck this up, Lizzie. You can't fuck this up," she hollered, shaking, tears in her eyes as she scurried to the edge of the hissing portal. "I'm not going to leave them behind."

"Scarlet, no!" I drew back and fired as she shoved it straight for me.

CHAPTER FOUR

I dove to the floor as my switch star slammed into the portal. Energy shot out, singing my arms and numbing my teeth.

The brightness blinded me for a moment. I lay clutching the floor, blinking against the dots. Horrified, I saw the portal zoom straight over me and down the stairs.

"Son of a—" I took off after it, with Scarlet right behind.

She hit me with a blast of power as we dashed headlong for the runaway gateway to God-knew-what. I felt it like an electric punch to the back. Coins popped underfoot. I grabbed for the railing as she tried to throw me down the stairs.

"Duck!" I screamed at Phil, who hit the deck as it zoomed past him.

"Red Skulls! Defensive positions." Grandma hollered from behind him, her voice clear above the fray.

Witches dove under tables and behind the bar as the portal swooped low, zapping two outlaws, the stereo system and a cowboy strumming a guitar.

Phil was still on the floor. I dropped to my knees next to him. "What do we do?"

He swung a fist straight through me and into Scarlet. She went down in a heap. He sat up, breathing hard, grey hair wild. "I'd never hit a lady, but she was about to hex you."

"She's not a lady anymore," I said, urging him behind the nearest overturned table. "I don't know what she is anymore."

The portal zipped over the bar, shattering glasses and exploding the long gold mirror. A ghostly piano player plopped down on the bench and began playing the *Wabash Cannonball* as cowboys and outlaws went after the portal, guns blazing.

"Fire in the hole!" Grandma hollered as a wave of spell jars blasted the portal. It shimmered, turning purple and then back to blue.

Our biker witch reinforcements poured into the bar, led by Pirate.

"Let 'er rip!" Grandma hollered. This time, the portal shook under the onslaught.

Grandma dove behind our table. "Lizzie, we need one last blast of juice," she said, digging a jar out of her pack as the piano banged and witches scrambled to re-load.

"You ready?" she asked as I drew a switch star and focused all my energy, all my love, all my desire on blasting that deadly gate to hell where it belonged.

"Ready."

She gripped my shoulder. "Hold back until I tell you," she said, standing up. "And...fire!" She threw the jar like Roberto Clemente.

The portal shot sparks as each spell slammed into

it.

"Go, Lizzie!" I threw and as the portal turned purple, my switch star tore a hole straight through it.

The biker witches and the outlaws cheered as it folded in on itself, sparking and hissing. It collapsed in on its own energy until it disappeared with a loud crack, sucked back to wherever it came.

I knelt on the floor, sweating as Phil and I stared at each other wide eyed.

"I'd say we did it," he said, in the understatement of the year.

I forgot and tried to embrace him. Naturally, I went straight through. "Damn it." The air was warm and smelled like bubblegum, which made me smile.

"Don't curse," he said, grinning as wide as I was.

Yeah, well I was hanging around the biker witches too much.

"Did we lose any?" Grandma asked, finger jabbing as she counted the witches. She exhaled. "We didn't lose anybody."

Just a few outlaws and the blackjack dealer. I clapped her on the shoulder, as relieved as she was. We always seemed to lose somebody.

The biker witches were dusting off, hugging, sharing whiskey bottles and greeting the reinforcements. It was a reunion all over again.

"Wait." I scanned the bar. "Where's Scarlet?"

She stood at the bottom of the stairs, Phil's coins sizzling on her ghostly flesh, a death spell in each hand.

I approached her slowly, one hand on my switch stars. But much of the fight had already gone out of her.

She stood, bewildered. "What happened to me?"

she asked, almost to herself. "What did I do?"

"It's okay," I said, stopping a few feet away. "You're back with us now." I imagined a shimmering white tunnel above her head. I could feel it, open and ready.

"But," she stared at the path above her, torn.

"Go, Scarlet." She deserved warmth. She deserved peace. "Go to the light."

Fear glanced across her features, replaced with a firm resolve. She nodded to me, accepting at last. "Thanks, Lizzie."

"I'll never forget what you did for me," I said.

She smiled faintly and then tilted her face toward the light.

Scarlet rose up, becoming one with it, and at that moment, I too felt peaceful.

The bar had gone quiet as the biker witches, both alive and dead, stood watching.

"You should go too," I said to the rest of the ghosts.

They murmured among themselves, not moving. Carl shook his head slowly.

He walked up to me, the steel chains of his biker boots clinking with every step. "I wasn't lying when I said you needed us, Lizzie." He stopped, studying me. "There's a revolution brewing in hell."

"I know." I was going to have to face it. "But it's not your war."

He seemed surprised at that. "Of course it is. When each of us died, we were given a choice. Go to the light or wait to make a difference."

I stood, not sure what to say, as I looked out on the bar full of ghostly biker witches.

"We're your last line of defense," Carl continued, "and I don't mind saying, I think you're going to need our help."

"From ghost bikers?" I was still trying to wrap my head around it.

Grandma chuckled. "Is there any better kind?"

"What about them?" I asked, as a table full of cowboys broke out into an off-key rendition of *The Yellow Rose of Texas.*

One who could definitely use a shower and a shave guffawed. "Peace and light ain't what we're after."

Obviously. "Then what are the rest of you waiting for?"

"A good fight," said his buddy. The men at the table cheered and stomped their boots against the dusty wood floor.

Yeah, well I could probably arrange that.

A tussle broke out between the outlaws at the bar. "We'll just have a little fun here until you need us." Carl grinned as Betty handed him a shot.

"How will I know how to find you?" I looked out at the motley crew of outlaws and bikers. It wasn't like we'd be fighting demons in the middle of the desert.

"You'll find us," he said, toasting me before downing his whiskey. "You might not need us right away. But when the time comes, we'll be here."

"I'm glad," I said, and heaven help me—I was.

Enjoy more of Lizzie's adventures with the biker witches in the Accidental Demon Slayer series by Angie Fox

Date With A Demon Slayer

Chapter One

"What do you mean you sent my anniversary present back?" I stared at the silver haired biker witch. She wore chaps, a leather jacket with fringe, and had an obnoxious rhinestone skull do-rag knotted around her neck. Sue me when I felt the urge to yank it tighter.

Yes, my Grandmother's gang of witches was…unusual. Word had it, they'd been a regular coven before a demon had kept them on the run for thirty years. After that, they'd had to move fast, stay on the road. They'd started riding Harleys. Then came the biker nicknames, the tattoos, and boyfriends named Lizard Lips. The rest was history.

At the moment, I was tempted to call Ant Eater by her real name. Mildred.

Her eyes widened behind her green tinted hippie sunglasses as I glared at her. She held up her hands. "I'm telling you, Lizzie, it looked like another box of empty beer cans."

That got a definite frown from the hunky shape-shifting griffin to my right. "The package was addressed to me," he growled.

Damn. I always liked having him on my side. Luckily, I'd been smart enough to marry him. Dimitri stood a foot above the tallest one of us, a wall of muscle and grit. And I'd never get enough of my husband's lyrical Greek accent, even now, with Ant Eater pulling one of her stunts.

"Fairy mail usually requires a signature," I said.

Fae paths were strictly regulated. Reliable, too. Fairy postal workers could find anyone, anywhere in two to three business days. It was the best way to get things while we were on the road.

Ant Eater shook her head. "If you want to return something, you just gotta tell them it isn't for you." She blew out a breath. "I should have looked at the whole *who it was addressed to* thing," she said with a wince, which was as close to an apology as we'd get. She shot a glare at the blonde witch closing in on her left. "I was trying to save our asses. I don't care if Frieda collects what she drinks," she said, turning up the volume, "but if that woman doesn't stop ordering beer cans on eBay, we're going to be buried in rusty Schlitz cans."

"Those cans are vintage," Frieda said, as if we were dissing her children. "You show me a 1954 Schlitz that doesn't have rust." She brought a bright pink painted fingernail to her chin. "And if we're cleaning up, maybe I should toss all those bras you have hanging down by the creek."

That earned her a glare from Ant Eater. "Do it and you die."

"What the frick, people?" I asked. And when did this become my life?

Yes, I'd run off with my grandma's gang of biker

witches. They'd taught me how to fulfill my destiny as a demon slayer. They'd also saved my butt more than once. In return, I'd hoped I could calm them down a little. I'd been a preschool teacher in my former life. I'd made my peace with chaos.

This was a whole new brand of it. And somewhere along the way, they'd gotten me into wearing leather pants. And bustiers.

I wasn't quite sure how that happened.

In any case, we didn't need to be fighting about beer cans. Or dirty undies. I got that riding Georgia's winding back roads could make a person spit dust, but, "No unpacking. We're only stopping for dinner."

Frieda snorted. "Damn, I hope you get more than that."

"That's rude," I told her, ignoring Ant Eaters low chuckle. Although, frankly, I'd been hoping the same thing.

A year ago, on this very night, I'd married the mostly sweet and always sexy Dimitri Kallinikos. We'd said our 'I do's' at a gorgeous estate on the coast. Of course, the Earl of Hell crashed the wedding, but you know, these things happen.

This year, we found ourselves toning it down a little.

Okay, a lot.

At the moment, we stood in a field off Route 9. We hadn't seen anyone for miles.

It was me, my sexy-as-sin husband and about thirty biker witches, who were busy tossing back beers, making campfires, and setting up dart boards against some pine trees by the creek.

I turned to Dimitri. "You want to help me with this one?"

But he'd retreated several steps and spoke urgently on his phone, tracking my present no doubt.

We were headed out of New Orleans after defeating a necromancer who'd had a hard time letting the dead stay that way. We'd earned a break. And when we saw a neat looking old restaurant, we stopped. Never mind that it didn't open for another hour. Or that chains blocked the driveway. No doubt they did that to keep out trespassers. It was no problem to park the biker witches in the woods next door.

The restaurant looked like it had been some kind of plantation house before. I loved the white columns out front, the long winding drive, the brick and iron entrance gates, dripping with lush green vines.

It was perfect for what I had in mind: a date night with my husband. Alone.

Frieda followed my gaze, which had pretty much moved to Dimitri's ass. "You think he got you some sexy lingerie?" she asked.

Little did she know I was already wearing a hot red number I'd picked up in Baton Rouge.

Ant Eater barked out a laugh. "He's got to do something to make up for the dinner." She nudged me. "A hoity-toity place like that is going to serve boring steak and chicken. They won't even have squirrel. Do you know how easy it is to hunt squirrel around here? Your grandma's already caught a half a dozen."

Lovely. We could always count on Grandma to lead the charge.

Then again, the biker witches had agreed to give us a night to ourselves for our anniversary. They could eat raccoon livers for all I cared.

"Just don't get too comfortable," I told them, heading off to join Dimitri. Left to their own devices, there was no telling what the witches would do. "No enchanted animals, no beer can sculptures, and try not to hang your undies in view of the restaurant."

"What part of camping out don't you get?" Ant Eater hollered after me.

Dimitri ended his call and shoved the phone into his pocket. He kissed me on the head. "No worries. We're going to have an amazing night. And," he wrapped an arm around me, "I just arranged for your gift to be delivered after dinner." I loved how he always tried to make things special, even out here.

"I don't know what I did to deserve you," I said.

I nestled against his warm chest.

Behind us, a group of biker witches let out whoops and *atta-girl* cheers.

I leaned my forehead against my man. "Someone must be tapping the pony keg."

Dimitri brushed a kiss over the top of my head. "I think they're cat-calling us."

We weren't even doing anything yet. I felt my lips quirk as I looked up at his handsome face. "You had your chance to run." I was stuck with the biker witches. He signed up for this when he married me.

"Didn't notice." The side of his mouth cocked in a half-grin. "As soon as I saw you, I had to have you."

I leaned up and touched my lips against his. It was supposed to be a thank-you, maybe even a little bit of a tease. But then his mouth slid over mine, and I forgot all about that. I pressed against his solid chest as he deepened the kiss. Mine. His hands slipped down my back, cupped my butt as I ground closer to him.

Oh yes, I couldn't wait to be alone with this man.

"Time out," my Grandma called, jogging over to us. Right. I pulled away. Although Dimitri still managed to keep a hand on my ass. Is that true love or what?

Grandma had tied back her long gray hair into braids and was grinning like a mad woman. "Before you disappear," she said, slightly out of breath, "we've got some anniversary presents to give you." She held out a hand as a smart aleck witch named Creely caught up to her. The heavily tattooed witch barked out a laugh as she gave Grandma a recycled jelly jar filled with pinkish-blue goo. Grandma waggled it at us like a tease. "This is to ramp up the passion. Get all wild and crazy. Right?"

"Like we were before you interrupted us," Dimitri said.

"At least we caught you early," Creely said, tossing a red Kool-Aid dyed lock of hair out of her eyes as she reached into her bag again.

Grandma shoved the Passion Spell into my hands as Creely handed her a second jar. This one was filled with greenish-brownish sludge and reminded me of a swamp I'd go out of my way to avoid. Grandma held it up proudly. "Break *this* jar if you want to hold off the passion. Like if you just ordered one of them pricey ten dollar hamburgers from that restaurant over there and you want to get your money's worth." She handed it to me.

I tested the lid, making sure it was sealed tight.

"Guard that," Creely said, "he's going to try and hide it."

Grandma let out a guffaw.

"Speaking of that restaurant," Dimitri said, eyeing the mansion, "I just saw them open the driveway gate. We should think about heading over."

"Wait," Grandma held up a finger. "One more treat

for you tonight." She drew a small baby food jar from the leather pouch at her belt. It twinkled with a thousand tiny sparks, like trapped stars. "I just perfected this," she said holding it up and admiring her work. "It's a new and enhanced sneak spell." She winked. "In case you want to get off somewhere. Alone."

Ah, like we were about to do before she interrupted us. "This is great," I said, looping all three spells into the demon slayer utility belt at my waist. "Thanks."

"We appreciate you thinking of us." Dimitri gave Grandma a Greek double kiss on the cheeks, which must have surprised her because she started blushing.

He looked at the spells on my belt and his smile wavered. He had to be thinking about my limited success with spells in general. Still, these were simple. And they were good for us. I was sure it would all work out.

"Go have fun," Grandma said, ushering us out of camp. "Pretend we're not even here."

They'd be hard to miss. A cemetery stood between the house and us but that's not much when you're talking about biker witches. Not to mention the huge bonfire they'd started putting together.

You know what? It wasn't our problem.

Dimitri offered me his arm. "Want to go?"

I brushed a kiss along his jaw. "I do."

* * *

Since a hike through the cemetery wasn't my idea of a romantic time, we doubled back and walked along the road. The historic home seemed to glow in the soft evening light. I leaned close to Dimitri. Something told me tonight would be different. Fun.

I was just about to tell him so when I heard an anguished voice behind us.

"Lizzie!" It was my dog, Pirate.

Ever since I'd come into my demon slaying powers, Pirate could talk to me. It was one of the side effects.

Only those in tune with the paranormal could understand him, which included Dimitri and every biker witch on the planet.

"Hold up," Pirate said, when I had the gall to keep walking. "Stop. Don't leave me!"

He dashed up next to us like he was on fire.

My wiry Jack Russell terrier stood about as tall as my shin, but he didn't take that into account when it came to being fierce. He was mostly white, with a dollop of brown that spotted his back and covered his left eye. Hence his name.

"Pirate," I said, trying to be tactful, "this is our anniversary dinner. We can do it without you."

He turned in a circle and sat down on the dirt shoulder in front of us. "I don't understand."

"Go back," I said.

Dimitri leaned down and gave him a scratch between the ears. "The witches need you to guard their camp."

Pirate cocked his head as we made a detour around him and started walking again. "I get it," he said, following. "You're trying to keep all the steak for yourself."

"Restaurants aren't for dogs," I reminded him, as we passed through the gates and began up the winding driveway.

The weathered brick and stone had to be original. I was willing to bet the thick, gnarled oak trees on either side of the path were as old as the house. Moss clung to the trunks and dotted the lush grass. It felt like we were entering another world.

Pirate dodged around us and trotted out ahead, nose to the ground. "I think you need me more than the witches do." He sniffed at the packed earth. "This place doesn't smell right."

"It's gorgeous," I said. The pillars of the house stood tall and imposing. Yes, they'd been painted and re-painted over the years, but they were one-of-a-kind, with exotic flowers and creatures carved into the bases and up the sides. "Look. A gargoyle." I pointed toward a carving at the top. A thick white spider's web clung to its wings and stretched up to the antique brass lamp over the front door. Age had tarnished the lamp's ornate detailing, but it still hung with an air of majesty. I wondered just how many distinguished visitors had passed through this entryway.

Pirate growled low under his breath. His neck bristled as he stared at a rocking chair on the wide wrap-around front porch.

Dimitri moved up behind the dog. "What is it?"

Pirate remained perfectly still, staring. "I don't know."

I opened my demon slayer senses. Usually, I had an insane attraction to danger—anything that could attack me, skewer me or chop me in half. I focused my attention on the chair and the space that surrounded it.

My powers reached out like fingers through the mist, searching.

A shadowy presence lurked near the chair, possibly a lingering memory or a very weak entity. It was difficult to say, really. Ghosts weren't my specialty.

I expanded my reach and searched inside the

house, down long, crumbling corridors covered with fresh wallpaper. I felt a certain note of desperation inside, along with unresolved chaos. Upstairs, I could sense shadows of darkness and pain. But nothing demonic.

"I think it's okay," I said.

The bronze marker by the front door said the house had been built in 1830. I ran my fingers over it as it bled green onto the white brick underneath. "Anything this old is bound to have a few odds and ends lurking about."

Dimitri's shoulders relaxed. "Then let's eat."

He pushed open the large black door and we entered a narrow foyer. Rich burgundy wallpaper with gold vines scrolled past ornate sconces. It reminded me of a garden maze I'd once visited.

Tonight had to turn out better than that little adventure.

A round-faced woman with curly red hair scurried out of what appeared to be a dining room to our left. She wore a pretty green dress and if I didn't know better, I'd have thought she was one of the patrons. "Welcome to the Peele House Inn," she said with a fat Southern accent. Her smile faltered when her gaze fastened on my skin-tight bustier, then my leather utility belt, my short-ish skirt. Then she really stared at my shiny, knee-high black leather boots.

"I picked this pair up in New Orleans," I told her, "as a treat, after…" Well, I probably shouldn't tell her about the trouble I'd had in that tomb.

She tried to recover and failed. "Are you with," she made a swirly motion with her hand, "*those* people," she said the last part as if it were a secret, "down the road?"

Ah. The witches. They always made an impression.

Our hostess took refuge behind a small wooden stand, which would have been comical except I was pretty sure the woman actually felt intimidated.

"Don't worry," I said, eager to let her know that we had not, in fact, brought any beer can collectibles or a pony keg to dinner. "We're not that way at all."

Dimitri wrapped an arm around me and ran a warm hand over my shoulder. "We're here tonight to celebrate," he explained, directing a saucy grin at me. "It's our first anniversary."

The hostess clasped her hands together. "Aww," she cooed. "Happy anniversary!" With newfound energy, she checked her book. "You're the couple with the reservation," she added, as if we'd done something special.

Dimitri nodded. "Slayer. Party of two."

It was how we ordered pizzas and everything. It was much easier than asking anybody to spell Kallinikos.

"I am so glad you came," our hostess said, with a sincerity you could only find in the South. "My name is Marjorie and I'm going to do everything I can to make your night unforgettable."

She led us to the room on the left. It boasted high ceilings and beautiful blue silk walls. Another couple dined at a corner table and, near the back wall, a gentleman sat reading the paper. She seated us at one of the remaining three tables, next to one of the big picture windows. "This is one of my favorite rooms. It used to be the parlor," Marjorie said, placing our menus on a table covered in a white linen cloth.

A fire burned in the white marble hearth. And, I realized with horror, my dog had followed us inside.

"I'm sorry. He's mine," I said, intending to go after him. Pirate had found a nice warm spot directly in front of the crackling logs and had begun to curl up and make himself at home.

Marjorie paused. "You know, if he's just going to lie down, it's okay." She gave a small, wistful smile. "We used to keep both a dog and a cat here when we operated the bed and breakfast."

Pirate planted his head on his paws and arched up his brows in that heartbreakingly hopeful way dogs do when they want to be completely manipulative.

It worked.

Marjorie let out a low cluck. "Aren't you precious?" She left us, to go pet him.

"You have to understand—" I began, before I realized I'd lost her attention.

I didn't want to make a commotion. Although the other diners didn't seem to notice, or care.

"We don't want to reward his behavior," Dimitri added.

"Nonsense." She scratched Pirate behind the ears, which started his tail wagging. "I could never say 'no' to a face like that." She ushered Dimitri and I back to our seats. "Now I'm going to get your sweet puppy a bowl of fried gizzards, on the house. You two look over the menus."

I could swear Pirate grinned as he watched her go. "A cute face and a wagging tail will get you a long way in life," he said happily.

No kidding.

I opened my menu. "They get a decent crowd in here for such a quiet road," I said.

Dimitri hummed a response as he studied the wine list. Soon, I forgot all about the other patrons, as well as my dog. We ordered wine. We gorged ourselves on lobster ravioli, steak, and fresh baked bread.

I was fawning overly a particularly delicious side of mushroom risotto when Dimitri leaned over the table, grinning at me. "Look," he said, glancing toward the fireplace. "Pirate found a friend."

I turned and saw the ghost of a matronly woman in an old fashioned dress, complete with a hoop skirt. She spoke to Pirate in soft tones while she rubbed at his ears. He licked at her pale fingers and she giggled.

"Always the charmer," I mused. Pirate had a particular affinity for spirits. And he could make friends with a doorknob, so I wasn't surprised at all when they began holding an animated conversation.

Dimitri reached for a slice of fresh bread. "I wonder what they have in common."

Pirate did have limited interests, seeing that he was a dog. "It's got to be food," I said, reaching for a sip of wine. "Or smelly things."

"Things that roll, things that make noise," Dimitri added.

"The mailman." I thought about it. "Did they even have mailmen back when women wore hoop skirts?" It didn't matter, I supposed. I was just glad Pirate had made a friend. The ghost seemed to need one as well.

Marjorie returned to re-fill our water glasses and slip us the check. "Whenever you're ready," she said, as if she were reluctant to interrupt.

I let Dimitri take the black folder. "You know this place is haunted," I said to our host.

"Very," she nodded, as if it were a grand secret. "Word has it that Hiram Peele himself has been seen upstairs.

I loved ghost stories. Even if most of the ghosts I'd

encountered kept to themselves. "So you called it the Peele House after Hiram Peele?"

Marjorie stood a little straighter, obviously proud of the house's history. "Yes. He's our original owner. Hiram Peele was a wealthy planter and he built this house in 1830 for his bride, a local preacher's daughter named Eva Fawn." she said, with all the finesse of a storyteller. "Men didn't often marry below their station in those days, but it was a true love match and Hiram was very close to her father. They were happy for many years until she died after falling down the grand staircase. It was so sad. He died the next night—in bed of a heart attack. Although most people say it was a broken heart."

Yikes. Maybe it had been despair I'd felt in the house instead of darkness. "Are they buried in the cemetery outside?"

"Yes. That's how they did it in those days." Marjorie held the water pitcher in front of her like a shield. "When my husband and I bought this estate, we thought the Peele's story might bring in the tourists." Her pale skin flushed at the neck. "But," she shook her head, "it's ended up being a bit much. Right after we opened, a newly wed couple took a tumble down the staircase. Both of them died," she said, her voice catching.

"What a terrible accident," Dimitri said, taken back.

Color rose in Marjorie's cheeks. "Then it happened again. About six months later."

"Did they? Not make it either?" I asked, not wanting to pry, but wow. Twice?

Marjorie shook her head 'no.' "The coroner ruled all four of the deaths...accidental." She made a subtle sign of the cross, but I noticed it. "We don't even like to go up to those rooms anymore. I know they said it was a fluke, but my husband and I just couldn't handle it if something else happened."

"I don't blame you one bit," I told her.

She nodded, accepting my sympathy. "It's a shame." She glanced at the dining room behind us. "As you might imagine, we could use the business."

I was about to tell her that it seemed like the other guests were enjoying their meals as much as we did. Only now that I looked at them, the couple dining at a corner table wore 1940's-era clothes. And had a pearly sheen. The gentleman eating alone had vanished.

After Marjorie left, Dimitri deposited a considerable sum in the bill holder. I was glad he could afford to be so generous. Then again, he was also eyeing me like he had an idea.

"What?" I asked, finishing the last of my wine.

His eyes flicked to mine. "She has private, quiet guest rooms upstairs."

A tingle of awareness warmed me. "Those are closed."

"Exactly." He placed a large, solid hand over mine. "We'd be all alone."

At last.

If we had the guts.

"No biker witches, no camping out," I said, warming to the idea. Even with a ghost or two it was worth it. Heck, I had demon slayer powers. I could handle myself. "A real bed."

Dimitri shrugged his wide shoulders. He was reeling me in. I knew it. He knew it.

"It could be an anniversary to remember," he said, tempting me more than he knew.

I ran my fingers along the edge of my wine glass.

"I do still have to give you your present," I mused. "Although you'll have to undress me to get it."

He stood a little too quickly as he reached into his wallet again and peeled off an additional wad of twenties. "We'll add it to her tip, enough to cover a room."

It would be a shame not to contribute to the upkeep of such a wonderful old home.

I stood faster than I'd intended, wobbling my wine glass. "Okay. But just a quickie."

He grinned. "Anything for you."

Oh my God, I couldn't believe we were doing this.

"Come on," I said, standing, taking his hand. "We need to get upstairs and naked." Soon. Before I lost my nerve.

Chapter Two

We waited until our hostess retreated into the back, then we raced up the stairs like we were on fire.

Oh my God. I fought back a giggle and Dimitri smothered me to his chest at the top of the landing. He might be as stealthy as a shape shifter, but I felt like an ox going up those stairs.

I covered my mouth, but still, my face hurt from grinning as he took my hand and pulled me down the hall. The air hung heavy and stale. The narrow, dark corridor offered the perfect place to hide.

Dimitri pushed open a door at the end and yanked me inside. Shadows clung to the corners of the room. A layer of dust coated the antique furniture. No one had ventured up here for a long time. We were truly alone. Free. In an old-fashioned Victorian bedroom. I ran a hand over the carved wood chest of drawers with its chilly marble top and delicately woven lace dresser scarf.

I couldn't believe I was doing this. I'd never let myself consider it before. Not in my un-wild, un-crazy teenage years. And certainly not in my responsible twenties.

Dimitri's voice sounded rough, hungry. "Come here," he said, with the same excitement I felt. He kissed me hard, backing me up against the bed. I squealed as he tipped me down on the mattress.

"Impatient much?" I asked, giving him a saucy grin.

Wait until he got a look at my sexy red bra and panties.

He shook his head, advancing on me, all alpha male and sexy. "It's been way too long."

Since we were back home and not sneaking around. Hiding.

Well, technically we were sneaking.

"Then come and get it," I said, sliding my hands inside his shirt as he came down on top of me. He was warm, solid. His masculine scent and his strong presence enveloped me. I would never get enough of this man.

I kissed him with everything I had and I swore the room itself started to spin.

He felt heavier on top me, not uncomfortable exactly. Still, he didn't usually press down so hard.

I slid my hands up his sides, tried to get around the front of his belt buckle. It took all my effort to pry it open. This was the man who'd fought demons for me. He'd gone to hell and back (literally) for me.

That in itself was so heady that I felt mesmerized. Captured.

A frantic barking sounded outside the door. Pirate. I couldn't hear what he was saying. He seemed far away.

Dimitri blazed a trail of kisses down my neck, to

my collarbone.

I couldn't see the top of the canopy anymore. It was dark.

Too dark.

"Wait." I tried to sit up. Something wasn't right.

Boom.

I felt like I'd been zapped by about a thousand volts of static electricity. The bed lurched. "Dimitri!" If I didn't know better, I'd think the entire room had spun off into oblivion. My fingers felt numb as I gripped his shoulders.

He was a dead weight now, struggling to move. He shoved hard against the bed and fell away from me panting.

Oh hell.

Blackness saturated the room, growing stronger. Heavier.

We had to get out of here. I struggled off the bed. My arms and legs tingled, like they were asleep as I forced my way to the door and yanked it open.

Pirate dashed inside. "Cut it out! In a jiffy! She says you can't do what you were doing!"

I didn't care what the owner thought. "Help!" I yelled down the stairs. "Something's up here!"

We needed people, noise, anything to fight back the darkness.

Pirate jumped up on the bed next to my husband. "There's nobody down there to call 911," my dog said, eyes wide. "We've been transported!"

"That doesn't make any sense." Dimitri drew a labored breath, working to buckle his belt.

"You can't do what you were doing," Pirate insisted. "I told her you were just wrestling on the bed. You always do that. But she said, '*not here!*'"

I braced a hand against the bedpost as electric shivers ran up and down my body. Why weren't we getting any help? And if we were transported, "Who in Hades were you talking to?"

Pirate let out a heavy sigh. "The lady of the manor. My new friend."

The matronly ghost from downstairs shimmered into view next to my dog. Her upper half anyway. She stood in the middle of the bed, her grey hair, pulled into a severe twist, shimmering with a light of its own. Her face drew tight with fear. "It's too late. He's taken you."

Dimitri rolled away from her. "Who?"

"The master of the house. He's pulled you to another dimension." She cowered, as if she were afraid of being struck. "He rules here."

Bruises blossomed on her cheeks, neck and forehead.

It felt like the air itself tried to suck the life out of us.

Cripes. We needed the biker witches. I ran to the window.

We'd taken a room at the far end of the hall, toward the back of the house. The witches should be right outside, past the cemetery. I threw open the velvet curtains and let out a choked cry when I saw an empty field.

"Ohhh biscuits," Pirate said, pacing the bed. "The lady's right. That ghost took us. We're in the wrong dimension. I'm in a freaky house with a bad guy."

"Run," Dimitri ordered. Never mind the fact he was too weak to stand.

The ghost let out a keening wail as she sank down into the bed. Her eerily high voice settled low in my gut. "He's coming."

"Who?" I demanded, then changed my mind. "*What* is the master of the house?" We had to learn what kind of a creature we were dealing with. Before it attacked.

"I can feel him." Pirate squeaked. "He's right below us!"

The ghost brought a finger to her lips. "Shh..." Her eyes held sadness. Bruises and blood marred her face. "My husband." Her gaze locked on the door. "He's a very pious man. He won't stand for fornication in his house."

"We didn't!" I protested. Not yet anyway.

From what I could see, her husband had been a violent man in life. And he'd morphed into something just as vicious after death. We needed a plan. Now.

Chapter Three

Stop. *Think.* If sexy vibes had caused all of this… I reached into my belt for the anti-passion spell Grandma had given me, the mucky brown and green one. I opened the jar and discovered it smelled just as bad as it looked. No matter. I poured the contents over my chest.

It hit me with a cooling rush of energy that calmed my nerves and settled my gut.

Dang.

I felt better. More like myself. I rushed over to Dimitri and dropped a big, wet handful on his bare chest.

"What the hell?" He jerked away. Yeah, it was nasty, but it did the trick. He rolled off the bed and onto his feet. "What did you do?" His legs appeared a bit unsteady, but the rest of him was gaining strength fast. "I feel better."

"The potion puts the whammy on any sexy thoughts." I told him. The smell alone would do it.

The ghost watched us, shivering. "You can't escape him. Don't fight," she whispered. "Then it won't hurt so much."

Screw that. I felt sorry for her but I wasn't going to stand here and be attacked.

A dark cloud roiled up from the floor between my boots. Cripes. I hopped up onto the bed. It seeped through the floorboards and filled the room.

A low growl echoed against every corner of the room. "Fornicators!"

"Fuck!" I said, nearly jumping out of my skin as Dimitri took my arm.

"Let's go," he croaked, as I slid off the bed and we hurried toward the door.

I reached to my belt for Grandma's Sneak Spell. I broke the jar against the hardwood floors, sending up a plume of glittering blue and silver smoke that felt hot in my lungs and made me cough.

Dimitri cleared his throat and gripped me tighter. "I'm never making fun of your Grandma ever again."

I fought for a clean breath. "That makes two of us."

Limbs stiff, we lumbered out into the hallway.

"Careful," he said, as we reached at the top of the winding staircase. The carpeting was slick with mildew. A layer of dust and cobwebs now coated the bannisters. Lord help us if we pitched down the stairs.

It had been so much fun to sneak up. Now, it could be an easy way for the phantom to snap our necks.

I had five switch stars, the weapons of a demon slayer. They were round like Chinese throwing stars, only much more deadly. They could slice and dice incubi, succubi, demons, imps, goblins, werewolves, and Frankenstein's monster, but they didn't work on ghosts. Damn. I really needed the biker witches.

Flames danced in the gas globes below. Taunting us.

My heart nearly beat out of my chest as we raced down to the foyer.

We made it.

Dimitri braced a hand against the wall, gathering his strength, while I pulled open the front door. A gust of frigid air blew in, ruffling his hair. "That actually felt good," he said.

"Oh, boy," I managed to choke out. At least if he was joking, he was feeling better.

Ghosts liked it cold, and it scared the bejesus out of me that the master of the house could control the weather in this...wherever we were. It was as if we'd entered the phantom's own particular brand of hell.

"Come on," Dimitri said, taking my hand as we escaped the house and ran for all we were worth.

I had one spell left—the one for passion. Fat lot of good that would do us. I had nothing for protection or defense.

We made it to the cemetery at the side of the house. A few hundred feet and we'd be—where? My breath caught in my throat. We were still in the wrong dimension, whatever that meant. Still, it's not like we could stop. We had to get as far as we could from the house.

The cemetery appeared to be as old as the estate itself. Narrow crypts thrust out of the ground, some tilted like they'd stood there for centuries. Smaller tombstones crowded the empty spaces in between, their crosses and weeping virgins reaching out to snag my legs and skirt.

Pirate dashed ahead of us, weaving in and out of stones. I followed his wriggling rump and stubby white tail until it disappeared into a rush of fog.

"Watch out!" I barely had time to get the words out

before a wall of black smoke rose up from the earth itself. Pirate flipped over backward to avoid it.

Dimitri cursed.

Another wall rose up on the left, and on the right. I spun to see the final wall go up behind us.

We were surrounded.

Pirate retreated until he hit my boots.

We stood in front of a limestone crypt. A harsh stone cross dominated the roof. Carved angels wept at the corners and the worn bust of a stern, older man stood on a pedestal under the limestone eaves. A faded inscription at the front, black with lichen, read:

Hiram Everett Peele
1796 - 1857
Eva Fawn Peele
1812 – 1857
Forever bound

"That's him." I said.

What to do about it was another matter entirely. Grandma might have answers—if she weren't in another dimension. Partying.

Cripes.

Think.

We had to find a way to beat the ghost and then somehow, hopefully, return home.

But I couldn't switch star an incorporeal entity. I couldn't spell him. Even if Dimitri shifted into his griffin form, his teeth and claws would be useless.

"Uh, Lizzie?" Pirate leaned harder against my boots.

The black fog had begun to take form.

"Stay close" Dimitri murmured.

The three of us stood together as I reached into my belt for the protective crystals I always carried. I laid them out around us in a circle, willing them to hold back the evil that chilled the very ground where we stood.

Steely gray eyes glowered down at us.

"This isn't going to be enough," I said, placing the last of the crystals.

The phantom loomed over us — at least seven feet tall — larger then he possibly could have been in real life. He wore an old fashioned suit with a thick black necktie and a heavy silver cross. His gray teeth glowed with an unnatural light. "Anybody ever tell you? Sin leads to damnation." Fire flickered at the edges of the phantom and I could swear I smelled brimstone.

He drew himself up like a demented preacher. "For the whoremongers," he announced, "for them that defile themselves with mankind. Let not sin therefore reign in your mortal body. Cast out your lust!"

I took one step back, then another, causing Pirate to stumble and dash behind me. "We weren't sinning, we're married!"

The ghost spat on the ground. "No virtuous woman wantonly inspires lust in a man." He advanced on me. "You are a sinful whore."

I hurled a switch star at his head.

It flew straight through and didn't come back. My weapons usually acted as boomerangs. Had the ghost vaporized it? Maybe it had gotten caught on one of the tombstones.

It didn't matter. The switch star hadn't stopped Hiram Peele.

"What do you want?" I demanded.

He sneered at me like I was a wayward child. "Hold still, now. You're going to get a good hard beating for the Lord."

"Back off," Dimitri hollered at the ghost, trying to shove me behind him.

"It'll make you a better woman," the ghost said, swinging a meaty fist down.

A thousand sharp pricks of energy slammed into me like debris from a hurricane. Pain lanced through my cheek. It was only a small portion of his wrath. My pathetic crystal ward glowed, absorbing what it could of his energy. But my hastily drawn circle wouldn't last. Not against this.

I swallowed back my shock. I'd never been personally attacked by a supernatural entity—based on who I was. The ghost didn't care that I was a demon slayer. He'd gone after me because I was a woman.

Dimitri surged for the ghost, but it was as if he hit a wall of energy. Hiram tossed him onto the ground.

"Stay away from her!" Pirate hollered.

Hiram's wrath surrounded us, swirling. Howling.

Pirate emerged from his hiding place behind me and braved the edge of the circle, his ears flinging back, "Leave Lizzie alone! She didn't do anything! Eva, too. She's terrified!"

The winds whipped Hiram's beard and hair. His eyes glared daggers into the black smoke to our right. "Don't you leave, Eva Fawn. You had to go and make friends, don't you? Now you're going to see what you made me do."

The woman's head shimmered into view, weeping. Cuts and scars crisscrossed her face until she was unrecognizable. Harsh winds tore at her hair as she screamed. And with every scream, he grew.

Dimitri watched, calculating. "Her fear is giving him power."

It was the classic abuse scenario. I'd be willing to bet the sicko succumbed to temptation with his wife and then beat her for it.

She'd given him her power in life and he was using it to hold her here.

"Leave!" I yelled to her. It was obvious she was in pain. "He can't hurt you anymore." I hoped. I thought.

A cut above her puffy, swollen eye opened up and blood poured down over her face.

Pirate let out a high-pitched doggie whine.

Frick. I tried to see outside the circle, but the ghost's wrath surrounded us.

"We have to help her," my dog pleaded. "She's hurting!"

I didn't know how. "She's been trapped here for more than a century," I told him. "She doesn't have anything else."

I wished she did. I wanted to help. The blood poured down her neck, her chest. She shook as her arms and hands came into view.

"She has me," my dog insisted.

"It's not enough," I told him. Yes, she'd crouched by the fire all night. She'd laughed with Pirate. I'd heard her. But I didn't see how a connection like that—with an animal no less—could change this.

And then, my dog did the unthinkable. He dashed out of the circle, through the choking black smoke and into the arms of Eva Fawn Peele.

"No!" I screamed. Dimitri held me back or I would have snatched my dog out of the air.

As it stood, I'd never seen anyone—ghost or human — more shocked than Eva when she reached out and caught him.

"I'm here! I love you! I'll help you!" Pirate wriggled in her arms, licking at her face, not caring that it was bloody and battered and awful.

The ground shifted. I stumbled, off balance, stunned as Hiram Peele hollered and lost the left side of his body.

"You got 'em!" Pirate said happily. "Look!" he said, snuggling tight in her arms.

No, she didn't have him. Eva had simply yanked part of his power supply. He turned to his wife in shock. Then his lip lifted into a cold sneer. "You will not —"

She kissed Pirate on the head, her eyes glazed with tears.

The phantom drew a sharp breath.

On the other side of our black hazed prison, bonfires appeared. Warmth flooded the air and I could see biker witches dancing, casting spells, and basically being their gorgeous, wonderful obnoxious selves.

We were back!

The ghost stared at his wife. It didn't appear he'd seen that side of Eva for at least a century and a half, if ever.

But it was a hollow victory. Yes, Eva had found something else to care about, the start of a loving relationship. But it didn't fix everything.

Hiram Everett Peele drew up to his full height, his face a mask of fury. Eva buried her face in Pirate's wiry fur.

"Drop that filthy animal." He stood over her. "Now."

Eva clutched at my dog, shaking.

Holy hell. Hiram was enjoying the fight. "Or have it your way," he snarled.

He shot out his hand and released a bolt of power straight into Pirate's neck. My dog yelped and fell to the ground.

"Pirate!" I screamed.

"No!" Eva cried.

His small body lay twisted on the grass. He wasn't moving.

Dimitri held me back. Barely. Oh my God. Pirate looked dead.

Hiram smirked as he sneered down on his wife. "Don't look at me that way, woman. This is your fault. You didn't obey."

Pain seared her eyes, mixed with fury. Rage. Her cuts faded away. Her bruises morphed to silky white skin. "No!" Her voice curdled as she drew out her hands like claws and launched a bolt of rage directly at her husband.

It hit him square in the chest and lit up the night. Needles of her energy pierced my skin as Hiram Peele, master of the house, staggered back, eyes wide with shock. He tried to speak, but no sound came as the light streamed from his mouth, nose and eyes.

She hit him again. And again. I squinted against the power and the light.

He broke apart, lost form as the cloud of smoke surrounding us began to break apart.

I ran to Pirate, who had started to roll over and open his eyes. I took him up into my arms as the phantom that was Hiram Peele screamed. He clawed and fought, but it did him no good. He was sucked back down into the grave.

Eva Peele stood in front of us. Tears streamed down

her face. She appeared utterly exhausted. And she only had eyes for Pirate. "Is he all right?"

Pirate lifted his head, although it had to be hard for him after such a hit. "I think I could use a belly scratch."

Eva let out a small, happy cry and stroked Pirate on the head and down the neck. Both seemed particularly pleased when he turned all the way onto his back to help her get to the soft fur under of his belly.

Meanwhile Dimitri inspected the place where the phantom had gone down. "We have to act. Now. There must be a way to trap him here for good."

I reached into my utility belt for a biker witch distress flare. It was long, small and had a double set of wings. "Emergency!" I hissed, before launching it up into the air.

It shot up high, leaving a glittery silver trail, until it burst into a red shower of sparks overhead.

Chapter Four

The biker witches arrived with pork ribs in hand.

"What have you got?" Grandma asked, ducking past a leaning tomb.

We explained, and in mere minutes, we had an army of witches working at breakneck speed.

"Take Two Toed Harriett back into the woods to gather more dioscorea if we need it," Grandma hollered to Frieda, as she poured herbs from her fanny pack into her palm and began mixing them with her fingers.

"That sounds like a disease," Dimitri said.

Grandma made a sign of the cross. "Protective herb. Should be strong enough to plant that abusing asshole back in the ground."

The biker witches each commandeered a small piece of land and began laying hands on it, chanting and sewing it with herbs. Dimitri brought up torches and supplies from camp. Meanwhile, Pirate managed to commandeer a discarded rib bone or three. He was looking better. Weak, but happy.

I scratched him on the head. "How's it going, buddy?"

His ears drooped. "She says she has to leave."

I looked past him and could barely see the outline of Eva Peele. It was as if she'd begun to depart already. "It's her time," I said, to both of them really. She'd earned her peace. "I'll bet she'll always remember you."

"She will." Pirate paused in his chewing. "She's more powerful than she thinks. She just needed the love of a pet to bring her out of her shell."

We both watched as the outline of Eva Peele took on a beautiful golden glow. She smiled. Happy. Then she lifted her chin toward the clear sky, scattered with stars, and began to rise.

"Thank you," I said, hoping she heard me as she drew higher.

Pirate nudged me. "She said to tell you the same thing."

We watched her until we could barely make out a perfectly round white orb as it ascended to the heavens.

* * *

An hour later, the witches had completed their work. Warmth filled the night. The haze had lifted and the ground felt solid beneath our feet.

Ant Eater walked over to me and slapped a hand on my shoulder. "Well, the master of the house is pissed. But he's not going to be able to hurt anybody again."

"Hiram Peele is still here?" I asked. I'd half-expected them to banish him. Where, I had no idea.

Grandma gave a low whistle as she joined us. "He refused to budge. So we locked him up in his grave." She glanced back at the old mausoleum. "As long as nobody disturbs him, he'll be fine."

"I'll let the owner know," I said.

"Want me to go with?" Ant Eater offered.

I shook my head. "Not necessary."

I took Dimitri instead.

We grinned at each other, same as before, as we walked up to the old mansion.

"Let's make a deal," he said. "Next anniversary we're going to avoid supernatural entities bent on killing us. I mean, first the wedding and now this." He squeezed my hand. "I don't want it turning into a tradition."

I kissed him on the cheek. "Deal."

Marjorie stood on the front porch. Her red hair glowed against the heavy bronze light over the door. She raised a hand in greeting. "Is it safe?"

Dimitri and I exchanged a glance as we made our way over to talk with her.

"What do you think you saw?" I asked.

She watched me as if she were trying to see into me. "I saw a bunch of vandals in my cemetery. Until the ghosts by the fire dropped their tea cups and bolted for the light."

She was more aware than I'd realized.

"They went to a better place." Dimitri said. "Hiram Peele has been put to rest as well."

"He was the troublemaker, wasn't he?" she asked.

I nodded and relief washed over her features. "This is going to sound crazy, but I could almost feel him leave." She paused. "Do you think it will be safe to open up the bed and breakfast again?"

"It should be." The house felt lighter. Clean. "Bring a priest through to bless the place. And don't disturb his grave," I warned her.

She nodded. "Not a chance."

"You might also want to hire some help," Dimitri told her. "I think you're going to have a lot more customers from now on."

We'd have the witches whip up a spell to draw some extra customers. Marjorie worked hard. She deserved it.

"Let's head out," Grandma called, approaching from the cemetery. "We're missing the rest of the barbeque,"

Our hostess frowned. "You *are* with those bikers?" She seemed genuinely confused. "But you said…" She halted. "But you're so nice."

"They are too," I said, as Grandma joined us on the porch. "The biker witches just took care of your poltergeist problem for you."

"Well darn it," the owner said, fretting all the more. "Now I wish I hadn't called the sheriff on them."

Grandma smiled and clapped her on the back. "No sweat, we get that a lot." She turned to me. "Ready to go?"

We said our goodbyes and headed off through the cemetery with Grandma. It looked like the other witches were back at their party already.

"They sure don't waste time," I commented, as we made our way through the graves.

Grandma snorted. "Yeah well when you get up there like us, you don't have a lot of time to fritter away."

"So are the police coming?" I asked when we'd almost made it. Music blared across the field. *You Really*

Got Me by Van Halen. Now that the crowd had spread out, I could also see they had a hog on the grill.

Grandma planted her hands on her hips. "Already took care of the law. The sheriff is drunk over by that tree. We hit him with a barbeque-craving spell. The rest is on him." She gave me a sideways glance. "Anyhow, it appears we're spending the night after all."

"Good." Dimitri wrapped an arm around me. "Let's go find your present. It should be here by now."

Grandma let out a curse. "That was for you?" She said. "I sent him away."

"Ask me if I'm surprised," Dimitri mused. He was used to fixing messes. "It's a good thing we have other ways to keep busy," he added, edging me back toward the pine forest.

Grandma hesitated. "You don't want to stick around and celebrate?"

"We will later," he said cryptically.

Grandma appeared confused for a second, before she started laughing.

I ignored her, and drew closer to my husband. "You're still in the mood?" I asked. "After all this?"

Not that I minded a romp in the forest with my man, but he'd been through a lot tonight.

He nuzzled my cheek. "Biker anti-passion spells don't last long on me. At least not when you're around."

Damn. "That just totally got me in the mood."

He turned to me, his sharp features accented by the moonlight. "I love you, Lizzie. I'll always want you, no matter what."

His words soaked through me, warming me like nothing else ever world. "That's the best gift you could ever give me."

And then I kissed him, contented to know that he was mine. To love, to hold, to grow old with. For better or worse. For the rest of our lives.

Enjoy more of Lizzie and Dimitri's adventures in the Accidental Demon Slayer series by Angie Fox

Some Like It Hexed

Chapter One

The Red Skulls biker gang, made up of Harley-riding witches, had never thrown a Halloween party before.

Sure, they'd gathered the coven at midnight on Samhain. They'd communed with the spirits on the other side. They'd reached beyond the veil in the light of the full moon.

But a party? With themed-out napkins and paper plates? I'd never seen it before.

I clutched the phone as my grandmother described the napkins she'd bought this afternoon, the ones showing green-skinned women with questionable fashion taste, riding broomsticks under a full moon. Aside from the fact that a witch flying like that would make an easy target for any demon, banshee, or evil warlock, I didn't get how this particular coven of powerful witches could act so blasé.

"Oh, and Lizzie, I need you to bring a snack to share," my grandmother instructed.

I gripped the phone tighter.

Grandma Gertie was the leader of the Red Skulls. She walked around in leather chaps with a sagging tattoo of a phoenix on her arm and purple sparkles in her hair. She ate pork ribs off the bone, drank whiskey straight out of the bottle, and hadn't touched an oven mitt since the Carter administration. "Whip up some of those cupcakes I saw in that magazine at your condo, the ones with the licorice legs that look like spiders. See if you can get gumdrops for the eyes."

Just because I read *Good Housekeeping* didn't mean I knew what to do with the recipes. I sent in the subscription card on one particularly optimistic day. After that, I enjoyed looking at the pretty pictures. It had been innocent. Harmless.

Until now.

"You seem to forget that I'm the anointed demon slayer of Dalea," I told her. There was only one of us born every three generations, for goodness' sake.

I'd learned about my powers on the night of my thirtieth birthday, when Grandma in her full biker glory showed up unannounced on my doorstep and informed me I wouldn't be teaching preschool anymore. She then inadvertently locked me in the bathroom to battle a demon with a bottle of air freshener. It had been a wild ride ever since.

"Are you fighting a demon right now?" she asked, her voice sounding even rustier over the phone.

"No," I groused.

"Then those should be some damned good cupcakes."

I groaned. Trapped. Like a rat.

So I headed to the grocery store, as requested, and even without my supernatural powers, I managed to figure out what size gumdrops made the best spider eyes.

If I take on a job, I do it right.

Then I returned home and did my best impression of Martha Stewart, if the homemade diva wore leather boots and a Kiss My Asphalt T-shirt.

After I'd finished baking, I dressed in a black leather dress, my demon slayer weapons belt, and a cute pair of spider earrings I found on a rack by the checkout lane.

It was time to party.

"Come on, Pirate," I said to my Jack Russell terrier.

I hoisted a box full of treats that would make my friends on Pinterest proud and led my dog out of the condo. I locked the door behind us since my sexy-as-sin plus-one, Dimitri, had gone into the city this afternoon to meet with visiting dignitaries from the griffin clans of Santorini. He was the liaison here in North America.

No doubt he would have found the idea of a biker witch Halloween party as odd as I did.

It was barely four in the afternoon.

Pirate trailed behind me, sulking. "I don't know why I followed you outside. I ain't going anywhere until you get me out of this straitjacket."

Did I mention one of the side effects of my awesome powers was that I could also understand my dog?

Sometimes it was a gift. Other times, a curse.

"You look darling," I told him. He did.

He was mostly white, with a dollop of brown on his back that wound up his neck and over one eye. I'd named him Pirate for that reason. And thanks to the Internet, I'd found him a little doggy pirate outfit, complete with a red-and-white-striped shirt and a black belt with a stuffed sword hanging from it. Precious.

"Admit it. I look stupid," he grumbled.

"That's because you're not wearing the hat," I told him, "but don't worry. I already packed it. We'll strap it on when we get there." Too bad the outfit didn't come with an eye patch.

"I'd better get a cupcake," he muttered as I picked him up and set him on the leather seat of my Harley.

Ever since I'd learned to ride, my furry friend had become a biker dog. Until recently, I wore him close to my body with what can best be described as a leather baby carrier.

A biker witch named Bob had made my dog a permanent doggy seat in front of me. Pirate liked being the first one to catch the breeze as we rode. I secured him snugly and fastened his canine riding goggles, also known as doggles.

Pirate stared at the box of goodies I'd strapped to the luggage rack of the Harley, as if he could make a cupcake fall out by willpower alone.

I'd tell him later I packed some yummy doggy dental chews.

"Okay, buddy," I said, climbing on behind him. "You ready?"

"Oh, yeah," he said, forgetting his wardrobe issues as I fired up the engine. Going on a ride always perked my dog up. Claiming a seat at the front of my bike was like sticking his entire body out the car window.

"Let's get this party started," I told him.

My dog threw his head back and howled in triumph as we blazed out onto the open road.

Chapter Two

The late-afternoon sun blazed in a cloudless blue sky as we drove up the Pacific Coast Highway to Long Beach and followed Grandma's directions through a quaint residential area near the water.

We passed a neighborhood of Spanish-style stucco houses with colorful tile house numbers. We saw a white-painted crab shack, an ice cream shop, and a crowded farmers' market. Palm trees lined the street, their leaves rustling as they swayed in the breeze.

This couldn't be right.

It was too...normal. And I wasn't detecting any clear magical hot spots.

The witches liked to party with fairies and necromancers. They hung at hole-in-the-wall bars with warlock bikers and banshee hunters.

Then again, the one thing I've learned about the Red Skulls over the years — there was no telling what they might do. These were hard riding, no-guff senior ladies who'd been in love with Harleys for longer than I'd been alive. They seized every day with no apologies and seemed determined to eke every bit of pleasure from life.

Even still, I was really surprised when Grandma's directions led me to the Ocean View Senior Living & Rehabilitation Center.

This had to be some kind of mistake.

I passed blue-painted benches under groupings of palm trees as I drove up the circle drive. I stopped my bike at the top and shut off the engine. "We're in the wrong place, little doggy," I murmured, rubbing Pirate on the head.

My dog's tail thumped against the seat. "It looks good to me." He eyed an older gentleman in a heavy jacket sitting on a bench by the door. "See that guy? I think he wants to pet a dog." Pirate tried to leap off the bike and I was glad I'd strapped him in good.

"Hey mister!" Pirate hollered. "I'm cute and I'm soft. You want to pet my head? I'll let you rub my belly."

The man smiled. I doubted he was a warlock, which meant he didn't understand my dog's actual words. Still, Pirate was about ready to spring out of his skin with excitement. No way to miss that.

"You are shameless," I said, returning the man's grin as I reached into my back pocket for my cell phone.

Pirate craned his neck to look up at me. "I have learned to ask for what I want. Not everybody can say that."

"I'm going to call Grandma," I said, dialing. Hopefully, we were close to the fairy highway that would take us to the secret magic party.

Just then, I saw Grandma's second-in-command walk out of the front entrance.

"Ant Eater?" I kicked on my engine and pulled my bike up closer to the witch with knee-high black boots, a black greaser wig, and a red cape. She wore black leather chaps and the most obnoxious belt buckle I'd ever seen. "What are you supposed to be?"

She waved at me, her red cape trailing in the breeze. "Elvis." She grinned, her gold tooth gleaming. "You can't park here. This lane is for pickup and drop-off only. Go along the side of the building. You'll see a line of bikes. We're just grabbing a couple of things. Party's already started."

"At a senior center," I said, as if maybe she hadn't noticed.

The Red Skulls were one of the most powerful covens on the West Coast. They practiced a dynamic, healing white magic that could be stunning in its complexity—even if they did tend to use items most of us could find around the house, or on a drive through town.

Ant Eater waved at two witches carrying a giant black cauldron in from the side parking lot. People were going to notice.

I dismounted and pulled her aside. "Why are you doing this here, of all places, on the eve of Samhain? Surely you could have found a more private place for a ritual." Even my condo would have been preferable to this.

They couldn't possibly expect to go undetected here.

Skinny Loretta passed us. She wore a Minnie Mouse costume and carried a karaoke machine.

"Put it by the piano," Ant Eater instructed. "We may need it." The gold-toothed witch turned to me. "Who said anything about a ritual? This is a party!"

"I'll be right in," I told her. I had to see it for myself.

Pirate and I drove the bike over to the side lot. Then I unstrapped him and grabbed my cupcakes.

"I hope they have bacon treats," he said, shaking off.

We made our way toward the front door. It hurt to break it to him, but, "I doubt they'll have doggy snacks on the food table."

"Who said anything about dog food?" Pirate balked.

I noticed the biker witches didn't even pause at the large front desk just inside the doors. I signed my name and hoped they'd think Pirate was a service dog.

"It'd help if you wore the hat," I told him.

"Only if you can catch me," he said, ready to flee. Stubborn dog.

We set off down the hall, with me trying to hold my cupcake box as evenly as possible and Pirate glancing back at me, as if he expected me to swoop down any minute to plunk a tricorn hat on his head.

I would have, too, if I thought I could get away with it.

Handrails lined the hall on either side, and groupings of chairs dotted the corridor.

My dog took it all in, even as his little legs churned so fast that his striped shirt looked like a blur. "We should have brought Flappy," he said, whipping his head from side to side, trying to see inside the rooms as we passed.

"No dragons in the senior center," I told him. "I saw a sign."

Besides, the dragon had been on a growth spurt lately. I doubted he'd have fit through the front door.

"Don't worry. I'll smuggle home some treats for him," Pirate said, taking the lead as we made a sharp left.

Ant Eater pulled open the doors to a rec room. A warm enchanted breeze whooshed out and I drew up short. I should have expected it. I should have known.

And yet? I paused for a moment to take it in.

While Pirate dashed forward — heading for the snack bar, no doubt — I savored.

The entire room sparkled with magic. Bob sat at the piano by the door, pounding out old show tunes. A pair of round yellow smiley faces bobbed from his head on springy wires. Next to him sat a woman in a wheelchair much like his. She giggled as they came to a double glissando and swept their hands down the keyboard.

"I haven't been able to play since '57!" she hollered to me.

A wisp of a woman struggled to pass me in the doorway. I stepped back and as soon as she crossed the threshold, her gait changed and her shoulders lifted. She raised a hand and caught the beat as she began to boogie out to the dance floor.

Unbelievable. "I see what you're doing here," I said to Ant Eater.

She merely grinned.

The two witches I'd encountered outside had planted their black cauldron in the middle of a snack table that lined the left wall. They busied themselves mixing herbs while another member of the coven poured a jug of what appeared to be orange soda into the cauldron.

I'd bet anything the drinks were spelled.

Abandoned wheelchairs and walkers mingled with

the black and orange streamers against the walls as residents swing danced and boogied.

"This is great," I said. My words died on my lips. "Ohmigosh." I pointed to a couple in the corner, making out. "They need to get a room."

Ant Eater followed my gaze. "Oh, that's Mr. and Mrs. Levinson. They already share a room."

I gasped. "They should know better."

Ant Eater shot me a squirrely look. "Like we never caught you naked in the garden with Dimitri."

I almost dropped my cupcakes.

"Ahem. I need to put these snacks out," I told her, clutching the box, ignoring her toothy grin as I escaped to the refreshment table.

I hated when Ant Eater was right.

I placed the spider cupcakes between a plate full of caramel apple slices and a bowl full of Chex mix with candy corn mixed in.

A few paces away from the snack table stood Creely, the witch who wore her Kool-Aid-red hair in ponytails. From her shoulders to her knees, she wore a sphere with glass tiles glued all over it. Oh my. She'd come as a disco ball. Creely had a rapt crowd of about a dozen circled around her.

"Abracadabra and all that jazz." She grinned.

As she spoke the words, she waggled her fingers at a pair of spectacles in her palm. Slowly, they lifted into the air. The crowd oohed and ahhed as the glasses began to spin in lazy circles.

They clapped at her cleverness.

Only it was no trick. It was straight-up bona fide magic.

"Want to see how it works?" she asked teasingly. "You just might."

Oh my. She couldn't be planning to share her little secret.

Or could she?

A large black banner proclaimed this party as the *Witches' Bash.*

Before I could worry about it too much, something short and furry bounced off my leg.

"Oh, hey. Excuse me," Pirate said, his chin down, chewing. He glanced up, saw me, and swallowed whatever he'd been eating. Whole. "The plate fell," he said quickly. "I was just cleaning up," he added, before I could get a word in edgewise.

"Why don't you go see if Bob needs help on the piano?" I asked. It was on the other side of the room from the food.

Although the last thing we needed was a dog singing party tunes.

A witch named Frieda clattered up on platform heels. She wore a black catsuit and a pair of furry kitty ears on her head. "Sooo," she drawled, hands on her hips, "what do you think?"

"I never could have imagined it," I said. It was the God's honest truth.

Grandma walked up on my other side. She'd colored her skin green and wore a witch's hat and a flowing black dress. She looked like a bad napkin. "A witch?" I asked her. "Really?"

She planted the end of her broomstick on the floor. "If the hat fits." She grinned. "Where's your costume?"

I pointed to my web earrings. "I'm a spider."

"You're not even trying," Frieda said.

"Hey, I baked for this party," I told her. "And besides, I have to tell you. I don't think anybody here realizes you're serious."

Grandma had an Elphaba impression going on. Frieda had drawn a kitty-cat nose and whiskers on her face. All-powerful witches didn't usually do that.

"Of course they know about us," Grandma said, reaching to the snack table behind her and handing me a drink. "It's right there on the sign."

Technically, yes. "But it could be seen as a joke."

Grandma sobered. "I don't joke about magic."

Okay. How to explain... "Most people don't believe," I told her.

Grandma shrugged. "The ones we want do." She took a long drink from her cup, and then wiped her mouth with her hand. "Make no mistake. This is a recruitment event."

"You want people to join the Red Skulls?" I asked, trying to get it through my head. It couldn't be as simple as that.

"It's a respectable life choice," she said, somewhat defensively.

Hmm... So that's why she'd traded in her usual leather chaps for the Wicked Witch of the West ensemble. "I figured you were here to help some nice people have a good time."

"We are," she said, looking out over the crowd, "but you know we've lost some members over the years."

Yes, to demon attacks and battles with banshees, as well as a particularly unfortunate trebuchet accident.

Grandma slapped me on the back. "We could stand to muster some new blood. Speaking of which..." She flagged down a kind-faced old woman with gray dreadlocks and a large pink feather in her hair. "This is Rosette. She was a great witch back in the day."

"Pish," the woman said, waving Grandma off. "I only dabbled. A little of this, little of that." She fingered the sleeve of her flowing pink sparkly gown. "I picked up a few tricks over the years, but nothing like these ladies."

"Perfect recruit," Grandma concluded.

Rosette pursed her lips. "I have my hands full here. Anyhow" — she took one of my hands in both of hers — "you must be Lizzie the demon slayer. Your grandma is so proud."

"I love your accent," I told her. It was a melodious Cajun Creole.

"Isn't that sweet?" she said. "Your grandmama didn't tell me you were coming." She held up a finger. "If you have any special talents you want to lend to the party, you just let me know."

I didn't have any magic, and I wasn't about to start tossing weapons. "Um, no thanks," I told her. "Did you organize this?"

She nodded. "I told your grandma we have lots of people here at Ocean View who have...how should I say it? Magical tendencies? It's always good for folks to try a new hobby."

Sure, like witchcraft.

Grandma grinned. She quickly started coughing, though.

I patted her on the back. "Hey, ouch." That didn't sound good. I took her drink from her while she caught her breath. The cup smelled like lemonade, and it was nearly empty. "Is this pink lemonade or yellow? I'll get you some more."

"No need." She reached down the front of her dress and into her bra.

"Grandma," I protested, as she withdrew a small

silver flask.

"I've got more right here," she said proudly unscrewing the flask. "Here. Hold this steady." She placed the cup in my hand while she poured a yellow liquid into it. Bits of herbs swirled, and a faint smattering of bubbles clung to the bottom.

"What's this?" I asked, sniffing.

Grandma gently but firmly removed it from my grasp. "It's for my back. And my legs. And my joints." She rolled her eyes. "I'm not feeling so hot today."

She took a sip, before trying to force another, larger gulp.

"Are you sick?" I asked. I'd never seen Grandma have a health issue that didn't have to do with getting shot with magic or possessed by a demon.

She leaned heavily on her broomstick as she brought a hand to her head. "I think it's getting worse," she said to her friend, not to me. "I might need to lie down."

"Of course," Rosette said, flashing me a worried glance. "You can rest in my room."

That or we could simply try this on another day. "Maybe I should take you home," I said, as we escorted her out of the party.

"Nah," Grandma said, fighting my grip, waving to her friends and pretending nothing was wrong. "I'm one of the hosts."

This didn't feel right.

When we made it out of the rec room, I opened up my demon slayer senses. Bits of biker witch magic clung to the beige hallway. That was to be expected. I ignored them. Instead, I focused my energy on anything new or unusual.

My gifts didn't merely help me hunt down and

destroy hell spawn, they gave me the ability to sense danger in many forms. I was insanely attracted to anything that could chop my head off, eat me, or leave me crying for my mother.

It had been a bit of a curse when I first started. Now I used it to my advantage.

Rosette led us down a side corridor, done in mauve wallpaper. Grandma clung to the balance rail along the wall. I wished she'd have held on to me, but I wasn't going to push it. We passed doorways with gold nameplates and various fall wreaths, poster board pumpkin cutouts, family pictures, and other personal decorations.

I willed my mind to calm, my breathing to grow even. I opened my mind and searched with my powers like fingers reaching through cold, dark water.

A sharp, tingling magic churned in the air. I pressed harder, trying to get a lock on the source. One thing I knew for sure: it didn't come from the Red Skulls.

It was too…cutting.

I didn't want to criticize Rosette's home, but, "Grandma, do you feel that?"

"I don't know," she said, stumbling against Rosette.

For a second, I thought they were both going down. I moved in behind them, but her friend caught her.

"It's the next door," she said to both of us. "And yes, there are stirrings in the air," she said, glancing at me. "The land here is not good. Come inside and I will explain."

We escorted Grandma into a tidy, colorful room with a homemade quilt on the bed and pots of herbs lining the windowsill. It smelled of orange peels and lavender incense. A small altar occupied a sturdy wooden table next to her nightstand. Candles, playing

cards, beads, shells, and airline bottles of rum crowded a small hand-sewn depiction of a skeleton in a top
hat smoking a cigar. The pull string for a nurse's call
dangled near the bed.

Grandma collapsed into the mattress and closed her
eyes.

I didn't like the flush of her skin, or the way her
limbs tangled on the bed, unmoving. "Are you okay?"
I asked. We might need a nurse.

"I'm fine," she said, eyes closed. "Rosette, you tell
her."

Wooden beads clattered around the old woman's
neck as she motioned me to a small purple velvet
chair. I pulled it up close to Grandma while Rosette
settled herself into an orange-and-pink-painted rocking chair near her altar.

She folded her hands on her lap as she began. "I
came here because these people needed me. I also
needed a place to live," she added, practically.

"Rosette may not be the queen of spells" —Grandma chuckled, her breath rattling in her chest—"but
she's been doing magical outreach for as long as I've
known her." She cleared her throat. "It's important to
keep good magic flowing on bad land," she added,
still not opening her eyes. "Rosie does that. She acts as
a conduit for good, healthy energy. Otherwise, people
get sick easier, they get hurt. They just don't feel as
good."

"Like you feel right now?" I asked. "If this place is
affecting you, there's no shame in leaving." Rosette
would understand. "Thanks for the hospitality," I
said, standing. "I'm sure the rest of the party will be
great, but we should go."

"Sit your ass down," Grandma groaned. "I don't

want to bug out. It'd make me feel worse, not better."
She cracked her eyes open. "Have you ever considered the fact that I'm just old?"

"No," I answered immediately. Honestly. She'd
never shown her age, not really.

Until today.

Rosette ran her hands along the arms of her rocking chair. "Your granddaughter is right. You do not
look so good." She reached underneath her altar and
slid out a wooden box painted with red *X*'s. "If you
please, I have a healing draft that might help."

"No, thanks," Grandma said, waving her off. "I just
took an elixir and I don't want any magical interac-
tions."

"Ah." Rosette nodded, holding the box.

I could feel the power swirling inside the box. Rosette may not consider herself a talented spell caster,
but Grandma was right—her friend possessed a gift.

Since that was the case, she had to be feeling what I
did.

Maybe I was too used to trouble finding us, but,
"This entire situation feels wrong."

Rosette watched me, her expression grave. "I will
prepare extra protective herbs for this room." She
clutched the arms of her rocking chair as she stood.

"You do that," I said, ignoring Grandma's huff of
indignation.

She cracked open her eyes, struggled up on an
elbow. "I like how you're suspicious. Hell, I trained
you that way. But let me tell you something about the
human body. Things start slowing down at seventy-
seven, even with a daily dose of herbal magic." She
began to cough, and then fought it off with a hard
swallow. "What we're doing here is important. We're

pumping up the vitality of this place. Yeah, I joked about a recruiting event. It would be nice to find a few new members. But we're mainly here to load everything from the people to the walls with positive energy. It'll make it easier for Rosette to do her job the other three hundred and sixty-four days of the year."

"On Samhain, the veil between the living and the dead is the thinnest," Rosette explained, opening a drawer on her nightstand. She removed three small jars: mugwort, basil, and dragon's blood. All three acted as protective herbs, and had most likely been enchanted beyond their natural organic abilities. "Tonight, we can conjure good forces that will protect this place long after I'm gone," she said, carefully pouring out the herbs into an earthenware bowl. "I'm not getting any younger, either."

"That's a large undertaking," I said, watching her unwrap a small animal's skull.

It would be a tall order, even if the woman didn't look as if she were about a hundred years old.

"I do just fine." She straightened as she glanced over at Grandma. "Oh"—her expression softened—"she has fallen asleep." She lowered her voice. "I'll finish my conjuring when she is awake. For now, let's leave her to rest."

I hesitated.

I didn't want to leave her, period.

"This room is mine. It is protected," she assured me. Rosette drew the homemade quilt over Grandma, taking extra time to tuck it in around her. "We have been friends for many years. I wouldn't leave her unless she was safe."

I focused my energy and searched the room for myself.

Dark magic mingled with the light.

It would kill me if anything happened to Grandma, whether by otherworldly means or by something as simple as getting old.

I pulled Rosette's rocking chair closer to the bed. "I'm going to sit with her if that's all right."

"Of course, my dear," she said, lowering the shade. "She's lucky to have you."

The older woman paused. "I do not wish to imply your grandmother has any issues, but this weakness surprises me. It's not like her to have it or to hide it. You may want to ask some of her coven if this is a new issue or if she has been suffering for some time."

Good idea. I appreciated her honesty. Besides, learning more about the problem would help me isolate it, and figure out how we could tackle it. In fact, it would be easy enough to ask Frieda right now. That way Grandma wouldn't get upset about it, or try to stop me.

"Will you stay with her?" I asked Rosette. "It won't take me more than a few minutes."

She nodded. "If she wakes, I'll let her know you will be back soon."

"Thanks," I said, slipping out the door.

Unfortunately, that's all it took for things to go to hell.

Chapter Three

I returned to the rec room to find the party in full swing. Bob spun tunes on the karaoke machine. Mr. and Mrs. Levinson had stopped making out in the corner long enough to stand next to a television on a wheeled cart, singing "Cotton Eye Joe" on full volume. A conga line snaked past them.

The women had kicked off their shoes and were dancing barefoot. Men were wiping sweat off their foreheads. The hot bartender didn't have a shirt on.

Hey, wait…

I grabbed Frieda off the conga line. "Where did that guy come from? You shouldn't be serving alcohol to retirement home residents."

The rhinestones on her red cat collar twinkled. "What? Because they're not twenty-one?" She chomped on her gum, the heat from the dance floor wilting her blond bouffant hairdo at the edges. "These people aren't senile. They just need a little extra help sometimes. And Kellen the bartender sure gets your blood pumping," she added, as if daring me to protest.

"I'm a married woman," I said, although if any-body had abs to rival Dimitri's, it was that guy.

Frieda pursed her lips in appreciation. "He's Stella Howser's grandson." She broke into a grin. "Turns out he likes Bob's dandelion wine."

My mouth fell open. "You drugged him?"

"It only gave him a buzz, lowered his inhibitions, same as a regular drink. He's a big boy." She gave a low chuckle. "Besides, there aren't any side effects. We even spelled it so it won't interfere with anyone's meds. It's safer than conventional wine. We'll keep him here until it wears off and he'll go home feeling like the bee's knees."

I'd have to trust her that meant something good.

"Fine," I gritted out. It wasn't our biggest problem anyway. "Listen to me," I said, making sure I had her attention. "Grandma isn't feeling so hot. She's taking a break right now in Rosette's room."

"I was wondering." She frowned. "I saw you leave."

"Has she been feeling out of sorts?" Granted, I hadn't seen her in about a week. "She looked fine last weekend."

Frieda played with the gold tag of her cat collar. "We all have our days," she said apologetically, as if they weren't allowed to get sick, as if I expected them to be superhuman.

Maybe I did.

Guilt wound through me. "All the same, I'd feel better if you talked to her. See if you can get her to be one hundred percent honest about her symptoms."

I may have expected Grandma to push herself a little too hard before, but I'd make up for that now. If she were still asleep, I'd let her sleep. If she needed anything, I'd make sure she had it.

"I'm on it," Frieda said, slipping out of the party with me. She didn't bother with her shoes, which was just as well. I didn't know how she walked in those platform sandals anyway.

"This way," I said, hurrying down the corridor, anxious to have it settled. I couldn't shake this feeling of dread.

Yes, I was the cautious one, the planner. But when push came to shove, it also helped me root out trouble.

I stopped midway down the hall. "It's this one." A black wreath hung on the door, festooned with white ribbons, smiling skulls, and mini wooden coffin lids.

In other circumstances, I would have thought it adorable. Now? It made me even more nervous.

We knocked softly and entered.

Black candles flickered between pots of herbs on the windowsill. The curtain had been drawn up. An orange sunset blazed across the sky, and I gave an involuntary shudder at the darkness seeping into the room.

A twisted red candle flickered on the nightstand, next to the empty bed.

My breath caught in my throat. "Grandma?" I called, hoping she was simply in the bathroom, although the hollowness in my gut told a different story. "Rosette?"

My voice echoed off the walls.

"You feel that prickle?" Frieda asked, her voice low, her tone urgent. "The energy that feels sharp as a woolly cactus? That's black magic."

It skittered up my arms, like invisible spiders.

Oh my God. *Keep moving. Keep searching.* I checked the bathroom, the closet. I even looked under the bed. "They're gone."

Frieda stood rooted to a spot near the ad hoc altar. "Holy hell, Lizzie. There's something in the bed."

I turned. The discarded, rumpled quilt covered most of the bed. A pillow lay askew. Then I saw it. A quivering lump, no bigger than my hand, near the center of the mattress.

Jesus, Mary, Joseph, and the mule. "What the hell is that?"

I drew a switch star, knowing my demon slayer weapons would be useless against a non-demon.

The switch star warmed in my hand. It resembled a Chinese throwing star, only the blades on the ends spun and glowed pink when my fingers clutched the handles. I hoped it would be enough. It was the only thing I *could* do.

"Back away. I've got this," I said.

The room grew much, much darker than the approaching dusk outside the window. The air heated, practically sizzled. My hair stood on end.

It felt like we were being sucked into a black hole.

"Do it," Frieda hissed.

Right. Only I needed to see what I was firing at.

Every second we hesitated, the black magic grew stronger. It was impossible to know what to do, what kind of evil we faced, until I reached out with sweat-slicked fingers, grasped the edge of the quilt, and yanked it as hard as I could off the bed.

A voodoo doll quivered on the sheets, as if it were alive.

It wore a black dress. Long gray hair streamed out from under a witch's hat, and there, on the arm, was a hand-drawn tattoo of a phoenix.

Thick needles pierced it at the neck, the chest, and straight through the left eyeball.

It gave one final shudder as the head began to bleed a thick black sludge.

Chapter Four

"We've got to find her," I told Frieda.

"Where?" she pleaded.

That was the question. We had no idea where to look.

I focused and reached deep down inside. I tried to feel my way through the dark magic swirling around us to learn where Grandma could be.

It clung to me like tar, hot and sticky, blinding.

"I'm going to at least take some of the pins out," Frieda said, reaching for the doll.

"Don't touch it." I said quickly. "We don't know what kind of voodoo we're dealing with."

We might only make it worse.

Suddenly, I felt it stronger—as if merely speaking of the dark magic drew it to me. It seeped close, searching for an opening. It wanted to twist its way inside me, to weave its way into my very soul. Every instinct screamed at me to run. Instead, I let it stalk me while I searched for the source.

I stood my ground, waited, drew it closer than I

would have otherwise dared. It surged like a dark wave rolling onto the beach — a massive swell of power that felt very, very wrong.

Frieda swayed under the assault. "I feel dizzy." She tried to lie down in the bed.

"No." I touched her on the arm. She felt ice cold. The magic slid over our skin and suddenly I knew why I felt the rush of the waves, the pounding of the shore. It was coming from the beach.

"This way," I said, escorting Frieda from the room. She couldn't come with me, not in the shape she was in, but I wasn't going to leave her alone in that place.

When it came down to it, I wondered if anywhere was safe. Grandma had felt sick before she entered Rosette's room. Frieda succumbed afterward.

I led her to a plush chair in the hallway. "Sit. I'll fix this. I'll be back soon."

I spied an exit at the far end of the hall. Halfway there, I almost collided with a kind-faced, middle-aged nurse as she exited one of the rooms. "Hi. Sorry." I reached out to steady us both. "Will you take a look at my friend?" I asked, pointing out Frieda. "She's not feeling so well."

"Of course," she began, trying to lead me back from where I came.

I dodged past her. It hurt to leave Frieda, but I didn't have time to wait while the nurse checked her out. Besides, I had a feeling I'd be helping her more by getting to the bottom of this. "Is that the way to the beach?" I asked.

The nurse smiled, somewhat taken aback by my exit. "Yes, but those doors will beep if you leave. It's best to go back through the building and around the —"

"Gotcha." I ignored the nurse's protests as I dashed down the hall and blew out the back door.

The alarm blared a harsh *scree-scree-scree* behind me. I hurried across a patio and down the stairs toward the beach. Sea grass rose up on either side of the narrow steps. I pressed forward, my boots pounding the wood below.

Black magic pierced the air and I watched in horror as the sun sank below the waters of the Pacific. Samhain was upon us, the night when the veil was the thinnest between the living and the dead.

I opened up my demon slayer senses and felt the irresistible pull of wanton destruction and death. It had been no coincidence that we found ourselves here on this night. Now I just had to figure out who had drawn us here and what they wanted.

I followed the magic along the shore, my heart pounding as I struggled to move quickly through the sand.

If I hadn't left Grandma, if I'd have stayed in the room with her…well, it might have been me caught in the snare. I wished it was.

Then I saw the flicker of torches ahead, in a cove past the water. My mouth grew dry.

It had to be them.

I climbed the rocky outcropping, scattering pebbles, unsure of my next move. Somehow, I'd have to bridge the gap. I needed to figure out a way to navigate the dark waters ahead if I had any hope of making it to the secluded cove.

One hand braced on my switch stars, I pressed forward, trusting the universe. I'd make it possible. Somehow. And just when I thought I'd step off the edge and plunge into the ocean, I came upon a narrow pathway.

The sandy soil felt soft under my feet.

I pulled the Maglite out of my utility belt, chancing a quick look. The path was barely as wide as a person, and left no room for error. At the same time, it seemed solid, and it snaked along the edge of the water.

That was all I needed. I prayed it went as far as the cove.

A woman's voice uttered a low chant, barely discernible amid the breaking of the waves.

I killed my light. It was too much of a risk. Then I stepped onto the path.

I was on my own, unless Frieda somehow recovered and rallied the others. I didn't have high hopes for that. Whatever attacked Grandma had struck Frieda as well. It might have even made it to the other witches by now.

The chanting grew louder. The pounding of drums echoed over the water and I doubled my pace, moving as quickly as I possibly could. I didn't know much about voodoo rituals, but everything I'd seen made me think they were obsessed with death. Sacrifice.

I turned the corner and stared in horror.

Torches illuminated a small cove amid the cliffs. Inside the grim circle of light, Rosette pounded on the drums, chanting, while in the center of a blackened circle of ashes, Grandma stood, battling for her life.

A twisted, blackened entity hovered over her, poised to strike.

She watched it like the predator it was. All the while, she chanted age-old words of magic. "*Modestro tolomus avanhara.*"

The ancient spells spilled from Grandma as she wound her hands through the air. Black ooze trickled down her forehead.

She had no spell jars, no backup.

I drew a switch star.

"Stop!" Rosetta called, missing a beat on her drum.

Grandma spun to look at me, losing her focus on the entity. She cried out as it slammed into her shoulder.

Oh my God. "Grandma!" I dashed down the embankment.

"Don't cross the ashen line," Rosetta warned, attempting to block me. I ducked around her, aiming the switch star for the entity. I had no idea what part of it to target or if it would even work against a creature that was more black magic than flesh and blood.

But I focused my strength, my will, my positive focus that I could defeat this monster, that I could free Grandma. That everything would be all right.

I let loose my switch star in a blaze of pure energy and light.

It struck the being and exploded in a surge of power that made me weak in the knees. The force of it knocked Grandma to the ground. She rolled away and came up in a crouch, ready to go again.

I watched in horror as the creature broke into at least a dozen writhing, fiery pieces. They spewed like a volcanic explosion into burning chunks on the beach.

I might have just made it worse.

My switch star winged back to me like a boomerang.

Rosette charged the nearest chunk of molten magic. "*Halo mancha verno ta!*" she shouted. "Away with spirits bold and soiled!" Rosette stomped on the fiery mass, sending up a wave of purple sparks. "Away!"

she shouted, her shoes smoking, as if she could banish it by force of will alone.

It fell to ash under her feet.

Holy smokes. I took the next one. "Away with spirits bold and soiled!" I hollered. The slice of magic felt soft under my feet, as though I could sink straight into it. "Away!" I insisted, ignoring the quicksand feel of it, how the chunks of burning soot broke into purple shards of energy. They snaked at my legs, burned ribbons up my knees. "Away!"

Grandma held her hands over a half dozen or more of the splintering chunks. She chanted, forced out her power over them. One by one they sparked and crumbled. The final slice let out a crackling groan before it too disintegrated like ash.

I saw I stood on a circle of blackened soot. Nothing of the fire or magic remained under my feet, nor were there any more shards on the beach. We were left with the pounding of the waves and the crackling of the torches.

Rosette shook, rubbing her hands over her eyes.

I hurried to Grandma. She stood alone, speaking so low to herself it almost sounded like humming. I should probably leave her alone, but I had to know. "Are you all right?"

She stared past me, as if she could see entities I couldn't. "Yeah," she said, absently. "I think we got it."

I shivered. The air felt electric, charged with excess energy. "What was it?"

Grandma shook her head. Her hair tangled in her eyes and over her shoulders. She pushed it aside. "A voodoo curse come to life." She turned to her friend. "What are you playing at, Rosie?"

Grandma's friend wiped at her swollen eyes and swallowed hard, as if she couldn't quite believe we'd made it through. "It was supposed to be a love spell." She flinched as a purple spark crackled in the dead fire and launched into the night. "I'm so sorry." She hurried to where the spark had ignited. "Away!" She stomped, reaching into her pocket and sprinkling what appeared to be dirt and herbs onto the fire. "Away!"

"That felt like the last of it," Grandma said, rubbing a boot in the ashes.

"I never meant…" she began, stumbling over her words. "It should have been simple. One spell." She crossed her arms over her chest, still stomping. "I needed a lock of my rival's hair." She swallowed hard. "You weren't even supposed to notice."

Grandma stared at Rosette as if she didn't quite know what to make of that. "Spell work is dangerous on this kind of land," she said, going with what she knew. "Any kind of negative emotion can make it go dark, turn it into a curse," Grandma warned, too late. "I told you that you were powerful."

She didn't say the rest—that Rosette would have to be very angry with Grandma for it to have gotten this far.

She ran a hand over her tear-stained cheek. "The doll was to make you sleepy, not sick. Once I had your hair, it was supposed to be over. I don't even remember kidnapping you to the beach."

"I know," Grandma said, "I saw it in your eyes. You weren't there. Until it began the attack."

A tear escaped. "Then it was too late."

"You took control of the drums," Grandma said. "You did your best to cage it."

"Until your granddaughter blasted it," Rosette said, her voice thick with gratitude. She turned to me. "You're a good girl, Lizzie."

"I try," I said. It wasn't always easy to stay on top of this crowd.

Grandma smiled. She knew.

Rosette poked at the remains of the fire with her feet, as if she refused to believe she could conquer her demons.

Grandma went to her old friend. She stood in the dead fire with her and touched Rosette's arm. "Stop your stomping. It's over." She tilted her head. "Now tell me. Why am I your rival?"

Rosette stared down at the ashes, her dreadlocks shielding her face before her gaze found Grandma's. "Remember? You stole Eddie Turner. At the Independence Day party in 1976."

"Ah." Grandma clucked with sympathy. I could tell she was having trouble figuring out just who this Eddie Turner might be.

Rosette blinked back fresh tears as she avoided Grandma's scrutiny. Instead, she looked out to the ocean. "He was sweet on me. I could tell. It was only a matter of time before he asked me out," she said, a flush creeping up her cheeks. "Then you took him to the movies. You asked him out. You made him like you."

"Aw," Grandma said gently. "I didn't know you liked him."

"No doubt you had a love spell," Rosette challenged, as if daring her to deny it.

"I've always used something better," Grandma said. "You want to know my secret?"

"No," Rosette said, wiping at her eyes, looking

back to the mess on the beach. "I'll stick to protective magic. It's the only thing I'm good at."

"Don't say that," Grandma soothed. "It's hard to do positive conjuring on bad land. It took our whole coven to put on the witches' bash. The bad magic kept trying to seep up and taint it, like it corrupted your love spell." She shook her head. "I won't deny you made a mistake in judgment." Grandma held her hands up over the beach and glanced at me. "It's gone, isn't it?"

I opened up my demon slayer senses, gave it a thorough search. "Yes." The only remnants were the ashes on the beach, and even those would be gone with the tide.

"I'm so sorry." Rosette sniffled as she began dousing the torches. "I should have kept Eddie in my past. I haven't seen him in forty years, and I've been avoiding him ever since he moved into one of the apartments upstairs."

Grandma's jaw dropped. "At the Ocean View Senior Living Center?"

"Not even two weeks ago," Rosette said.

"That's fate," Grandma said, serious as a heart attack.

Her friend reddened at the cheeks. "I figured the Halloween party would be a good time to rekindle our acquaintance. One of the nurses said he was going."

"That's perfect," Grandma said. She'd regained her strength and the warmth in her voice. I could tell she had an idea. "But you don't need a love spell. You don't even need live chickens or naked chanting to get his attention. You can get Eddie on your own."

"Impossible," Rosette huffed.

"You want to try it?" Grandma prodded. "Because I'd be damned pissed if you voodooed me, stole a lock of my hair, and got me attacked by a nasty-ass spirit and then turn scaredy-cat when it comes to getting the man at the end."

Rosette stood still, the light from the last torch flickering over her features. "I can't believe you'd want to help me after what I did."

"You're a good person, Rosie," she said, softly. "You get that, right? You didn't set out to hurt me. Jealousy can be as dangerous as black magic. It fuels the bad and gives it an opening to hurt us. That's why you have to be careful. Pish! I don't need to lecture you. You saw the consequences up close and personal tonight. But we need to be very clear. One mistake doesn't wipe out four decades of doing the right thing."

Tears filled her eyes and her mouth twisted into the first smile I'd seen from her since Grandma got sick. "Thanks. I suppose you're right."

"You bet your ass I am," Grandma said, leading Rosette away. "Now I know just the thing to get that man off the fence."

Chapter Five

We walked Rosette back inside. Frieda still slept in one of the tan chairs in the hallway. But her color was good and she seemed to be snoring comfortably. I shook her awake.

"Oh my," she said, her eyes fluttering open. "I had the strangest dream."

Grandma and I helped her up while Rosie ducked into her room for an emergency lipstick-and-hair-arranging session.

"You okay?" Grandma asked.

Frieda stood straighter. "Yes, of course. What do you need?"

Grandma clapped the blonde biker witch on the arm. "If you're feeling up to it, I'd like you to go to the second floor and make sure a man named Eddie Turner comes down to the party."

"You got it," she said, straightening her black cat-suit and fluffy ears.

"And you," Grandma turned to me. "Get me one of your fancy cupcakes."

"Right." I went to go show Frieda where to find the elevator. Then I headed into the party to grab a cupcake and to have a word with Bob at the karaoke machine. "We're going to need a love song coming up," I said, patting him on the shoulder.

He merely grinned.

I returned to the scene of the crime with the cupcake just as Rosie emerged from her room. She'd changed into a fresh purple gown. A gold scarf wound in her hair and her cheeks flushed with natural excitement.

"You look good," I told her.

A shy smile tickled her lips. "I feel good," she said, glancing at Grandma.

I handed her the cupcake. "I think you're supposed to give this to Eddie."

Grandma nodded. "Tell him you picked it out special."

Rosie looked down at the cupcake, as if it would come alive and bite her. "But isn't that forward?"

"Then you're going to ask him to dance," Grandma said. "A slow song."

Her friend blushed all over again. "I can't."

"Come on," Grandma said, coaxing her down the hall. "You said you wanted to pay me back. This is how you do it. You reach outside yourself and you be happy. I won't accept anything less."

"He's going to think I'm a fool," she said breathlessly, her fingers digging into the paper surrounding the bottom of the moist cupcake. "He's going to say no."

"And what's the worst thing that can happen?" Grandma asked, as we neared the party.

Rosie swallowed as she looked from Grandma to

me. "The worst is over," she said, as if realizing it for the first time.

I opened the doors and Grandma nudged her inside. "Go get 'em, tiger."

Rosie took a few confident steps, and then slowed as she saw an older man in a blue sports jacket. It must be Eddie. He'd made it to the party.

He stood at the edge of the dance floor, watching the others have fun. The biker witch Creely spun in the middle, a human disco ball, as others danced around her.

As if drawn by a force more powerful than him or her or anyone else in the room, the man in the blue sports jacket turned and saw Rosie through the crowd.

She made her way to him and shyly greeted him, handing him the cupcake. He barely looked at it. He was too busy noticing Rosie.

I caught Bob's eye and gave him the thumbs-up. He nodded and changed up the music. A slow, sultry melody captured the room. "At Last" by Etta James.

I felt a wet nose on my knee and smiled down at my dog. He'd lost his pirate outfit and was instead wearing a crocheted hot dog and bun on his back that really did make him look stupid.

"Where on earth did you get that?" I asked, picking him up.

He tried to shake it off and failed. "Mrs. Levinson said she could take my pirate costume off. I never expected the bait and switch."

Ah well. "At least you get to be food." It was his favorite thing. "Look," I said, as we watched Eddie lead Rosie out onto the floor.

"Aww," Pirate said. "Now, that's nice."

It truly was. Eddie gazed down at Rosie as though he'd never seen anyone so lovely. She beamed and she was beautiful.

I remembered that feeling, when I'd first realized I belonged with Dimitri. It was astounding in its pure joy and simplicity.

Grandma joined us, appearing quite satisfied. She had every right to be.

"What did you do?" I asked. I could see the change in Rosette already.

She smiled knowingly. "Not a damned thing," she said, leaning on her broomstick. "Some things are better than magic."

Enjoy more of Lizzie's adventures in the
Accidental Demon Slayer series by Angie Fox

Southern Spirits
Available now!
Book 1 in Angie Fox's brand new
Southern Ghost Hunter series

When out of work graphic designer Verity Long accidentally traps a ghost on her property, she's saddled with more than a supernatural sidekick – she gains the ability see spirits. It leads to an offer she can't refuse from the town's bad boy, the brother of her ex and the last man she should ever partner with.

Ellis Wydell is in possession of a stunning historic property haunted by some of Sugarland Tennessee's finest former citizens. Only some of them are growing restless – and destructive. He hires Verity to put an end to the disturbances. But soon, Verity learns there's more to the mysterious estate than floating specters, secret passageways, and hidden rooms.

There's a modern day mystery afoot, one that hinges on a decades-old murder. Verity isn't above questioning the living, or the dead. But can she discover the truth before the killer finds her?

About the Author

New York Times bestselling author Angie Fox writes sweet, fun, action-packed stories. Her characters are clever and fearless, but in real life, Angie is afraid of basements, bees, and going up stairs when it is dark behind her. Let's face it. Angie wouldn't last five minutes in one of her books.

Angie earned a Journalism degree from the University of Missouri. During that time, she also skipped class for an entire week so she could read Anne Rice's vampire series straight through. Angie has always loved books and is shocked, honored and tickled pink that she now gets to write books for a living. Although, she did skip writing for a few weeks last year so she could read Lynsay Sands Argeneau vampire series straight through.

Angie makes her home in St. Louis, Missouri with a football-addicted husband, two kids, and Moxie the dog (who so far, doesn't talk...at least not in real sentences).

To receive an email each time Angie releases a new book, sign up for new release alerts at www.angiefox.com

Printed in Great Britain
by Amazon.co.uk, Ltd.,
Marston Gate.